...ned to any branch of the

# LOOKING AT THE STARS

www.totallyrandombooks.co.uk

# JO COTTERILL

# LOOKING AT THE STARS

THE BODLEY HEAD

LOOKING AT THE STARS
A BODLEY HEAD BOOK 978 1 782 30018 2

Published in Great Britain by The Bodley Head,
an imprint of Random House Children's Publishers UK
A Random House Group Company

This edition published 2014

1 3 5 7 9 10 8 6 4 2

Copyright © Jo Cotterill, 2014
Cover illustration and title lettering © Grady McFerrin, 2014
Photograph of girls © Lee Avison / Trevillion Images

The right of Jo Cotterill to be identified as the author of this work has been
asserted in accordance with the Copyright, Designs and Patents Act 1988.

All rights reserved. No part of this publication may be reproduced,
stored in a retrieval system, or transmitted in any form or by any means,
electronic, mechanical, photocopying, recording or otherwise,
without the prior permission of the publishers.

The Random House Group Limited supports the Forest Stewardship Council®
(FSC®), the leading international forest-certification organisation. Our books
carrying the FSC label are printed on FSC®-certified paper. FSC is the only
forest-certification scheme supported by the leading environmental organisations,
including Greenpeace. Our paper procurement policy can be found at
www.randomhouse.co.uk/environment

MIX
Paper from
responsible sources
FSC® C016897

Set in Goudy Old Style

RANDOM HOUSE CHILDREN'S PUBLISHERS UK
61–63 Uxbridge Road, London W5 5SA

www.randomhousechildrens.co.uk
www.totallyrandombooks.co.uk
www.randomhouse.co.uk

Addresses for companies within The Random House Group Limited can be found
at: www.randomhouse.co.uk/offices.htm

THE RANDOM HOUSE GROUP Limited Reg. No. 954009

A CIP catalogue record for this book is available from the British Library.

Printed and bound in Great Britain by Clays Ltd, St Ives plc

*For my daughters*

| Lancashire Library Services | |
|:---:|:---:|
| 30118128240706 | |
| PETERS | JF |
| £12.99 | 03-Feb-2014 |
| | |

We are all in the gutter,
but some of us are looking at the stars.

Oscar Wilde

# 1

The day the soldiers came, we cheered. We weren't supposed to, of course; if Potta had seen us, he would have been furious; but we couldn't help it. Jenna and I were on our way back from the reed beds, our arms full of plants for use at home, when we saw the dust rising up in the distance. The road was empty apart from a woman walking towards us with a basket balanced on her head. The dusty, scrubby track wound off into the distant mountains, with only the occasional tree to break up the landscape. Usually there was nothing to be seen at all, but today there was a low cloud growing bigger and bigger by the minute.

'Horses?' I was puzzled.

'Wagons?' suggested my sister.

The woman with the basket turned to look behind her. 'Soldiers,' she whispered. 'The liberators!'

I felt an excitement rush through me at her words, though I didn't know what to expect. Jenna and I watched the dust clouds approach, and before long we could hear the noise of the vehicles too. The woman stood with us and tugged at her headscarf to cover her face.

Then the cars and trucks were upon us, one after another, kicking up tiny stones and more clouds of dust as they passed, making us cough. Soldiers riding on the roofs, smartly attired in beige and brown, with foreign badges on their caps, smiled and waved at us. Of course, to begin with I tried not to look at them, but there were so many smiles and waves and cheerful shouts that after a while I couldn't help but smile back. And then I waved, and the soldier I waved to looked so delighted that suddenly I couldn't stop waving, and then I was cheering, and the woman next to me was cheering, and Jenna was cheering too – and then the woman unwound her headscarf and brandished it in the air! I gasped at this public breaking of rules, but when no one came running to arrest her, I looked around furtively and unwound my own scarf too.

'Amina!' cried my sister. 'What are you doing?'

'Being liberated!' I cried, my green scarf mixing in the air with the black of the woman's. 'Come on, Jenna!'

But my sister was more cautious than me and kept a tight hold on her own navy scarf.

'It's like a story, Jenna,' I said, exhilarated. Excitement bubbled through me. 'Once upon a time there was a kingdom ruled by a tyrant. But then a flight of angels arrived to rescue the people!'

'Hardly angels,' said Jenna, though she was smiling. 'Where are their wings?'

The engines roared like avenging dragons. I could almost imagine them breathing fire. The smiling soldiers blurred in the haze and the dust and the intoxicating scent of freedom.

'Remember this day,' said the woman as she gazed at the seemingly endless procession of vehicles. I wasn't sure if she was talking to me or to herself, but she repeated it. 'Remember this day – the day liberation began.'

'I will,' I said impulsively, and she turned to me and smiled.

'Everything will change now,' she said. 'You'll see.'

\*

Eventually the procession came to an end, and we put our scarves back on and went on our way. I glanced behind at the woman, whose name we didn't know, and there was a lightness in her step that I was sure hadn't been there before. I felt the same way. After five years of living under the Kwana, we were about to be rescued! No more stupid headscarves, no more stupid rules about going out without escorts, no more flogging in the streets. The life I could remember only as a kind of dream – life before the Kwana – would return!

'How long do you think it will be before we can go back to school?' I asked Jenna eagerly.

My sister, her headscarf tightly in place, made the sort of tutting noise my mother was so good at. 'Mini, why do you always ask things like that? How can I know the answer? How can anyone?'

'What are you talking about?' I asked. 'The soldiers are here, aren't they? Everyone's been saying for months that things can't go on the way they are. Look at the riots in the big cities! The rest of the world has finally realized what Ranami has been doing to our people. Our glorious leader and his glorious Kwana army – huh!'

'Ssh!' Jenna looked crossly at me. We were nearing the edge of our village. 'Can't you hold your tongue? You'll get us into trouble!'

I was frustrated. 'Aren't you even a *little* bit excited, Jenna? I mean, don't you *want* things to change?'

'Of course I do! But I don't think it's a good idea to talk about it.' Jenna unwrapped one arm to gesture at our village. 'Are things different here yet? No. So it's still not safe.'

My gaze swept over the approaching rows of homes. Talas wasn't all that big compared with Gharsad, the nearest city, but it felt big to me. I'd never lived anywhere else; never set foot outside the area. It was as familiar to me as my own hands. The buildings were made out of stone, brick, wood, metal – anything people could find or buy at market. Some were grand affairs, with several rooms, gardens and verandas. Others simply consisted of one main room where everyone slept, ate and washed together. I could remember when this particular street had been half the length it was now – over the years, new people had come, bought a piece of stony ground, and built their home on it, stretching the street further and further. We'd been promised running water and electricity when the Kwana came to power, but it never appeared. Maybe, I mused, the arrival of the foreign troops would mean that we finally got those things.

The thought made me smile. Running water, in our own house! Being able to turn on a tap and fill up a cup, just like that! It would be heavenly.

It was a mistake to smile in the middle of the street, as I should have remembered. 'You!' called a harsh voice to our left, and Jenna and I stopped sharply. My gaze flicked across instinctively, and my heart sank. Four men were sitting outside a café, staring at us. All of them were dressed in the dark green jackets of the Kwana local military, and all had rifles propped up against their chairs. A large poster of Ranami, his expression stern and forbidding, adorned the wall of the café, its colours faded from the sun. The man who had called to us was tall, with a thick moustache and a badge that indicated he was one of the commanding officers. He stood up now, frowning.

All this I took in faster than I can describe, and I cast my eyes to the ground, biting my lip. My arms tightened on the collection of reeds and I felt cold from fear in the hot sunshine.

I heard the man walk over, his boots crunching the fine pebbles. 'Young women,' he said, his voice low, 'are not permitted to make a spectacle of themselves in the street.' He spat at my feet, and I saw a tiny globule attach itself to my little toe. It made my guts lurch. He walked round behind Jenna, and I heard her gasp, but I didn't dare raise my eyes. Then he was back behind me. 'Young women should behave properly,' he hissed.

I felt a deep twinge of anger. I had only been smiling! How could that be seen as improper behaviour? But I didn't dare speak; I knew enough of the Kwana not to risk making things worse. Besides, these men didn't need an excuse to pick on people: sometimes they did it just for the fun. It was useless to wish I'd done something differently.

I felt the man's hand on my head, which made me shiver, but he was only pulling at the edge of my headscarf. 'Not even dressed properly,' he said with a sneer.

I reached up to my scarf, realizing that I hadn't tied it tightly enough when I'd put it back on. Thank goodness the Kwana hadn't seen us waving to the foreign soldiers! I gulped at the thought of how we might have been punished.

The soldier smacked my hand away. 'You should not need reminding,' he told me. 'You are old enough to know better. What would your glorious leader say?'

One of the men still sitting at the café table called over, 'You could make sure she won't forget, Hamsi.'

I heard Hamsi laugh softly, and I squeezed my eyes shut. Maybe, if I was lucky, I'd only get a slap across the face, or a kick in the back. The Kwana were supposed to follow strict rules on what punishments were suitable for which crimes, but some of them liked to make up their own punishments . . . I hoped that Hamsi was one of the ones who followed the guidelines. Maybe if I showed that I was sorry . . . I dropped to the dirt, feeling the sharp stones dig into my knees. Hamsi laughed again. 'It's too late to beg.'

There was a tug at my throat, and then a sudden rush of air about my ears as Hamsi pulled away my headscarf. I swayed slightly, off balance, and dropped my reeds. My shoulder-length black hair hung in straggly tendrils about my face. I felt suddenly very exposed. Yes, I'd taken off my scarf to wave at the soldiers, but that had been my choice. Here, with a man removing it for me, in front of other men, I felt humiliated, and my cheeks burned.

The three men at the table laughed, and one of them muttered something to the other two. 'Maybe we should give her something to hide under that headscarf,' Hamsi said, his voice raised so that his colleagues could hear. 'Something that will remind her to keep it on.'

I felt dizzy with panic. What did he mean?

Then I heard a long scraping noise as Hamsi removed the knife from the sheath on his belt, and I started to tremble. I felt my hair being gripped tightly in a clump on top of my head, and I gasped as my chin jerked upwards, exposing my neck. The knife flashed dangerously close. Was he going to cut my throat? I screwed my eyes shut again and started to pray – to the gods, to my parents, to anyone who might help me.

A radio crackled harshly and a voice came out of it. I couldn't make out the words, but one of the men called sharply to Hamsi, and my hair was suddenly released. Hamsi, losing interest in me, strode back to his companions, and then, without a word or a glance, they were all gone, walking purposefully down the street towards the central square, their guns carried tightly in their hands and Hamsi's knife back in his belt.

I bent forward, shaking with relief, glad that I was already on my knees – otherwise I would have fallen. 'Amina!' My sister was speaking urgently. 'Amina, are you all right? You must get up, quickly, in case they come back.'

I struggled to my feet, trying to gather up the dropped reeds in my wobbly arms. They were covered in dust and would need a thorough soaking before they were clean enough to weave. My sister's face was pale as she picked up my head-scarf from the ground and helped me tie it on. 'I'm sorry,' I said. 'I was only smiling . . . I'm really sorry, Jenna.'

'I know,' she said. Then she sighed. 'Trouble again, though. Come on, let's get out of here.'

We started off again, trying to ignore the stares from passers-by. Talas was a busy place, even on the outskirts, and several people had witnessed my humiliation. It was too much to expect anyone to come to my rescue, though. Everyone knew the penalties for getting involved with something that wasn't your business.

We kept our heads down all the way home. There was no chance of my getting caught smiling again – the euphoric feeling from earlier had completely evaporated. Foreign soldiers here to liberate us? So what?

Only Mamie and Vivie were at home when we arrived, which was to be expected. Potta was at work and my older brother Ruman was at school – the school that had been forbidden to girls ever since the Kwana came to power.

Jenna swiftly explained to Mamie what had happened in the street. News travelled fast in Talas, and my mother would find out from some gossipy neighbour if we didn't tell her. Mamie brought me a drink of water and relieved me of my bundle of reeds, instructing Vivie to take them out onto the back porch. My nine-year-old sister did as she was told, though I could see she was bursting to ask for more details.

I sat for a moment, drinking my water and feeling the trembling subside. 'What happened?' asked Mamie quietly. 'Why did they pick on you?'

'I was smiling,' I said with a shrug. 'I looked too happy.'

She gave a sigh. She knew as well as I did how the Kwana didn't really need a reason to show off their superiority. 'You must pay more attention to your surroundings, Amina. Why were you so distracted?'

My gaze went automatically to my older sister. Jenna looked hesitant, and I knew she was wondering if we should tell Mamie about the soldiers. But she'd find out anyway. 'We saw the liberators arrive,' I said in a low voice. 'The foreign soldiers. In their trucks and cars and everything – oh, Mamie, it was such an amazing sight!'

'Hush!' said Mamie, alarmed. 'How— Where were you?'

'On our way back from the reed bed,' I said. 'They were just coming along the road, just – *there*. Out of the dust, truck after jeep after car after—'

'It would have been better if you hadn't been on the road at that time,' said Mamie. 'Still, I suppose as long as you kept your heads down and didn't look at them—' She caught the involuntary glance I exchanged with Jenna again, and her jaw dropped. 'What did you do? Tell me, quickly!'

12

'We – we waved at them,' I admitted reluctantly. 'That's all, I promise.' It wasn't all, and Jenna knew it. We'd cheered, and I'd taken off my headscarf, which was about the worst thing I could have done in front of strangers, but I couldn't bear to get into any more trouble.

'You waved at them?' said Mamie, appalled. I heard Vivie give a little gasp, and suddenly I felt cross. It was all so unfair! Why should welcoming the soldiers who had come to free us be such a bad thing?

'You'd have done the same if you'd been there,' I said rebelliously. 'It was amazing – the most amazing thing I've ever seen. And it made us feel . . . happy. Hopeful!'

'Amina!' cried Mamie.

'Well, it did,' I went on. 'Everyone's always saying how much we need help to come from outside. Everyone hates the Kwana. Now the help is here – why shouldn't I be happy? Why shouldn't I wave to them and let them know I'm pleased they're here?'

'That's enough!' snapped Mamie sharply, and her eyes were fearful. 'You stop right there, Amina

Ambrose, before you get us all into trouble.' A thought occurred to her. 'Did anyone else see you doing this?'

I stared at the floor, mutinous. 'There was another woman on the road. She stood with us – she cheered too.'

'A woman? What woman?'

I shrugged. 'She had a black headscarf, but I didn't know her.'

'Married,' said Mamie, her eyebrows drawing together. 'I don't know whether that's a good thing or a bad thing. She could be married to a Kwana – she could report back to him . . .'

'She said that we should remember this was the day liberation began,' Jenna said unexpectedly. I felt grateful to her for backing me up. 'She seemed really happy to see the soldiers.'

Mamie sighed. 'Well, there's nothing we can do about it now. We'll have to hope that she is what she appeared to be. You know the Kwana have spies everywhere.'

There was silence. There was more I wanted to say, but I knew it wasn't a good moment. Not for the first time I was in trouble for speaking out too much.

Why couldn't I just hold my tongue and be a good girl, like my older sister? Jenna kept her head down and her mouth shut, and she was rarely in trouble. Sometimes I envied her. My mouth seemed to open of its own accord, and words and thoughts came out without my control. I should have been born a boy – then it wouldn't have mattered. The thought made me bitter.

Potta and Ruman came back at about the same time. My father looked tired. 'There was trouble on the road,' he said. 'I had to come a different way.'

'What kind of trouble?' asked Mamie.

Potta looked at us. Ruman was unpacking his school bag; Jenna, Vivie and I were sitting quietly in the corner, weaving tiny flower decorations out of pieces of reed. I tried not to look curious. 'Protests,' said Potta. 'More students out, clashing with the Kwana.'

'Students from your university?'

Potta shrugged. 'Who knows? I think so. I didn't stay to see. I had fewer in my class again today, though.'

Potta taught history at Gharsad university, and I

knew his job had become more difficult recently. The Kwana, not content with ruling people's day-to-day lives, wanted to rule their minds too, and their education. Potta was no longer allowed to teach parts of the country's history that the Kwana deemed 'unacceptable'. Instead, he was forced to stick to a new curriculum that they had created. We all knew he hated doing it, although he would never dare say so. But I saw the way he frowned when he looked at his books now, and heard the annoyed mutters whenever Mamie asked him about work.

'Where are they all going?' Mamie wanted to know.

'Joining the underground movement, I suppose,' said Potta. 'It's so dangerous – they're young, idealistic. They think that they'll be able to work with the foreign troops . . . You know they passed by here today?'

'Yes,' said Mamie. Her eyes flicked across to me and Jenna. 'Amina and Jenna saw the jeeps on their way back from the reed beds.'

Potta stared at us. 'You saw them?'

I nodded.

'How many were there?'

I was surprised. I thought he'd be cross with us for being in the wrong place at the wrong time. 'Loads,' I said. 'Hundreds.'

'One hundred? Three hundred? Be precise, Amina.' Potta sounded urgent.

'I – I don't know,' I admitted. 'I didn't count – I'm sorry.'

'I thought there were about one hundred and twenty,' said Jenna in her soft voice. 'But I lost count after I got to seventy-six.'

'A hundred and twenty!' my brother suddenly exclaimed. Ruman was fifteen and as tall as Potta now, though he was thin and wiry where Potta was more thick-set. His dark eyes were shining under his mop of black hair, which never stayed lying flat no matter how often he combed it. 'I wish I'd seen it! It must have been incredible.'

I felt a rush of warmth for my brother. He knew how I'd felt.

'They're on their way to Bremir,' said Potta thoughtfully. 'I wonder . . .' Then he seemed to remember we were all listening, and his face changed. 'You must remember,' he told us, 'that things are still the same.'

17

'How can you say that?' asked Ruman. 'Everything will change now.'

'Perhaps,' Potta replied. 'But not yet. For the moment, everything is the same. If liberation *does* come . . .' He hesitated.

'*When* it comes,' said my brother.

'*If* . . .' repeated Potta, 'then we will change accordingly. But the Kwana are still in charge in Talas, and until that changes, we go about our lives as usual. Ranami is still our leader, don't forget.'

'Not for long,' muttered Ruman, and Potta turned on him, suddenly furious.

'Don't you know how dangerous it is to go around saying things like that? Have you forgotten what brought the troops here in the first place? The Kwana are *strong*, I keep telling you – look what happened in Bremir and in the west of the country. All those people shot because they dared to protest! I will *not* have my son risking his life and the lives of his family because he can't keep his mouth shut!'

Ruman's face flamed red with embarrassment, and I felt for him. He and I had the same problem: we couldn't help asking 'What if?' and 'Why?' and whereas it was more acceptable for a boy to ask questions, it wasn't safe for *anyone* to question our leader. He pressed his lips together tightly, picked up a text book and went out to sit on the back porch.

Jenna, Vivie and I exchanged glances and went back to our work.

Mamie made Potta a cup of herb tea and murmured soothing things. They talked quietly for a while, too quietly for me to be able to hear the words, but just before the sky darkened outside, I heard Potta say something that chilled me from the inside out:

'There are bad things to come, my Mia. There may be salvation at the end, but things will get worse before they get better . . .'

# 2

The reeds that Jenna and I had carried home needed several washes the next day before they were clean and flexible enough to use for our work. She and I spent most of our days weaving baskets and mats to sell at market. It was boring work, but essential: since Potta's salary as a professor had been reduced, we'd had to find other ways to make money, and I was grateful that we weren't forced to beg or to run after tourists in the big cities like poor children, trying to sell them cigarettes or postcards.

It was a task we had learned long ago from Mamie, whose fingers had roughened so much they resembled reeds themselves. Jenna was better at weaving than I – her long fingers moved like lightning, and her skill had almost surpassed Mamie's. Jenna's baskets sold for twice as much as mine. I envied Jenna her slender fingers – mine were short and stumpy, and I often had to start over again due to a clumsily snapped reed or a too loosely tied knot.

Working in silence didn't come easily to me, and I was soon speculating on the events of the day before. 'Do you think the soldiers have reached Bremir yet?' I asked.

Jenna shook her head. 'How should I know?'

'I wonder what they'll do when they get there. Do you think they'll just drive straight up to the gates of the palace and demand to see Ranami? Or maybe they'll surround the city and take everyone hostage.' I wasn't quite sure what the word 'hostage' meant, but it sounded glamorous and exciting.

Jenna looked around uneasily. Our porch was fairly private, but there were houses on either side. 'Mini, I don't think we should be talking about this.'

I lowered my voice, just to be on the safe side. 'I'm only wondering,' I said. 'Nobody cares what I think – why would they? I'm just a *girl*.' I said the last words sarcastically. The Kwana had taken away everything women had had – jobs, rights, freedom – when they came to power. Mamie had been a teacher, like Potta, but she'd had to give it up, and Jenna and I had been told to stop going to school. I hated it – it was another reason why I couldn't wait for things to change again.

'*You* might be just a girl,' said Jenna, her soft voice sounding crosser than usual, 'but what about Potta and Ruman? You could get them into trouble if someone heard you. It's not just about *you*.'

I bit my lip. She was right, of course. One member of the family could get everyone into trouble. 'I have to talk about *something*,' I said. 'You know I do. I can't work without talking.'

My sister smiled. 'You can't work when you *are* talking,' she pointed out. 'If you just concentrated a bit more, you'd get better results.'

I looked down sadly at the mat I'd been weaving. The work was nothing like as fine as Jenna's – my corners were sharp instead of rounded, and the places where one reed ended and another began were too obvious.

I sighed. 'I could tell you a story while we work. That's safer than talking about the soldiers, isn't it?'

'You know Mamie doesn't like you telling stories,' said Jenna.

'Mamie's not here.' I glanced around quickly to

make sure this was true. 'Besides, if I tell a story about basket weaving, maybe it'll improve my own skills . . .'.

Jenna laughed. 'That would be clever. I'd like to see that happen.'

'Good.' I wriggled on the mat and composed my thoughts. 'In a land far away, there was a young girl locked in a tower by a magic spell. She wasn't allowed to talk to anyone and she wasn't allowed to read. Instead, she was forced to weave, day in and day out. If she stopped weaving – except to sleep – a terrible blackness would fall on her.'

'This sounds very gloomy, Mini,' commented my sister.

'It was all the fault of the evil wizard holding her prisoner,' I explained. 'He wanted her all to himself. He didn't want to share her with anyone. And he sold the things she made for lots of money so that he could bring her beautiful gowns and sparkling crowns.'

'You've stopped working,' Jenna pointed out.

Hastily, I began to plait the reeds again. 'And the girl grew into a beautiful woman with amazing skills. Everything she wove became a masterpiece. Kings and queens from around the world bought her creations and placed them in their palaces for everyone to admire.' I glanced down, hoping that, by some miracle, my own weaving would now be sublime. 'Hmm.'

Jenna smiled. 'I don't think it's working.'

'I'm just not good at this. I'm never going to be as good as you.' Then I brightened as a new idea struck me. 'I'd be much better at *selling* them. Think, Jenna – how amazing would it be if we could have our own stall at the market, instead of getting someone else to sell for us? You could make the goods and I could sell them!' I raised my voice in an imitation of the stallholders'. 'Fine quality baskets! The neatest mats in Talas! All hand made and unique! Orders taken!'

Jenna laughed. 'You *would* be good at that,' she agreed.

'I'd love it,' I said enthusiastically. 'We could sell them at decent prices, and keep the profits – and we could choose when to work too! Just think – maybe important people would order from us, and we'd become known as the best in the area! Just like the girl in the tower! Well, *you'd* be the best,' I conceded, 'but I'd handle the deals. I know just how I'd do it too. I'd name a price, and then the customer would look like *this*' – I made a disapproving face – 'and he'd say, "That's too much," and offer me a much lower price. And I'd make *this* noise' – I sucked in air through my teeth – 'and say that we were really far too busy to take on any new work right now, and—'

'Stop, Mini.' Jenna was laughing, though, her face even prettier than usual, lit up by a smile. 'You're dreaming again!'

'I can't help it,' I said with a sigh. 'I just want things to be different. Maybe not go back to the way they were before the Kwana, because everyone says the country was unstable then, but I can't help longing for change. Don't you dream of it too?'

The light in my sister's eyes faded and she looked serious again. 'No,' she said quietly. 'I don't. All I dream is for everyone to be safe, and for us to be happy with what we have.'

I stared at her. 'Really? Honestly, in your heart of hearts, you don't want things to be different?'

Jenna took a breath. 'Don't you think it's better to be content with the world rather than rail against it all the time? I mean, I know things aren't perfect, but how can you go through life wishing for something you don't have? How can you be happy that way?'

I was baffled. Jenna was my sister and my closest friend. I loved her like no one else, but I didn't understand her mind at all. How could she dismiss the desire to have a better life so easily?

She reached out and clasped my hand. 'I just want you to be happy, Mini,' she said with a smile. 'I just want everyone to be happy.'

The sun was fully down before we stopped weaving. Long before then, my fingers had started to bleed from tiny cuts caused by the sharp edges of the reeds, but I bit my lip and said nothing about it. It was my own fault for not being more skilful, and it was something I was used to. Jenna, despite her skill, also suffered from the hairline cuts, and we were both glad when Mamie came out to tell us that tea was ready. We washed our hands and rubbed them with oil, to help the cuts to heal, before we went inside.

Vivie had spent the day buying food and supplies with Mamie, and she had also helped to prepare the tea. 'Here you are,' she said to Potta, handing him a cup. He smiled at her and I felt mildly irritated. Vivie was the youngest, and Potta and Mamie still treated her like a baby sometimes. She got the nicest treats and was hardly ever scolded for speaking out.

Ruman was back from school and was already sitting on the floor next to Potta. There was soup and rice and bread, but we had to wait until Potta and Ruman had served themselves before we girls were allowed to eat. This was traditional, even before the Kwana took charge, so I hardly noticed it.

Potta was looking puzzled at something Ruman had said. 'I don't see why Ranami would want this,' Potta said, shaking his head. 'It makes no sense. We have never needed to be identified in this way before – why now?'

Ruman shrugged. 'My teacher said it was to teach us all that different backgrounds made no difference in our society, and that it would show us that we were already superior to our invaders, who squabble amongst themselves and yet seek to purify the world.' He frowned. 'But he didn't sound convinced when he said it. He sounded worried.'

'What's going on?' I asked, forgetting my place as usual.

Potta frowned at me. 'Have you been asked to speak, Amina?'

'No,' I muttered.

'We should explain to the girls,' Mamie offered. 'Tell them, Ruman.'

My brother's chest expanded with pride at being able to tell us something we didn't know. 'At school today,' he began, knowing how this phrase annoyed me because I couldn't attend, 'we were told that from next week, every family must display the letter of its heritage. Letters will be allocated by officers and local leaders, who will instruct each member to display the letter on his or her chest.'

Jenna and I exchanged glances, and I was relieved to see that she looked as confused as I felt. Letters of heritage? What were they? Visions of 'Dear Sir . . .' rose before my eyes.

Ruman had obviously noticed our expressions. 'Don't you know what letters of heritage are?' he asked smugly.

'No,' I said, unable to stop myself adding, 'and I bet you didn't either before today.'

'Amina!' snapped Mamie. 'Do not insult your brother!'

I lowered my gaze, my cheeks scarlet. I didn't *mean* to get into trouble; my tongue just ran away with me.

'A letter of heritage,' said Potta, 'is a badge with a letter of the alphabet on it. It indicates your genetic heritage – your family history. Over the years, the letter may change as your family merges with another. It's an ancient way of tracing a family, but no one has really used the letters in a practical way for decades.'

'What letter are we?' asked Vivie, and no one told her off for speaking without permission.

'We are letter H,' said Potta. His eyes flicked momentarily to Mamie. 'We are *all* letter H. It is a noble and traditional family letter, going back many centuries.'

I didn't really understand. What did the letter actually *mean*? What *was* our family background? Some other children had grandparents living with them still, but ours had died a long time ago. I couldn't remember them – what had they been like?

But I knew better than to ask any more that evening. Instead, I ate hungrily, my mind racing, and as I reached for the bread, I saw a glance pass from Potta to Mamie again. There was something in it that I didn't understand – a curious intensity. As though an invisible secret was travelling between them.

As I lay between Jenna and Vivie that night, I

wondered about the meaning of that look. It was the sort of look Potta sometimes gave Mamie when we asked about the soldiers or questioned our leaders. It was a look that said they knew more than we did.

I wondered what it could be.

# 3

A week later, we received our badges, and Jenna and I painstakingly sewed them onto our shirts. 'Letter H is a good letter, Potta said so,' I said, admiring my blue and yellow badge. 'I wonder which letters are not so good and why. And how will we know?'

Whenever we went out, we saw badges of all colours and letters. Some, like ours, were yellow and blue; others were red and blue or orange and green. At first we pointed the different colours out to each other with some excitement, but then the novelty wore off and I began to notice other differences.

'Fs are scruffy,' I whispered to Jenna one day. 'They always look like beggars, and their children have runny noses and flies in their eyes.'

'You can't say that,' Jenna argued. 'We've only seen two families with the letter F.'

'Yes, and they both looked scruffy,' I persisted. 'And they lived at the scruffy end of the street.'

Next door to us lived the Strame family. Their children were all younger than us, the oldest being only five. Their letter was H too, which made me feel kindly towards them. 'It's nice when you see other people wearing the same letter as you,' I commented to Mamie one day. 'It's like they suddenly become friends; you feel like you can trust them.'

Mamie frowned. 'A badge can't tell you that kind of thing about a person,' she said. 'You shouldn't go so much by outward appearances, Amina. Haven't we always taught you that it's what's on the inside that matters?'

'Yes,' I said reluctantly. 'But surely these letters are sort of a help in identifying the people who are from the same background?'

'Why is that a help?' Mamie turned to look at me. She and I were on our way to visit a family who lived a few streets away. Mamie was friendly with the mother and liked to take round tea and bread sometimes. Normally she took Vivie with her, but Jenna was teaching Vivie how to weave a square mat, and Mamie had said she should stay and work. Vivie had been most annoyed that I'd usurped her place. 'The world is made up of lots of different sorts of people, Amina. If we only valued the ones who were like ourselves, it would be a sorry kind of place.'

'Mmm,' I said, not at all sure she was right. I would be quite happy not to share the world with people like the Kwana!

The Masih family had lived in this particular street for a long time. There was a mother, father, aunt, grandmother and five children, all squashed into a house smaller than our own. I liked visiting them, though, because the children knew many songs and rhymes and the whole family loved to sing. Of course, they had to be careful not to make too much noise in case the Kwana accused them of disturbing the peace.

As their house came into view, Mamie caught her breath. Daubed on the outside wall in black paint was an enormous letter Q.

I was astonished. 'Why's that there? Are they letter Q? Why would it be written on their house?'

Mamie was shaking her head. I saw her glance up and down the street, as though checking to see who was around, before she knocked on the door.

It was opened quickly by Noori, the eldest girl. I was pleased to see her because back at school we had been friends; now she had a horrible job collecting rubbish in Gharsad, so I hardly ever saw her. 'Hello, Noori!' I said in delight. 'I thought you'd be out.'

Noori ushered us in, glancing up and down the street just as Mamie had done. 'I don't work any more.'

'Why not?'

'I'm not allowed.'

I was about to ask why, but Mamie was busy greeting Noori's mother, aunt and grandmother, and I was distracted by Noori's twin brothers, who were only a year old and learning to walk. Laughing at their efforts, I only just heard Noori's mother say to mine: 'You shouldn't have come. It's not safe any more.' But then she caught me looking over, and told us all to go out the back and play. I started to tell a story to Noori's brothers, but they kept trying to climb on me and I laughed so much that I couldn't finish the tale. Before I knew it, it was time to leave.

On the way home I remembered what Noori's mother had said and asked Mamie why it wouldn't be safe to visit them.

Mamie's face was tight with anger. 'The letters,' she said sharply.

'Letter Q? Is that bad?'

'Some people think so,' Mamie replied. Then she pressed her lips together and wouldn't say any more.

She wouldn't explain even when we got home. 'You're back early,' Jenna said, surprised.

'We didn't stay long,' I said, 'but I don't know why. There was a big letter Q on the wall of their house, and Noori said she's not allowed out any more – not even to the shops.'

'What? Why?'

'Mamie won't tell me,' I said resentfully, flicking a glance at her. 'But Noori's mum said it wasn't safe to visit any more, so I think letter Q must mean something really bad.' I felt a pang. Noori was a friend – although not one I saw very often – and I didn't like to think of her in trouble. And her two little brothers were so sweet, falling over each other and everyone else in their eagerness to walk.

'Bad like what?' asked Vivie, all agog. She'd obviously forgiven me for stealing Mamie away from her earlier.

Mamie, preparing dough for the evening meal, put

a pan down with such a bang that it startled us. Eyes blazing, she turned to us. 'Now you listen to me,' she said, her face close to ours; her breath rasping our cheeks. 'The letters mean *nothing*, you hear me? I don't like them. They will divide us. No good can come of comparing yourselves to others like this. And never – *never* – believe that you are better people because you wear a certain letter of the alphabet. You might as well try to label people by the length of their fingernails or their preference for rice over bread. I will not have my children believing such rubbish. Do you understand me?'

'Yes, Mamie,' we said, shocked by her tirade. But what shocked me more was the look in her eye. Mamie was angry, yes; but more than that – Mamie was afraid. And she made no reference to the letter Q and what it might mean.

A week later, Ruman came home from school with a black eye. 'An A punched me,' he told us that night. 'Called me a filthy H.'

Vivie was outraged on his behalf. 'You should tell someone!' she said. 'He shouldn't be allowed to get away with that.'

'His father is in the Kwana,' Ruman said. 'No one will stand up to him. Even the teachers are afraid of him.' His face darkened. 'In lessons, we're ranked by letter now. It doesn't matter that I might be cleverer than another boy: if his letter is better than mine, he gets a higher mark. It's pathetic.'

Mamie opened her mouth to speak, but a look from Potta silenced her. I wondered if she was again going to tell us that no one was better than anyone else. Whatever she felt, it didn't seem to be what other people thought.

'If things go on like this,' said Ruman, his tone becoming bitter, 'then I stand no chance of reaching university. My teacher says that soon only certain letters will be allowed to study.' He glanced at me. 'Look at how they banned girls from school. That was only the beginning.'

I felt touched that he cared about my education. I missed school so much – I would have given anything to have the lessons he had!

Ruman had sunk into a sigh, one hand gingerly stroking his injured eye. I raised my hand. 'Yes, Amina?' said Potta. His expression was anxious.

'When can we expect to be liberated?' I asked.

'I mean, the soldiers arrived ages ago, and everyone says there's fighting in Bremir. If we all refused to wear these silly badges, the Kwana couldn't make us, could they?'

'It is not as simple as that,' Potta replied. 'Things do not change overnight. The soldiers are not *here* in our village. And although there are rumours of fighting, no one really knows what's happening.'

'Why not?' I asked. 'What about the radio? Aren't people reporting what's going on?'

'The news is tightly controlled,' Potta said. 'Yes, there is radio, but the official stations are only saying that Ranami is our great and glorious leader and that he will squash the invaders like ants. The same in the newspapers. You don't understand how difficult it is to get reliable information.'

'Can't you ask—' I began, but Potta interrupted.

'It's too dangerous, Amina. I can't be seen to question the leadership. In Gharsad, the Kwana are everywhere – they're actively recruiting more members. And they have spies too. There was a young science professor at the university who started to ask questions. He's disappeared – no one knows what's happened to him.'

'Don't frighten them,' said Mamie abruptly.

'I can't pretend everything is fine,' Potta argued. 'I have a job; I have responsibilities. What would happen to all of you if I were arrested for making trouble? All I can do is keep my head down.'

He sounded just like Jenna! I knew he was worried, but it was so frustrating. Wasn't it worth a bit of risk to find out what was going on? I saw Ruman frowning too. 'I hope the soldiers are trying to assassinate Ranami,' he said. 'Only once he is dead will we be free.'

There was a collective gasp from the rest of us. 'You must not speak those thoughts out loud,' Potta said in a shaking voice. He had gone pale. 'Promise me, Ruman.' He went over and took my brother by the shoulders. 'Promise me you will keep those thoughts locked inside your head.'

Ruman snorted. 'We're inside our house, Potta. Who do you imagine will hear me?'

Potta shook him – once, twice. 'You are a fool,' he said fiercely. 'Did you not hear me say the Kwana have spies everywhere?'

For a moment I thought Potta was accusing one of us of spying for the Kwana! But his eyes went to the door. Did he think there was someone outside, listening? Just standing in the street with their ear pressed to the crack? Surely Potta was exaggerating.

I could tell that Ruman thought the same by the way his lips pressed together disbelievingly. But he didn't argue back, which was a relief. Much though I identified with my brother's rebellious spirit, I didn't want to see a yelling match between him and my father. Inside, I felt a trembling fear. Things seemed to be disintegrating around us, piece by tiny piece.

'I shall make some more tea,' said Mamie into the awkward pause.

That night, as Vivie and Jenna breathed softly and deeply and Ruman mumbled in his sleep, I heard Mamie and Potta whispering.

'. . . nothing to be done now,' Potta said. 'We agreed.'

'Yes' – Mamie sounded tearful – 'but that was before we saw the effects on the children.'

'Even more reason,' Potta said urgently. 'Do you want to put them in danger?'

'No, of course not!'

'Then there is nothing else to be done. We decided

our course, my Mia. I still believe it to be the safest one – for all of us.'

I heard Mamie sigh, and there was a pause, followed by some faint kissing noises. I screwed up my nose.

Ruman stirred and turned over, bumping his elbow on the floor. His eyes jerked open and his gaze met mine. I wanted to say I understood how he felt, and that if I were a boy, I'd be standing up to everything too. But I didn't dare speak in case Mamie and Potta heard me. So instead I gave Ruman a smile that I hoped conveyed the right feeling. His expression was unchanged for a moment, but then he smiled back. His hand snaked across the floor towards me and we linked fingers for a moment. Solidarity in the silence.

Then he withdrew his hand and turned over. I stared at his back and thought about what Mamie and Potta had said.

What had they decided to do? And why might we otherwise be in danger?

# 4

The next Thursday, Jenna and I took our latest creations to market. Ruman was at school, Potta at work, and Mamie was teaching Vivie how to make vegetable dyes. Vivie was keen to dye some reeds so that she could make multi-coloured baskets. Mamie did not believe the reeds would 'take' the dye properly, but she humoured Vivie.

Jenna and I were carrying six baskets and ten mats between us. Jenna was the expert when it came to balancing them on her head; I was forever forgetting to keep my head up, and consequently we had to stop three times on the way for me to pick up the items I had dropped.

Jenna sighed impatiently. 'Mini, you ought to know how to do this by now. If you keep dropping them, they'll get dusty and dirty and we'll never be able to get a good price.'

'I know, I know,' I said irritably. She said this to me every time we took baskets to market. 'I don't do it on purpose, you know. I was thinking of a new story.'

'You and your stories! Can't you just think about what you're doing?'

'That's so dull,' I argued. 'And I can't stop myself imagining. Ideas come to me all the time, just flying out of nowhere.'

'Your ideas get you into trouble,' said Jenna, though her voice was kind. 'Honestly, Mini, don't you remember what Mamie said? Stories aren't important. Having enough to eat; keeping safe – those are the important things.'

The load on my head wobbled and I was prevented from replying as I tried to stop the baskets toppling again to the ground. I didn't know how to explain anyway. I could no more stop myself imagining than I could prevent the sun burning my skin.

As we drew closer to the market, Jenna frowned. 'Something's different.'

I gazed around. The street, as usual, was packed with stalls and people. Brightly coloured canvas marked out one stall from another, and the scent of food and spices was in the air. Everything looked the same and smelled the same. But Jenna was right – there *was* a difference. Usually, people shouted and grinned at each other cheerfully. Market days were an opportunity to chat; exchange gossip; catch up with acquaintances and the latest news. Women took the chance to move around more freely as they did the shopping, and wives helped their husbands on the stalls. Today, however, there seemed to be less noise than usual. People were still buying goods, but they didn't smile so easily. Their eyes shifted from side to side, and often flicked to the badges on other people's chests. As we passed a sweet stall, its tabletop spread with the usual honeyed treats, the stallholder, Partan, glanced at our badges and immediately turned aside, pretending to busy himself with a box of candies. I had raised one hand to wave at him – he knew us well – but my hand stayed arrested in mid-air. I found myself feeling embarrassed for an unknown reason.

'It's quieter,' I said to Jenna under my breath. 'And nobody is smiling. Did you just see—'

'Yes,' she interrupted. Her forehead creased in anxiety. 'Maybe they're expecting trouble.'

'Trouble? What kind of trouble?'

'*I don't know, Mini!*' Jenna snapped, startling me. 'But I think we'd better sell our things quickly and go home. I don't like it here today.'

We threaded our way through the unsmiling stall-holders. Was it my imagination, or were there fewer women out and about today too? Certainly, I didn't see the baker's wife or Piralla, who helped her brother on the shoe stall. The men and boys conversed in low tones, their eyes darting suspiciously sideways whenever anyone passed them. Unconsciously I moved closer to Jenna, almost tripping on her heels. She let out a hiss as my foot caught her ankle. 'Sorry,' I whispered. But the eerie atmosphere had disturbed me so much I kicked her twice more before we reached our usual trader.

Davir and Lakma had bought our baskets for the past three years. They sold all sorts of household items: rugs, lamps, pans, matches, oil and suchlike, and to begin with they had taken a few of Jenna's baskets as a favour to Potta. The baskets had sold so well that Davir had asked for more, and so Jenna and I had been able to contribute to the family's earnings quite substantially over the past couple of years. Both of us felt proud that Mamie could buy better quality goods because of our hard work. We weren't allowed to sell the baskets and mats ourselves, of course, but Davir had always given us a fair price. Jenna and I were very fond of his wife, Lakma, who had a smile that lit up the whole market and showed her pronounced dimples. But Lakma was nowhere to be seen today, so Jenna was forced to address Davir, who was tall and slightly stern.

'Sir,' began Jenna in the traditional way, though I heard a tremor in her voice, 'my sister and I have brought our latest offerings in the hope that they will please.'

I wanted to ask where Lakma was but didn't dare. Davir had always been pleasant to us, but he wasn't a friendly sort of person in the way that his wife was.

Davir seemed even taller and sterner than usual. He was frowning. A large green and yellow M was fixed to his shirt. Jenna began to unload the baskets from her head, but Davir suddenly spoke. 'I am sorry,' he said, rather more loudly than was necessary, 'but these goods are of inferior quality.'

I saw Jenna's jaw drop and felt mine do the same. 'In-inferior quality?' she stammered, confused. 'But they are the same as the ones we brought you last week.'

'They are not the same,' said Davir, fingering the rim of one basket and carelessly tossing it aside. 'These are less well made.'

Less well made? What was he talking about? I felt baffled – it was as though he hardly knew us, and yet we'd been visiting the market every Thursday for the past three years! If anything, the baskets we had today were even better than the ones we'd brought last week, since Jenna had perfected a new weaving technique and had made two really beautiful square baskets with lids. We'd both hoped that Davir would offer more money for such obviously high-quality and unique items.

'But—' said Jenna.

'I will pay you two per basket and one per mat,' said Davir loudly.

I gasped. 'Two and one?' cried Jenna, and her voice was high with shock. 'But we usually get eight and three!'

Davir shrugged. 'Demand has fallen,' he said. 'And, as I said, these are inferior.'

He was wrong – he was completely wrong. Why

was he lying like this? I glanced from side to side, shamed by the curious and contemptuous looks of the other stallholders and customers. Again, I couldn't see any women, and being surrounded by men made me nervous.

'Please,' said Jenna, and something in me twisted to hear my sister beg, 'please – can't you at least make it four and two?'

'Two and one,' snapped Davir. 'And that's my final price. You'll take it if you know what's good for you.' His eyes flicked to the badge on my chest, and I felt a white-hot anger. This was because of the letter we wore! Suddenly it was so obvious!

'That's not fair,' I said in a low voice.

Jenna shot me a look as she bent to pick up the basket Davir had tossed aside. 'Shut up, Amina. We will take the money. What else can we do?'

I was seized with a sudden rebellion. 'Sell them somewhere else,' I said without pausing to think. 'Not everyone will have a problem with our letter.'

'Somewhere else?' Jenna's voice was almost a squeak. 'What are you talking about? We don't know anyone else!'

What she meant was we hadn't been properly

48

introduced to another home-goods trader. And since we were girls, it wasn't really done for us to introduce ourselves.

Davir was looking down at us as we scrabbled to place our baskets back on our heads. I wanted to make a rude remark about his letter, but I held my tongue. You never knew who might be listening, and I hadn't forgotten Jenna's words the other day about how she might be beaten for my bad behaviour. Instead, I drew myself up and met his gaze, trying not to look nervous. 'Thank you for your offer,' I said politely, 'but today we will trade elsewhere.'

His lip curled but I didn't wait for an answer, turning aside and setting off down the street. Jenna hurried after me. 'Mini, think for a moment! We can't just go up to people. I know what Davir offered was unfair—'

'Unfair?' I interrupted. 'It was laughable! How dare he treat us like that?'

Jenna's eyes were wet with worried tears. 'But maybe it's just a temporary thing. Next week he might go back to offering us a good price. We should take what he offers, Mini.'

'No,' I said, grabbing her arm as she turned to go

back. 'No, Jenna, we shouldn't. He can't do that kind of thing. You *know* your baskets are the best in the market. Someone else will offer us a better price.' I hoped I sounded confident. Inside, I wasn't at all sure that I was doing the right thing, but anger made me stubborn.

'How,' asked Jenna plaintively, 'without Potta here to make the right introductions?'

'We'll have to do the best we can,' I said. My whole body felt taut with apprehension. What I was suggesting was strictly against the rules, but I would do it anyway. I marched along the row of stalls until I found another one selling home goods. This one had a few reed mats but nothing like the beautifully woven baskets we carried. The trader, his back to us, was unpacking a crate of lamps to set out. 'Excuse me,' I said in a voice almost without a tremble, 'I know I am only a girl and have no right to address you.' The trader turned to look at me. I lowered my gaze and went on. 'My sister and I have some fine-quality goods that we would like to show you.'

The man glanced at Jenna and frowned. 'By the colour of her headscarf, she outranks you,' he said. 'Why are you speaking for her?'

I cursed the stupid Kwana rules that meant we were visibly ranked by age and status. Just by looking at us, anyone could tell that I was thirteen and Jenna fourteen. Vivie, only nine, had an orange scarf, whereas married women wore black. Until we were married, everyone we met would know exactly how old we were. Boys didn't have to put up with this! I could see Jenna open her mouth to reply, and I just knew she was about to apologize for bothering him and to ruin our chances of trading. 'She's a mute,' I said rapidly. My sister's lips closed again, pressed tight in anger. 'She hasn't spoken since the traumatic event three years ago when she witnessed her twin sister being flogged to death.' Jenna's eyes widened at my outright lie, but she was sensible enough to hold her tongue. I was pleased with my quick thinking.

The trader sighed. He had a kindly face and for a brief moment I wondered if he had daughters at home. 'I am sorry for that,' he said, 'but as you can see, I am fully stocked and do not need any more goods.'

'Won't you just look at them?' I said hopefully, holding out a basket that Jenna had made and carefully concealing my own, less impressive effort. 'I can see that you don't have any baskets, and ours are the best in the market.'

The trader shook his head. 'I am sorry.' He turned away. 'I wish you fortune elsewhere.'

I would have tried again, but Jenna tugged at my sleeve and made urgent gestures about leaving, so I sighed and moved on.

'You idiot!' whispered Jenna once we were safely out of sight. 'Why did you say all that about me being a mute?'

'How else could I get round the stupid rules?' I whispered back. 'I thought it was pretty good, considering. If you want me to do the talking, we have to explain why.'

'It didn't work anyway,' said Jenna. 'This is hopeless.'

'Don't give up so easily,' I told her. 'There are at least four more places we can try.'

But as the sun moved across the sky, our luck went from bad to worse. Two of the traders were at least polite to us, but neither would look at our wares. The third ignored us completely, and the fourth actually yelled at us to go away because we were 'putting off' his customers!

It was nearing the time for the midday meal, and Jenna and I would normally have been home by now. Sweating and dusty, we sat down to rest for a few moments. Behind us, plastered across the stone wall of a building, twelve posters of Ranami frowned down, as though disapproving of our existence.

'I can't understand it,' I said. 'This used to be a really friendly place, everyone smiling and chatting to each other. Now no one meets your eye and hardly anyone smiles. And where are all the women?'

'Maybe that's why everyone's less friendly,' said Jenna perceptively. 'Because there aren't so many women.'

I considered this. 'That could be true. The women are usually the first to smile. I wonder where they all are?'

'Maybe they've been told to stay at home,' said Jenna. She gazed uneasily at the stalls across the street. 'Maybe we should have stayed at home too. Maybe everyone knows something we don't.'

'Potta would have told us,' I objected. 'He wouldn't have let us come if there were rumours of trouble.'

'Potta works in Gharsad,' said my sister with a

shrug. 'Not here in Talas. And maybe – maybe it's only this morning that bad news has come. Oh, I don't know, Amina! It's all maybes and possiblies.' She got to her feet. 'I don't want to stay here any longer – it doesn't feel safe. I think we should go home.'

'What about our things?' I felt guilty. 'I'm sorry, Jenna. I honestly thought we'd be able to sell the baskets elsewhere. I know mine aren't anything special, but the ones you make are the best in the market. Maybe you were right – we should have taken Davir's offer.' My stomach rumbled.

My sister looked at me for a moment, hesitating. 'We could go back to him. Apologize and see if he'll still pay us.'

I met her gaze and knew how much she hated the idea – just as much as I did. 'Do we have to?'

'No,' said Jenna, 'but if we don't, we'll have to take everything home again and tell Mamie what happened.'

I got to my feet. 'No, we need the money – anything we can get. You're right. And then we can get out of here.' A stallholder close by was staring at us, and his open hostility made me even more eager to leave. Was his piercing stare for the badges on our shirts or because we were female? He leaned towards a customer and exchanged a few words, and then the customer turned to stare at us too. Only it wasn't a customer, it was the trader we'd first spoken to, who had believed my story about Jenna being a mute. Had he seen us talking together? We had better move along before I got us into any more trouble. I hoisted my baskets onto my head, my face burning with embarrassment.

As soon as Davir saw us coming, in our dusty state and with our baskets and mats starting to droop in the heat, the corner of his mouth turned up in a sneer. 'Not so easy after all, then?' he said.

'No,' said Jenna humbly. 'I am only a foolish girl, but—'

'That you are,' Davir broke in rudely. 'A pair of foolish girls. And I suppose you have come back to beg?'

I bit my tongue and kept my eyes down.

'Yes,' said Jenna in a small voice. 'We were headstrong and foolish and we hope you can take pity on us.'

There was a slight pause. Daring to glance

upwards, I saw, to my surprise, that Lakma was now behind the stall too, although standing well back from her husband. Her eyes met mine for a split second, then she looked quickly away. I was struck by the anxious expression on her face. Was she nervous for herself or for us? Where had she been all morning, and why had she now appeared? But my wonderings were swept away by Davir's next words.

'I will give you six for the lot,' he said smoothly.

For a moment I thought I hadn't heard him correctly. He couldn't have said six. That would be ridiculous! He must be joking, mustn't he?

My sister put out a hand to steady the baskets on her head, which had given an almighty wobble. 'For . . . the lot?' she said faintly. 'For *all* the baskets and mats? *Six?*'

'Six,' repeated Davir. 'And that is generous, given the state of your goods now they have been dragged around the market.' As Jenna hesitated, he spoke again. 'The longer you wait, the lower the price.'

I was in an agony of frustration. Only biting as hard as possible on my lip prevented me from bursting out with the unfairness of it all. How dare he treat us like this!

'All right, all right!' said Jenna, and I could tell she was close to tears. 'Take them.'

I could hardly bear to look at Davir as we unloaded our baskets and mats. He passed them back to Lakma, who began stacking them on the shelves. How could she stand by and watch her husband behave like this? 'Lakma,' I whispered, but she shook her head so fiercely that I didn't dare say anything more.

Jenna's face was wet by the time Davir handed over the six coins, not even bothering to look at us. A customer had arrived, and we were brushed aside as though we were sandflies.

'Six!' said Jenna in despair as we headed away from the market. I took her hand, but she shook me off. 'I can't believe it! Six!'

'He's a heartless wolf,' I said.

'How are we going to survive?' Jenna said, but I knew she wasn't expecting an answer. 'Six!' she kept repeating all the way home.

I didn't know what to think. I'd visited the market every week for most of my life, but it was suddenly an alien place. The rules and traditions, so clear in my head, wavered and broke into shuddering pieces.

It was like seeing a person taken apart and put back together in the wrong way, their arms attached to their knees and their eyes on the back of their head. For an absurd moment I wondered if I had stumbled into a dream. Surely what had just happened couldn't be real?

By the time we were halfway home, I had almost convinced myself that I was still asleep and that none of the morning's happenings existed in reality. Because the alternative was just too frightening and baffling to contemplate.

# 5

Mamie and Vivie were on the porch, trying to dry the dyed reeds without losing the colour. 'Isn't there some way we can fix the colour so it doesn't come out?' I heard Vivie say as we drew nearer.

Mamie's mouth opened to answer, but then she caught sight of us and jumped to her feet. 'Where have you been?'

'We were at market,' said Jenna.

'All this time?' cried Mamie. 'What happened? Was there trouble?'

'Not exactly—' Jenna started to say, but I interrupted her.

'What have you heard, Mamie?' Perhaps if I delayed the telling, it wouldn't be so bad.

She embraced us both, one after the other, and I could feel that her arms were trembling. 'Kwana officials came through the village just after you left. They said that people were causing trouble in the towns – there were fights breaking out. They said that if we knew any family members who had been involved, we were to turn them over. Anyone caught hiding a criminal would be taken away.' Her voice had risen in pitch, and I could hear the strain behind it. 'I'd never have let you go to market today if I'd known. I wanted to come after you but I didn't want to take Vivie in with me.' She let out a shaky breath. 'I am so glad you have come back safely.'

Jenna and I exchanged glances. 'That would explain it,' she said, and I nodded.

'Explain what?' asked Mamie quickly. 'Did you see anything?'

'Not exactly,' I said. 'But the market was . . . different . . . today. It was uncomfortable. And most of the women stayed away.'

'Then what kept you so long?' cried Mamie.

I glanced at Jenna, knowing that she should be the one to tell the story, but wanting to spare her the shame. After all, if I hadn't refused Davir's first offer, we could have brought home a lot more money. 'Davir wouldn't give us a fair price for the goods,' I said quietly before Jenna could speak.

'Why not?'

'He said they were of inferior quality,' said Jenna.

Mamie snorted. 'What rubbish! They are exactly the same quality as the ones we usually take. Not to mention the two new baskets that Jenna worked so beautifully.'

'We tried to show him,' said Jenna hesitantly. 'But he said he would only give us two for the baskets and one for the mats.'

Vivie, who had been watching us with wide eyes, exclaimed, 'But that's not fair!'

'I know,' I said. 'I told him so.'

'You told him so?' said Mamie, a sudden expression of fear crossing her face. 'Oh, Amina, were you disrespectful?'

'He was disrespectful first,' I said, scuffing the ground.

'She only wanted to get us a fair price,' Jenna said. 'But Davir wouldn't raise his offer.'

'So you took his money?' said Mamie. 'After all, two and one would still be enough to buy us . . .' I could see her calculating how many meals that would supply, and I couldn't bear it.

'We refused his money,' I said. 'I mean . . . *I* made Jenna refuse. She wanted to take it but I thought it was insulting, so I dragged her away. We tried to sell the baskets and mats to other traders.'

'Other traders?' said Mamie faintly. 'Other traders that you didn't know?'

'It was the only thing we could do,' I said defensively. 'I thought we could get a better price elsewhere . . .' I trailed off.

'But you didn't,' said Mamie, unblinking. 'Did you?'

I shook my head, suddenly speechless.

'But you haven't brought the baskets back with you,' said Mamie. 'So . . . how much did you sell them for in the end?'

There was a pause.

'How much?'

Vivie looked from Jenna to me and then back to Mamie, as if she sensed a storm coming.

'Six,' I said.

'Six for each item?' said Mamie.

'No,' said Jenna. 'Six . . . for everything. Six in total. For the lot.'

There was another pause. 'I see,' said Mamie flatly. Then she turned and went into the house.

'Six for the whole lot?' whispered Vivie. 'Oh, Jenna. That's awful.'

The atmosphere remained strained for the rest of the day. Jenna and I went quietly out onto the back porch with Vivie, to do some more weaving. Who knew if we'd be able to sell these goods in the future? But at least it was something to keep us occupied and stop us just sitting around staring at each other and wondering what else was going to go wrong.

'Do you think Potta is all right?' asked Vivie in a whisper, glancing at the door to make sure Mamie couldn't hear. 'If there is fighting in the towns . . .'

'I'm sure he's fine,' said Jenna. 'He's at the university — there wouldn't be fighting there.'

I wasn't so sure. Hadn't there been student uprisings in the past? And Potta himself had said that students were sometimes the most fiery opponents of government because they were being taught to think for themselves.

'Mamie was so worried about you,' Vivie confided. 'When the Kwana came through, she wanted to set off into market straight away to bring you back. I said I'd go with her but she wouldn't take me. Said I should go next door to the Strames' but I didn't want to.' Her lip wobbled. 'I thought if she went after you, then all of you might not come back and I'd be left on my own.'

'But we did come back,' I said hastily, fearing a tearful outburst from my little sister. 'And we're all fine, see? So there's no need to worry.'

'But Potta's still out there,' said Vivie. 'And Ruman.'

'They're men – they can take care of themselves,' I told her.

Jenna caught my eye but said nothing. Vivie blinked and nodded valiantly, and we all got back to weaving in silence, keeping our thoughts to ourselves.

By the time Potta and Ruman did come home, I had almost convinced myself that they'd both been caught up in violent clashes and arrested. I felt shocked when I heard their voices inside, with Mamie. And after relief at knowing that they were safe came anxiety: what would Potta say when he knew that Jenna and I had sold all our wares for such a pitiful amount of money?

Mamie called us in, and I was glad, for the mat I had been weaving was so uneven it would all have to be unpicked, and my fingers were sliced worse than usual with careless reed cuts. We washed our hands and quietly went into the house.

Ruman and Potta sat together on the floor, their expressions serious. We sat opposite and I tried not to wince as my fingers started to throb.

'Mamie has told me what happened at the market today,' Potta began, and his eyes seemed almost black in their intensity. I didn't dare speak, even though I wanted so much to be able to apologize. 'I don't want you going there again – not for a while, not while everything is so unstable.'

I felt relief mixed with worry, for if we didn't sell our goods, how would we have money to buy food?

'There isn't much confirmed news,' Potta went on, 'but Gharsad is full of rumour and speculation, and the university is rife with it. Yesterday there were riots in Bremir again, and more to the west of the city. Not the big, organized riots that we have seen put down by the Kwana, but spontaneous fighting and looting. People are frustrated and desperate – even more so because the foreign troops are here and do not seem to have achieved much yet. And these letters of heritage do not help. Gangs are forming; vendettas are being carried out against selected letters. The Kwana—'

Mamie took a short breath. 'Potta, that is as much as they need to know.'

He shook his head. 'I cannot have my children running around believing they are safe.'

I almost laughed. Since the Kwana had come to power five years ago, I had never felt safe!

'The Kwana,' Potta said, lifting his head to look at us all, 'are coming down hard on anyone involved in rioting and looting. Those involved are beaten and shot, sometimes in the streets. The Kwana want to show that they are still in control – and, though it is only my personal opinion, I think this whole situation is playing into their hands. They want the people to be fighting each other, not the government. If ordinary people can't trust their own neighbours, then they can hardly coordinate attacks on the authorities.'

'We had a Kwana official come to school today,' added Ruman. 'He made us all line up, and then he went down the line pointing at our letters and saying

"trouble" to some of us. He – he said "trouble" to me.'
His voice shook slightly.

Potta put a hand on his shoulder. 'I am quite sure
that some of the looters and rioters are letter H,' he
said. 'Though, to be honest, I would be surprised if
any letter was exempt from the trouble.' He looked at
me and Jenna. 'I expect Davir was playing it safe
today, by trying to cheat you. He thought he could
get away with it since you were girls and couldn't
stand up for yourselves.'

'But he'd have known we'd tell you about it,' I
said in a small voice. 'And he respects you, doesn't
he?'

Potta sighed. 'Respect is something that may not
be around for much longer. No one knows who or
what to respect. What could I do in retaliation
anyway?'

I looked down. Something in me twisted painfully
to hear my father speak in such a defeated way. What
had happened to all the hope we had of the foreign
troops?

'Some of us still have respect,' said Ruman suddenly. 'Some of us still feel that the Kwana can be
overthrown, even with all this confusion.'

Mamie looked alarmed. 'What do you mean, "some of us"? You are a schoolboy!'

Ruman raised his head, and there was a light blazing in his eyes. 'I am fifteen, Mamie, not a child any more. And I can see that the people must work *together* if we are to effect any change in this country.'

I found myself nodding my head in agreement. Of course Ruman was right! It was what Mamie had been saying all along – the letters just made us question each other. They made us see the differences instead of the similarities! And how could people see the bigger picture when they were distracted by details?

Potta threw a nervous glance towards the front door. 'This is dangerous talk, Ruman, as it always was.'

'Someone has to take charge,' said Ruman fiercely. 'The people are acting like sheep, just as the Kwana hoped! Following each other around, fighting amongst themselves, instead of mobilizing against those who cause our suffering! We should be tearing off these stupid badges and uniting with our countrymen!'

My hand went impulsively to the badge on my

shirt and clenched it. Ruman sounded so passionate!

'Who gave you that idea?' asked Potta sharply.

'My teacher says it's obvious,' said Ruman. 'He says that it will take a few brave individuals to lead the way out of confusion.'

'Then your teacher is a fool!' Potta snapped. 'Haven't you heard a word I've been saying about the way the Kwana are dealing with the rebels?'

'At least they're *doing* something and not just sitting at home waiting to be rescued!' cried Ruman, eyes flashing. 'Their sacrifice will be remembered in years to come. They are martyrs to the revolution and they will be honoured!'

Potta was growing pale. 'Sacrifice? Martyrs? Are you mad?'

'Father . . .' Ruman's voice took on a pleading tone. 'Why have the gods given us tongues and brains if not to use them? Too long we have suffered under the leaders. Too long we have kept quiet. It is time to take back what is rightfully ours – our country, our lives! And we have a duty to stand up and be counted!'

'Duty? *Duty?*' Potta spat on the floor. 'You don't even know the meaning of the word! Our *duty* is to weather the storm. Look around you – this isn't just about you. You have sisters; a mother. They can't join the revolution. We have responsibilities.'

I wanted to say, *Yes! I can join the revolution! I would be happy to stand up and be counted!* My heart beat faster and my skin prickled as though a storm were coming.

Ruman's gaze swept over us. 'Every person must do as they see fit. That's what my teacher says. And those who don't stand up to be counted, well . . .' Somehow I knew what he was going to say, and my stomach clenched in anticipation. 'They are cowards,' he said with finality.

There was an icy pause and then Potta exploded. I jumped in shock. 'Get out! You are a danger to yourself and to your family! I will not have you under my roof with your insults! Get out!'

Ruman gave our father such a look that I quailed. Then he turned on his heel and walked out.

The rest of us hardly dared breathe.

# 6

I wasn't at all sure that Ruman would come back that night. Until today I could never have imagined that Ruman – our very own brother – would openly accuse our father of being a coward. It was practically the worst insult he could have come up with. And yet I felt I understood what he meant. Potta was keeping his head down, as he always had done, and my brother was frustrated. Still, I knew I would never have dared to accuse Potta to his face. Something in me was strangely thrilled by the confrontation, but at the same time I was aware of a deep sense of fear. And I knew that Jenna and Vivie were also frightened. Vivie stuck close to Mamie for the rest of the evening, so much so that Mamie tripped over her more than once as she got in the way. And Jenna was pale and looked at the floor, hardly seeming to hear anything anyone said.

Supper was a silent meal, and Potta's expression was blank as he ate. I shot glances at him occasionally, but the look on his face deterred me from saying anything. My normal tendency to chatter dried up entirely and I found it hard to swallow my rice.

When, an hour after sundown, Vivie suddenly burst into silent tears, Mamie sent us all to bed. Jenna, Vivie and I huddled together, even though the night was a warm one, rocking and stroking each other in an attempt to soothe our feelings.

Ruman did not return.

I did not expect to sleep that night, but somehow I found myself waking up at the usual time. For a moment I could not tell what was different – then I looked across the room to see Ruman's empty mat and it all came flooding back.

Potta, despite Mamie's attempts to make him stay at home, went to work as usual. Mamie at first told us that we should stay inside, but Jenna, Vivie and I soon bickered so much that she sent us out to the back porch to weave. However, within an hour we had run out of reeds, so that left us nothing to do again. 'We could go and get some more,' I suggested.

Jenna leaped at the suggestion. 'Yes, Mamie – it's not through the village, after all. We couldn't come to any harm out in the reed beds, could we?'

Mamie frowned. 'I don't like it. I don't want to let you out of my sight.'

'But Mamie, you said you wanted to visit Noori and her family,' I argued. 'And you said you didn't want us to come there either.'

'Certainly not,' said Mamie sharply.

'Well, if you're going to be out, then we might as well be too,' I said. Being cooped up with nothing to do was going to drive me mad. 'And we'll probably be back before you are.'

'We promise to stay out of trouble,' said Jenna. 'And we'll come straight home if anything happens.'

Mamie hesitated, and I saw her gaze move to Vivie. For a moment I felt a pang of annoyance. Vivie was nine years old; she wasn't a baby. Mamie had never worried about me or Jenna at that age. 'We'll look after her,' I said quickly.

Mamie sighed. 'All right. I suppose we have to continue as best we can for the moment – and after all, despite all these rumours, we haven't seen any fighting around here ourselves, have we? Nor have our neighbours. And I do want to visit Noori's family. But just promise me you'll stick together – and for goodness' sake, keep your wits about you. Don't stay out longer than you need – just go there and back.'

We all nodded. Mamie tied her headscarf even more tightly, and checked ours too before we set off in our different directions – her into town and us out on the dusty road towards the reed beds.

'Thank the gods!' I exclaimed when we were clear of the final houses of Talas and the endless posters of the stern-looking Ranami. 'I couldn't wait to get out of there!'

Jenna looked around but there was no one else in sight at the moment. 'Our house has never felt like a prison before,' she admitted. 'I hope Potta will come back with better news today.'

'And maybe Ruman will come back too,' I said hopefully. 'And he and Potta will make up.'

Vivie made a snorting sound. 'He was very rude to Potta.'

'He shouldn't have called Potta a coward,' I agreed, 'but I think he was right about the letters and about standing up to the Kwana.'

Jenna exclaimed, 'You would say that!'

'Yes,' added Vivie, 'you always want to make trouble, Mini.'

'I do not!' I said, stung. 'I just wish people would think for themselves more often, that's all. I hate all this "doing what everyone else does" stuff.'

'And that is why you will never get a good husband,' said Vivie unexpectedly.

I stopped dead and stared at her. 'A good husband? What are you talking about? What business is it of yours?'

Vivie shrugged. 'I heard Mamie talking to Cora Strame the other day. Cora said that it would soon be time for Jenna to marry, and then she said, "What will you do about Amina?" and Mamie sighed and said she didn't know because men usually wanted an obedient wife and she didn't think you'd be one.'

My jaw dropped in astonishment. *An obedient wife?* Jenna let out a little chuckle and I felt my cheeks heat up in response. I knew that I was only three years away from being old enough to marry, but Potta and Mamie had never said anything about it before, and I hadn't given the matter much thought.

Something in me felt quite hurt that no one would want to marry me. But on the other hand – I couldn't imagine being married at all! 'I don't want to be an obedient wife,' I said hotly. 'Being told what to do all day? No thank you!'

'Yes, because you have so much freedom at the moment,' said Jenna with an amused edge to her tone. 'You're always saying how nice it is to be able to do what you want.'

Despite myself, I laughed. She was right, of course. 'At least we got out of the house today,' I said, my good humour returning. 'That's something.'

But my smile faded when we reached the reed beds. The reeds, normally tall and stiff, were limp and drooping, their fleshy leaves blackened and withered. Vivie reached out a hand, wonderingly.

'Don't touch them!' I said sharply.

She withdrew her hand in shock. 'Why, what's happened to them?'

I shook my head. 'I don't know. But you might catch something.'

'Is it a disease?' wondered Jenna, her gaze sweeping the beds in dismay. 'Or blackfly?'

'Blackfly doesn't look like this,' I said. 'And

they've never had a disease before. Maybe they've been poisoned.'

Vivie's eyes widened. 'Poisoned? What do you mean? How could you poison a whole reed bed?'

I'd thrown out the word without really thinking, but as soon as I said it, a horrible idea occurred to me. 'What if it's not the reeds themselves that are poisoned?' I said, and swallowed.

'But you just said . . .'

'What if it's the water underneath?'

'The reeds get their water from the ground,' said Jenna. 'You can't poison the ground.'

'No,' I said, my brain racing ahead, 'but you can poison the well that shares water with the ground.'

Jenna's mouth dropped open. 'You mean . . . someone did it on purpose?' Her voice was a whisper. 'Amina, surely no one would . . .'

'There's one way to find out,' I said. 'Let's go and have a look.'

But we couldn't even get close to the well. Someone had attached streamers to pegs and roped it off. There was a sign attached to one of the pegs, and even Vivie could understand its meaning. We stood and stared.

'Where will people get their water now?' asked Jenna eventually.

'They'll have to go to another well,' I said. 'I suppose the one near us is the closest. We're lucky this hasn't happened to ours.'

Jenna's eyes met mine and I knew what she was thinking. We were lucky this hadn't happened to ours – *yet*.

It wasn't Mamie but Potta who met us on the front step of the house. He looked strangely pale, and a nameless fear clutched my heart. 'Thank the gods, you are back. Come inside.'

'The well was poisoned, so we couldn't get any reeds,' said Vivie.

'Never mind that now.' Mamie was inside, looking as shocked as Potta. 'You must listen – this is very serious.'

'What's happened?' asked Jenna.

'Is it . . . Ruman?' I said, gulping.

'It is Ruman's teacher,' Potta told us. 'The one who was talking about rebellion so openly.'

'Has he been arrested?'

'He is dead,' said Potta shortly.

We gasped. I felt my head spin. 'Dead? How?'

'Potta . . .' said Mamie.

He turned to her. 'They need to know. We cannot hide this from them.' He faced us. 'He was shot in the street by the Kwana this morning. Outside the school.'

A vivid picture of my old school flashed into my mind. It was a long, low building, with an enclosed playground in the front. A teacher was shot there? I couldn't imagine it. 'With-without a trial?' I whispered.

'Without a trial.' Potta met my gaze squarely. 'We are moving into dangerous times.'

'Where is Ruman?' asked Jenna. 'Does he know what happened?'

Potta hesitated.

'You might as well tell them,' said Mamie. 'You've told them everything else.' She sounded bitter.

'We don't know where he is,' said Potta, 'but there are rumours that he has joined some kind of underground rebellion.'

'Underground?' said Vivie, and I saw her eyes flick to the floor.

A whisper of a smile crossed Potta's face. 'Not

under the ground, Vivie. An underground movement is when a group of people meet and plan secretly together. There are groups springing up all over the place now.'

'I've never heard of them,' said Vivie.

Potta smiled properly now. 'Of course not. They're underground.' The smile vanished. 'There have always been people who worked against Ranami in secret. And even though the letters of heritage are confusing the issue, more and more people are joining the rebellion. Especially now that there is fighting between the Kwana and the foreign soldiers in our major cities.'

'Is there?' I asked in surprise. 'How do you know?'

Potta hesitated. 'There was fighting in Gharsad this morning. The university is closed – that's why I came home.'

My jaw dropped even further. Fighting in Gharsad! But that was only a few miles away! 'Then it's happening at last!' I cried. 'Like you said – liberation!' I felt a wild exhilaration sweep through me. Perhaps, by the end of the week . . . they would liberate Talas too!

Potta shook his head vehemently. 'No, no, no, you

don't understand. Just because there is fighting doesn't mean we're being liberated. The Kwana are strong, and they know this country better than the foreign soldiers do. And let's say the Kwana lose Gharsad – well, what about it? It's only one city in a big country. This . . . war . . .' He seemed uncertain over the word. 'You can't expect things to change for a while. Maybe not for months. Maybe years – I don't know. What I'm saying is that this situation could go on for a long time.'

My eyes met Jenna's and I could see my own shock reflected in hers. 'Years?' I said blankly. 'But I thought . . .' All of a sudden I thought I might cry. There was a lump in my throat, and I blinked fiercely. Panic made me bold. 'Then maybe we should join the revolution like Ruman said.' I heard Jenna gasp but I went on stubbornly. 'I mean, wouldn't it be better than sitting around waiting for things to change?'

There was a pause. Potta looked at Mamie. Then it was almost as if someone had let the air out of Potta. He seemed to shrink in on himself.

'Sit down,' said Mamie gently, and there was such tenderness in her voice that I looked at her, surprised.

Potta sat, and so we all sat too. He rubbed the back of his hand over his forehead and looked at us, as though debating something within himself. 'I do share some of your feelings, Amina,' he said quietly. 'I would like to see change. When the Kwana first came to power, I believed they were a force for good – they improved so many things about the country: gave us better hospitals and safer ways to travel. But their grip is too tight – we are being squeezed too far. However, you have to understand that the underground movements are dangerous. Not just because they're run by passionate people who can only see their own viewpoint. They're also dangerous to everyone around them – our leaders will do what they can to put down rebellion, even if that means arresting the families of those involved. Do you understand what I'm saying?'

'But that means . . .' I said slowly.

'Yes.' Potta looked at me. 'That means that if the rumours are true, Ruman may have put us all in immediate danger.'

I gulped, my eyes flicking instinctively to the door. In my head, I could already hear pounding on it, raised voices demanding that we all come out. Surely

Ruman wouldn't join a rebellion if he knew we might all be arrested?

'There's one other thing,' said Mamie, so softly we hardly heard her. 'I didn't want to say, but it can hardly make things worse.' She looked at me. 'Noori and her family have gone.'

'Gone?' I asked. 'Gone where?'

Mamie shrugged. 'I don't know. But their house is empty.'

'Didn't they leave a message?' I said.

'No. Nothing.'

There was a pause. I felt as though my head were filled with heat haze, making it hard to think clearly. Noori, gone? Just like that, with no word? Had they run away? Why? Had they been arrested?

'What are we going to do?' asked Jenna.

Potta was silent for quite a long time, and I felt the trembling fear in my stomach return. Potta *always* knew what to do – why was it taking him so long to tell us? Eventually he said, 'I think the best thing for us to do is remain calm. We have done nothing wrong. We will say that we do not know where Ruman is – which is true. We will say that we had an argument and he ran away. We have no part in this rebellion. I have to believe that justice and good will overcome, eventually.'

He sounded strong and firm, and part of me was reassured. But inside, a tiny voice whispered, *Keep your head down and stay out of trouble? Will that even work any more?*

I no longer felt safe in my house – for the first time in my life. But where could we go? And how could I persuade Potta that we needed to leave?

But by the next day it was too late anyway.

# 7

The officials did not even bother to knock. Instead, they simply pushed open our front door and kicked us as we lay asleep. 'Get up! Family Ambrose, you have some explaining to do.'

It has always taken me a while to return to consciousness, but Potta was on his feet in an instant, and through my groggy state I heard him say, 'What is the meaning of this? How dare you burst in upon my family in this way!'

There was a pause, and in that silence I heard the click of a gun being cocked. My body reacted instinctively, as though I'd been injected with ice. Suddenly I was fully awake.

'We've come to talk to you about your son,' said a voice, and the smooth tone of it made me shiver. I bit my lip, wishing more than anything that I'd spoken up the night before; insisted that we run away while we still had time.

We were herded out into the street, exchanging pale glances with each other. I pulled ineffectively at the hem of my nightgown, wishing it was longer. My knees felt unbearably exposed, and so did my head, uncovered by its headscarf. The streets were empty because it was barely even dawn – a faint sliver of light showed on the horizon. The air was still cool, and I shivered as I stumbled outside. The men were grim and silent, and none too gentle as they pushed us along. But what terrified me most was the look on Mamie's face. I had never seen her so drained of life. Her body sagged and her eyes flicked from one of us to another with a kind of desperation. It was almost as though she were trying to imprint our faces on her memory. That was when I realized that she believed we were all about to die, and the knowledge froze me to the spot.

One of the officials shoved me. 'Move. Over there, with the others.'

Jenna, Vivie, Mamie and I huddled together, flanked by armed men. Vivie clung to Mamie's waist, and Jenna and I gripped hands, standing so close that our shoulders pressed together.

'I don't know where Ruman is,' said Potta loudly. The blow to the back of his head caught us all by surprise, and Potta toppled to the ground like a felled reed, uttering a small groan as he did so. My knuckles turned white under Jenna's grasp.

'You will speak when you are spoken to,' said one of the officials.

I knew I should look away, but my eyes were fixed on the sight of my father on bended knees, holding his head. A redness seeped between his fingers.

'We have reports that Ruman Ambrose was involved in a riot last night,' said the man who had hit Potta. He seemed to be in charge. 'There is also an accusation that he poisoned the water supply two miles south of here.'

I heard Jenna gasp, and I knew she was thinking the same thing – there was no way that our brother, angry though he might be, would endanger the lives of innocent people.

Potta kept silent, but this seemed only to enrage the official further. Another blow to the side of the head made Potta reach for the ground to steady himself. 'Where is your son and who are his friends?'

Potta blinked hard, and I could see he was struggling to compose himself. 'I don't know,' he said. 'I told you. Ruman left our home two days ago and we have not seen him since.'

The official spat on the ground. 'You expect us to believe that he has not been in touch? Not sent a message to any of you?' His gaze swept across to us. 'Perhaps we should ask the little girls whether they have heard from their brother. That might prompt your memory.'

I was rigid with fear, and I knew the others were too. Vivie was making tiny whimpering noises. Mamie made an instinctive move forward, but one of the men grabbed her by the arm. 'Not you,' he said, in an amused voice. 'You're not a little girl.' The other men sniggered.

The chief official nodded towards us. 'That one. The smallest.' Vivie's arms clenched convulsively around Mamie's waist, but the next second she was torn away, her face white and tight.

'No!' Mamie cried, but received a slap in the face for speaking.

Vivie's eyes were fixed agonizingly on Mamie's, but

she made hardly a sound as she was carried over to the chief official.

Potta's face was grey as ash. 'Leave my daughter alone,' he said, but I saw his eyes blur with the effort of remaining upright.

The chief official put his hand on Vivie's head. 'Such a pretty child.' He bent down to look at her face. 'Such dark eyes and eyelashes – almost gypsy-like.' He traced a finger down the side of her cheek. It left a white streak, as though the blood had flinched away from his touch, even though Vivie had not moved. 'Where is your brother?'

Vivie stared straight ahead of her. 'I don't know.' Her voice was so quiet we could only tell that she had spoken by the movement of her mouth.

He gripped her chin and tilted it upward. 'Don't be afraid. Nothing will happen to you if you tell me the truth.'

'I don't know,' whispered Vivie, but her eyes flicked from side to side, and even though I knew she was speaking the truth, it looked like she was lying.

The official obviously though so too, because he suddenly grabbed her by the arms and shook her.

'Do you know what happens to little girls who don't do as they're told?'

Vivie bit her lip but didn't answer.

He struck her across the head, and the blow sent her flying to the ground, where she lay still. Mamie cried out, and Potta tried to crawl towards Vivie, but a kick from a nearby soldier sent him sprawling again.

The official turned back to us. 'Which of you will be next?' he said, and I could tell by his voice that he would not hesitate to strike again. Mamie tried to step forward again, but was restrained. I looked at Potta, groaning on the ground, and at Vivie's body, twitching slightly, and a sudden desperation took me.

'Ruman is hiding in Gharsad,' I said, the words bursting out of me.

It was as though I had flicked a switch. Everyone's eyes snapped to me, and a slow smile spread over the face of the chief official. 'Tell me more,' he purred.

'I heard from him yesterday evening,' I said rapidly. 'A friend of Ruman's brought a message. He is hiding out in a deserted building somewhere in the middle of Gharsad.' It was as though my mouth were acting of its own accord. I could no more stop the lies than I could fly.

'Where is this building?'

'I don't know – honestly. Somewhere near a . . . a bank, the friend said, but I don't know which one.'

'Who is he with? How many?'

'There are six of them,' I improvised. 'They're planning more riots.'

'Where? When?' The questions came fast and sharp, like bullets.

I shook my head. 'The friend didn't say. That's all I know.'

'Who is this friend who brought you the message?'

I hesitated. Whoever I named would be hunted down. It was safer not to name anyone. 'I'd never seen him before,' I said. 'He wasn't from Talas.'

'What did he look like?'

I shrugged. 'Short. Dark hair.' That could apply to almost anyone, I thought. Outwardly I hoped I looked calm, but inside, my brain was running at great speed. My body felt hot and cold and tingly. My hands felt as though they were twice their normal size.

The official smiled at me like a reptile. 'See how helpful you can be when you want?' He turned back to Potta, and there was something in the way he was standing that made me even more frightened. I rushed on, the words tumbling out as though, by speaking, I could somehow deflect the menace.

'Potta didn't know,' I said. 'I didn't tell anyone. Potta doesn't approve of what Ruman is doing – none of us do. Ruman is no longer part of our family.'

'Is that so?' said the official softly, without taking his eyes from Potta. And I knew, in that moment, that everything I had just told him had made no difference at all. He had come to make an example of us, and my lies, convincing though they might be, would not save us now. Words meant nothing. I could see the Strames gathering in their doorway, and a few more figures lurking round corners. I knew no one would step in to help us. The authorities were going to show us what power they still wielded – and it would ensure that other people didn't step out of line as we had.

'You should leave us alone,' I said, but my voice was losing confidence. 'We haven't done anything. Ruman's the one you're after. We're good citizens. We obey the laws.'

The official raised a hand, and the soldier nearest me reached out and clamped his grimy hand over my mouth. I tasted grit on my lips and fell silent. 'Good citizens don't keep secrets from their leaders. Good citizens don't raise sons to destroy the natural order. And good citizens need to be reminded who is still in charge.'

And during the whole time they were beating Potta, I tried to turn my head away, but the soldier's hand over my mouth kept me facing the terrible sight. All I could do was close my eyes and taste the salty dirt that ran into my mouth.

But I couldn't close my ears to my mother's screams.


Mamie sat in the dirt for hours, cradling Potta's head and sobbing more tears than I ever thought there were in the world. At first, Jenna, Vivie and I sat in the dirt too and watched her, although she seemed to be crying tears on behalf of us as well, for my own tears dried in the sun far too quickly.

There was no question that Potta was dead; his poor body was mangled almost beyond recognition. I could not have brought myself to touch him, but Mamie gathered him into her arms, oblivious to the blood and splintered bone, and rocked back and forth.

Villagers hurried past, casting fearful looks at us. Many of them were familiar. 'Why don't they stop?' I whispered to myself.

Jenna answered me. 'Because they are afraid.'

'But the officials have gone.'

'They are afraid of Mamie,' said Jenna. 'Look at her.'

I saw what Jenna meant. Such grief, such open lamenting, was frightening to see. It was too raw; too unrefined; too wide. Like a desert of grief. Utter despair, which could destroy whoever set foot in it. My own grief seemed tiny by comparison, and yet my heart ached as though someone were squeezing it tightly. Vivie had tried to embrace Mamie, but Mamie saw no one and nothing except Potta, and Vivie was pushed aside. Now she clung to me, crying in little whimpers and hiding her face.

As the hours went by and Mamie showed no sign of moving, I pressed Jenna's hand. 'What should we do?'

'I don't know. But we can't let her stay here all day. The sun is overhead; we need water.'

'And the flies . . .' said Vivie, giving a shudder. She was right: as the day brightened, the flies had come,

94

and now they buzzed around Potta's wounds in their dozens. Mamie seemed not to notice, but the sight of the fat black bodies turned my stomach.

'We must get her home,' I said. 'And besides, look at us. We're not dressed properly.'

Jenna looked around, but still there was no one to help. She nodded. 'All right.'

We got up, joints stiff and aching. Jenna took a few hesitant steps towards Mamie, then stopped. 'I don't know . . .' she murmured, her eyes fixed on the horrific sight. She turned and spread her hands help-lessly. 'I can't.'

'You have to.'

'I'll take Vivie,' she said, reaching out to our little sister. Vivie took her hands and huddled against Jenna's side. 'Please, Mini, can't you?'

I felt irritated. Jenna was the eldest; she should be the one to face it. She had a duty to look after Mamie. 'Jenna . . .'

'You're stronger,' Jenna said simply. 'Please, Mini.'

I stared at her. Stronger? What was she talking about? She was just making excuses and I knew it, but I couldn't make her take charge, and the sun was still rising in the sky. I made a noise of annoyance and walked over to Mamie, steeling myself.

It was much worse up close, and I could feel the bile rising in my throat. Trying to avoid looking at the remains of Potta's body, rippling with black flies, I put a hand on Mamie's shoulder. 'Mamie, we must go. Come on, now.'

She showed no sign of having heard me, so I shook her shoulder gently. 'Mamie. Mamie, can you hear me? It's Amina. It's Mini.'

She blinked. 'Mini?' Her lips were cracked and sore from the salt water that had dried on them.

'Yes, Mamie, it's me. We have to go now.'

She shook her head. 'Never, never, never.' She started rocking again.

I knelt down beside her, unable to avoid staining my nightgown with blood. 'Mamie, Potta is gone. We must go home. We need water and food. It is getting hot.'

But she continued to rock, shaking her head.

In desperation, I cried, 'Mamie, what about us? You still have three daughters – you have to look after us!'

She lifted her face to mine and I looked into the

inky depths of sorrow. 'But who will look after me?' she asked simply.

I had a sudden pain in my heart and I knew it was cracking right across, like a stone baked in the sun for too long. 'I will,' I said, swallowing. 'I will look after you. We will look after each other now. You and me and Jenna and Vivie – we will all look after each other. Like Potta would have wanted.'

At his name, her eyelids flickered as though trying to remember something long forgotten.

'Come on,' I said, and I stood up, holding out my hand as if to a child.

She reached out and clasped it, crusty blood chipping and crumbling to the ground. I swallowed again. 'That's it,' I said. 'Let go of him, Mamie.'

And she did, letting his body slump to the ground, but not without gently laying his battered head down. She whispered something too – at least, her lips were moving – but I didn't catch it. And then she took my other hand and got up jerkily, stumbling as she took the weight on two feet.

We left him there in the street. I knew it was wrong; at any other time I would have called for aid to have Potta's body bound and wrapped ready for burial. But we had to get Mamie home, and to be honest, I was frightened. I had never seen a body in such a way before, and the sight of it scared me. To think that *this* was what we were made of – flesh and bone and blood – and that it could be torn apart so easily, releasing the life inside to dissipate into the air and be gone for ever. A body was fragile in ways that I had never imagined, and I was revolted and terrified by what remained of Potta's.

Jenna and I supported Mamie into the house, and Vivie rushed out to the back porch, where she brought back the water we had remaining. We peeled Mamie's clothes off piece by piece, and washed the blood from her body. I am not sure she even knew we were there – she had gone deep inside herself. It was as though, having tried to cope with so much pain, her mind had turned inwards. Vivie stroked and kissed her constantly, uttering little whimpers and platitudes in a frightened voice: 'It's all right, Mamie, it's all right.' After some time, Mamie reached out in response and gathered Vivie into her arms, and Vivie sat quietly on her knee and placed her cheek against Mamie's.

I gazed at them and felt a terrible aching sadness

wash through me. Jenna reached for my hand and we exchanged a look. Then, without speaking, we quickly dressed, tied our headscarves into place, gathered up Mamie's bloodied clothes and went out onto the back porch. We didn't want to waste water by using it for washing clothes, so we put them in a bucket and pushed it into the corner.

'No one has come to see how we are,' I said dully. 'Not the Strames or anyone we know. You'd think . . .' I trailed off.

'They're too scared,' said Jenna. 'We're branded now: trouble. They won't risk talking to us.'

'What are we going to do?' I said. 'There's hardly any rice left, and we're going to need water before long.'

Jenna shrugged helplessly. 'I don't know. Maybe we could ask for help . . .'

'From who?' I asked. 'You just said no one will risk talking to us.'

'I . . .' She spread her hands. 'We'll ask Mamie. When she's . . . when she's all right again.'

We fell silent. Then I said, 'We should – we should take care of the . . . body.'

'You mean . . .'

'It's not right, leaving him there in the dust,' I told her. 'It's not respectful.' There was nothing in me that wanted to go back out to the road and look again on the crumpled remains of my father. My stomach heaved at the idea. But equally, I couldn't bear the thought of him lying there, slowly burning away in the sun and being eaten by flies and goodness knows what else. No one deserved that.

Jenna's face was pale. 'Maybe someone else . . .'

'Who?' I asked, and I felt irritation rise again. 'Who will do it if not us?' Why was Jenna always looking to others to take responsibility? 'He's our father,' I said fiercely, 'and I don't want to do it any more than you do, but there isn't anyone else.'

Jenna's eyes swam with tears. 'I know. I just . . . Oh, Mini . . .'

'Come on,' I said, grabbing her arm none too gently. 'We'll take the sheets from our bedding to wrap him up in. If we do it quickly it won't be so bad.'

Jenna gulped and nodded and, to my relief, followed me.

Vivie and Mamie were still sitting quietly together, their eyes closed. I hesitated, wondering whether to speak, but decided not to. Jenna took one sheet and

I took the other, and we carried them out into the street.

But there was no body there, just a deep red stain on the ground.

We looked helplessly up and down the road. 'Where is he?' asked Jenna.

'Someone must have taken him,' I said.

'But where? Why?'

'And who?'

Strangely, for this time of the afternoon, the street was almost deserted. Normally there would be people coming back from market, women visiting each other's houses, children playing in the dust. But there were very few people around, and those who passed us made obvious efforts to avoid speaking. There was no one to ask, and we had been inside our house for at least a couple of hours, so the body could have been moved at any time.

I felt baffled. Where was Potta?

'Maybe someone took him for burial?' Jenna said hopefully.

I couldn't believe that this was likely. Burials were undertaken by the family; no one else had the right to move a body. Unless the Kwana had come back, of course . . . My stomach twisted angrily. So it wasn't enough to kill him in the street; they had to come back to steal his body too? How could they treat people like this? We were no threat to them – how could it be right that they had the power to kill and destroy with no one to stand up to them?

There was nothing else for us to do, so we carried the sheets back inside. Mamie looked up as we came in, and I was pleased to see that some of the colour had returned to her face, though her eyes looked almost black with sorrow. Her gaze fell to the sheets in our hands.

I felt as though I should explain. 'We went to get Potta,' I said, hesitating. 'But he's gone.'

'Gone?' For a moment there was a flash in Mamie's eyes, and I wondered if it was sudden hope that perhaps Potta wasn't dead after all; perhaps he had crawled away . . . But then her eyes hardened again. 'So they have taken him completely,' she said, and her voice was hard too. 'I see.'

There was a pause. 'What are we going to do, Mamie?' asked Jenna quietly.

'We will leave,' said Mamie. 'There is nothing for us here and it is not safe to stay.'

I swallowed. I knew she was right, but it was frightening to hear her say it. 'Where shall we go?' I asked.

'Anywhere,' she said simply. 'Anywhere but here.'

'Now?' asked Jenna.

'Tomorrow,' said Mamie. 'As soon as it gets light.' She looked down at Vivie, whose eyes were wide with fear, and her arms tightened around her. 'We may have to walk a long way.'

Vivie nodded and then burst into tears.

'What about Ruman? Shouldn't we try to get a message to him?' I asked, but the look Mamie turned on me made the words freeze in my throat.

'I no longer have a son,' she said clearly. 'It is because of him that I no longer have a husband.'

I looked away, biting my lip.

We dined that evening on boiled rice, though none of us felt like eating, and Mamie only managed two mouthfuls before pushing it away. 'You should eat, though,' she told us. 'You will need strength tomorrow. We all will.' She looked around our room and I thought I might cry again because I knew she was saying goodbye to it – our home, the only place I'd ever lived.

We lay down to rest that night and I thought I

would never sleep, but I must have done because at some point I awoke with a deep, paralysing terror. In a matter of minutes, our lives had changed beyond return – nothing could ever be the same again. I had been able to fool myself that Ruman might return; that we could rebuild our family once more. But no one could bring Potta back from the dead.

# 8

We had not expected a checkpoint. I don't know how long it had been there – it could have been set up only the day before, for all I knew – but somehow we had all assumed that we would be allowed to walk out of our place of birth without question.

'We should have gone in the other direction,' I muttered to Jenna as we joined the queue of people waiting to leave Talas. 'Towards the reed beds.'

'And on to where?' she murmured back. 'This is the only main road anywhere.'

I knew she was right but I wished we hadn't come this way. Mamie had insisted that the road to Gharsad, which split off just before the city and led south, was our best option. 'We need to move further away from Bremir,' she said. 'Over the border, if necessary – out of the country.' I glanced at her now, wondering if she would change her mind and turn us all around, but her face was set and still. Vivie clutched her hand, nervous. I took a breath and hoped that there would be no cause for worry.

None of us had looked back as we left our house. I did not want to remember it as it was now: empty; without Ruman and Potta. And I tried so very hard to stop my eyes sliding across the road to the stained ground where Potta had died.

There were people heading out to Gharsad for work this morning as usual, as well as other families on their way out of Talas. I wondered how many of them were leaving for good, like us. One family had a donkey laden with bags and a tiny baby asleep on the top. I smiled shyly at a girl about my age who held the rein, but she looked blankly back, as though she barely saw me. I wondered if she too had seen someone killed in front of her. Ruman's teacher had been shot outside his school; Potta had been killed outside our house – how many others were there?

There were two other roads that joined this one; roads that came from villages further west of Talas. I was surprised to see more people coming along them, some carrying possessions like us. Were they running away from their homes too? Would everyone eventually be forced to flee the places they loved?

The checkpoint was a hasty affair, constructed out of bits of corrugated iron, bricks and planks. But it was an effective barrier, and there was only one way through – past the Kwana officials, of which there were at least six, all carrying guns. My heart thumped out of rhythm as I was seized with fright.

Mamie grasped our identity papers tightly and glanced across to make sure that our letters of heritage were all visible. 'Let me do the talking,' she said to me in a tight voice.

I nodded, taken aback that she would even think I could speak to the men. I might be foolhardy, but at that moment my tongue was welded to the roof of my mouth. Instead, I clutched my bundle of belongings more tightly – a few bits of clothing, a cooking pot and spoon, all tied in a sheet.

The queue moved agonizingly slowly as the Kwana officials scrutinized everyone's papers, and every now and then one of them would thrust out a hand to prevent someone from crossing the barrier. Jenna and I exchanged glances.

It was our turn at last. 'Papers,' said an official with

a large black moustache, and I gulped. It was Hamsi, the one who had caught me smiling in the street only a few weeks ago. Would he recognize me? Immediately I bent my head, staring at the ground. Mamie held out our papers. I heard a rustle as Hamsi looked through them, and then felt his gaze as he inspected our letters. 'H family?' he said. 'All of you?'

'Yes,' Mamie said. 'Myself and my three daughters.'

'Where is your husband?' asked the official.

Mamie faltered slightly. 'He is . . . he died. From a heart attack, last month.'

My eyes widened but I kept my gaze firmly on the ground. Why was Mamie lying? Unless she thought that we might be prevented from leaving if we spoke the truth . . . ?

Hamsi stared at Mamie for a moment, and then his eyes flicked over the rest of us. I felt my face grow hot with anticipation and I held my breath. But he did not comment, so perhaps he didn't remember me. Instead, he looked at our identity papers again. 'Hold on a minute,' he said, and turned to a colleague.

My heart thumped even louder. Was I about to be denounced as a disgrace to my family? Would he finish the punishment he started in the street, with his knife?

Several other officials were now scrutinizing our papers. Then one shook his head and pointed to something on one of the papers. Hamsi turned back to us. 'This paper has been forged.'

My jaw dropped, and I stared openly at him, forgetting myself. 'Forged?' I echoed. This wasn't about our previous meeting! Mamie trod heavily on my foot and I shut my mouth with a snap.

'I don't understand,' she said pleasantly. 'Which one?'

He thrust it at her. 'This one. Yours.'

She looked down at it, and in that moment I realized she already knew. There was something about the set of her mouth; her fingers trembled slightly. I remembered the whispered conversation in the middle of the night. Mamie and Potta talking about something they had done . . . it was too late to go back now . . . better that the children didn't know: was this what they had been discussing?

'Mamie?' I whispered.

She wouldn't look at me. 'You are mistaken,' she said clearly. 'I am an H, like my children and like my husband was.'

Hamsi spat on the ground. 'You are not an H. This paper has been tampered with. What letter are you really?'

'I am an H,' she repeated stubbornly.

He suddenly grabbed her arm, twisting it up behind her back. Mamie gasped in pain, and Jenna and I took an involuntary step forward. Vivie yelped. 'Do not lie to me,' he said softly in her ear. 'Your children will suffer too if you do.' Then he frowned at me. 'In fact, I think I have an overdue appointment with *that* one . . .'

I felt cold with fear. He *did* recognize me!

Mamie's eyes flicked desperately over us. Then she took a breath. 'I am a Q,' she said loudly, and her chin tilted up. 'I am a gypsy Q, and proud of it.'

A Q! Like Noori's family! Suddenly a whole lot of things started to make sense, but before I had time to think about them, Mamie swung her head back with such violence that she connected with Hamsi's nose. There was a crack, and he let out a cry and staggered backwards, releasing her. Blood streamed from his nose into his moustache and mouth, but Mamie didn't turn to look. She grabbed me with one hand and Vivie with the other, and pulled us fiercely through the checkpoint. 'Come on, girls,' she said, and we staggered along with her.

But the Kwana couldn't be shaken off that easily. We had taken barely five steps before Mamie was set upon by three other officials. One pulled her by the headscarf so that she choked; another took both her shoulders and put his knee into her back. 'No!' I shouted, but I was batted aside as though I were a fly.

The official with his knee in Mamie's back turned to glare at us. 'You'll get out of here, if you know what's good for you,' he said.

'What about Mamie?' I asked, trembling.

'She's coming with us,' he said. 'Gypsies are no longer allowed the freedom of the region.'

'But . . .'

He shoved Mamie to the ground and threw our papers at us. I clutched them convulsively. 'Go on – go!'

'Mamie!' cried Vivie, and Jenna grabbed her as she tried to get to our mother.

Mamie, her headscarf askew and her hair tumbling down around her face, twisted to look up at us. 'Go!' she said hoarsely before coughing again. 'You must go! Look after each other!'

The queue behind us, held up for several minutes

by the confusion and sensing movement, surged forward, and we found ourselves pushed along. Jenna and I reached for each other's hands instinctively, but I could hear Vivie shouting, 'Mamie! Mamie!' and when I turned, I couldn't see my little sister at all. Mamie was being dragged away by officials, but there was no way of reaching her; others were surging through the barrier now, impatient, and the Kwana were having difficulty holding them back. Shots were fired into the air, and people flinched and fell to the ground in panic.

'Come on!' Jenna pulled at my hand and we ran on, down the road, away from the shots and the confusion.

When we finally came to a halt, fifty metres beyond the checkpoint, we realized it was just the two of us. Of Mamie and Vivie there was no sign.

'Where is she?' Jenna twisted this way and that, trying to catch a glimpse of Vivie's orange scarf. 'I can't see her. We have to go back!'

'We can't,' I said, feeling sick with panic. 'It's too dangerous. We should wait. They'll throw her out soon – she won't be able to catch up with Mamie. She'll come after us.'

So we stood in the shade of a brown-leafed tree and waited, hearts thumping, staring intently at every person who passed us on the road. But Vivie did not come. 'I don't understand,' Jenna was muttering to herself. 'How could Mamie be a Q? Why didn't they tell us?'

I laced and unlaced my fingers, rubbing at the healing reed cuts. 'Remember how Noori's family disappeared that day? Maybe they were taken.' I tried to remember whether it was before or after this that I'd heard Mamie and Potta whispering in the night. When had they decided to hide Mamie's true heritage? 'Why is it so bad anyway? What's wrong with gypsies?'

'When we see Mamie next, we'll ask her,' said Jenna, but her voice was uncertain.

I looked at her, my head beginning to throb. *When we see Mamie next . . .* When would that be?

We waited some more. I didn't know what to do. Vivie was only little – still such a child. What had happened to her? She was so sheltered; she'd always been so indulged. At home, it annoyed me, but out here – I was terrified at the thought of my sister being left alone.

'She wouldn't leave Mamie,' said Jenna, over

and over again. 'She would stay with her, even if it meant . . . being arrested.'

I knew she was right. If it came to a choice between her sisters and her mother, Vivie would choose Mamie every time, no matter what the circumstances. But that was assuming the Kwana let her stay – surely they wouldn't want a child hanging around? And Vivie was an H, not a Q, so there would be no reason to send her to prison, or— The thought of my little sister in prison hit me like a sandstorm, stinging my eyes. 'We'll have to go back,' I said, suddenly determined.

'But you said . . .'

'I know. But we have to try at least. And Mamie . . .' My voice shook slightly. 'Mamie said we should look after each other. We have to find Vivie.'

Jenna nodded. 'Maybe she's waiting for us there. And things have quietened down.'

I reached for her hand again, and the contact brought me a little courage. 'Can you speak to them?' I asked.

Jenna took a trembling breath. 'I don't know. Can't you do it? You're so much better at thinking of the right thing to say.'

'They'll know you're older, from your headscarf,' I pointed out. 'Same as always.' Then an idea struck me. 'Take it off. We'll swap.'

'What?' Jenna stared. 'Swap scarves?'

'Of course.' I was amazed I'd never thought of it before. 'You're only a year older than me – who's to know just by looking at us?'

Jenna obediently took off her dark blue scarf and then wound my own green one around her head. 'It feels so strange to be wearing green again,' she said, with the tiniest hint of a smile.

I felt odd too, wearing a scarf that proclaimed me to be a whole year older than I was. But it also made me *feel* older. It was exciting and scary at the same time. I straightened my shoulders, determined to hide the fluttering nerves inside me. 'Come on.'

Hamsi was no longer there and I felt relieved. Of all the Kwana, he was the one I feared most. There was a younger official I didn't remember seeing before, so I went up to him, still holding Jenna's hand. He was sunburned, with tired rings around his eyes, and he was sitting on a bent metal chair, his rifle held loosely in his hands. The rest of the Kwana were checking papers, but this one seemed to be unoccupied. 'Excuse me,' I said, keeping my eyes lowered so that I could not be accused of being forward. 'I am sorry to address you directly, but we came through this checkpoint a while ago and we have lost our younger sister.'

The young official rolled his eyes. 'What do you mean, you've lost her?'

'She was with us at the checkpoint, but there was some' – I hesitated – 'confusion, and she didn't come through with us. We got separated.'

'What do you want me to do about it?' he asked. He didn't sound angry, just fed up.

'We wondered if she was still here.'

He waved an arm. 'See for yourself. There are no little girls hanging around. She must have gone back.'

My gaze caught Jenna's and I saw her shake her head. We both knew Vivie wouldn't have gone home – not on her own, anyway. Not to that place of death and blood. 'We have her identity papers,' I said desperately.

The official rolled his eyes again. 'Well, if she came through here, you must have missed her on the road.'

Had we? Surely not. But Jenna's hand tightened

in mine and I knew she was clutching at this hope. Maybe Vivie had got caught up with another family and had slipped by us? Could she be ahead of us rather than behind?

I didn't know what to do. The young man was looking away. 'Please . . .' I said hopelessly. 'Please, can you tell us where we should go?'

He snorted. 'How should I know?'

Tears stung my eyes. Mamie had been the one in charge; the one with the plan. Where would we go without her? 'Where is everyone else going?' I asked, and I couldn't help sounding upset.

He hesitated, and it struck me that he wasn't really so much older than we were. He glanced left and right before he spoke, and his voice was quieter than before. 'The camp at Altiers.'

'The camp?'

'The refugee camp. That's where most people are heading. There is aid provided for refugees.'

'Aid?' I felt like an idiot, repeating everything he said, but my spirits had risen. There was somewhere for us to go? Somewhere we could get help? Maybe Vivie *had* slipped past us. Maybe she would be with people going there too! 'Where – where is this camp?'

He leaned forward to speak, but one of his colleagues called to him in irritation. 'Lanso, we need a hand over here.'

Lanso snapped to attention, tipping over his chair in his haste to stand up. His gun tangled on his sleeve. 'Yes, sir.'

'Please . . .' I said.

'Just follow the others,' he whispered without looking at me as he hoisted his rifle strap onto his shoulder. 'It's a long walk though.' Then he hurried over to his colleague.

'Come on,' I said to Jenna under my breath. Two other Kwana had turned to look at us curiously. 'We should go.'

We didn't speak until we had walked a good few hundred metres away from the checkpoint and round a bend so that we could no longer be seen. Then we stopped and looked at each other. 'Do you think Vivie went past us?' Jenna asked.

I shrugged. 'I don't see how – but maybe we *did* miss her. She could be anywhere; we have no way of knowing.'

'If she went on ahead . . .' Jenna's gaze swept the road. 'We should catch her up!'

'If she didn't,' I pointed out, 'we'll be leaving her behind.'

We stared at each other. What should we do? Where should we go? 'I don't see that we have a choice,' I said finally. 'We can't stay here. We can't go back. We have to go on.'

'And look for Vivie,' said Jenna, nodding.

In my heart of hearts, I didn't believe that Vivie had gone past us. I had scrutinized every single person who had come through the checkpoint – but it was true that there had sometimes been small groups of people and other children. If Vivie had lost her headscarf or had been riding on a cart, or been blocked from view by someone else . . . well, maybe it was possible. And at least at the camp there would be people who could help us. *Aid*, the soldier had said. That meant help, didn't it?

'Yes,' I said. 'We will go on, to the camp, and look for Vivie on the way. And if we haven't found her by the time we get to the camp, at least there we can ask other people to help.' I felt better, having come to a decision.

'Maybe they could help us rescue Mamie too,' said Jenna. We both looked back. The dusty path wound round the small hill and disappeared. Jenna's eyes filled with tears. 'I don't want to go on without her, Mini. How can we leave her behind?'

'There's nothing we can do to help Mamie right now . . .' I swallowed as a sudden image of Potta's body flashed across my vision. Would they do the same thing to Mamie? My heart had already broken; surely it couldn't hurt any more than it already did.

'You mean we have to choose,' said Jenna miserably. 'Between Mamie and Vivie.'

We both knew there wasn't a choice. There was nothing for us to do here – we had to go on. After another moment or two we joined hands again and turned away from Talas, away from our mother and father, and possibly away from our brother and sister too. Where was Ruman? I wondered briefly. Our family had never spent more than a day apart before, and now suddenly six had become two. It was wrong – like losing an eye or a foot. Parts of us that had always been there had been ripped away.

I walked beside my sister, saying nothing, while everything inside me wept with grief.

# 9

We started with purpose and pace, both Jenna and I looking closely at the people we caught up with. Sometimes we hurried, seized by a sense of urgency. Maybe Vivie was round the next corner; with the next family group; sitting under the next tree. Our ears strained for the sound of her voice: a laugh, a wail. Whenever we saw a girl wearing an orange headscarf, our hearts thumped louder, and we ran closer. But it was never Vivie. Each time, our hopes were raised; each time, we were disappointed.

Before long, the sun was high in the sky, and Jenna and I were parched. Mamie had been carrying the bulk of the water and so we only had one small bottle between us. That was soon gone and my tongue felt hot and swollen in my mouth. Strange thoughts began to race around my head: would my tongue swell so much that it filled my mouth completely and prevented me from breathing? What would that feel like? Would I mind? Would it be so bad to die now, having lost so much already? How long did it take to die anyway? How long had it been before Potta—

*No.* I would not think of that – did not want to think of it.

I forced my thoughts away. They bounced to another mystery – Mamie's gypsy heritage. Why had she never told us? Was she ashamed of her background? Where were her family? Had something happened to them?

I also wondered about Ruman. Where was he now? Did he know what had happened to his father?

In between these thoughts was the constant worry about Vivie. I no longer thought she had been left behind with Mamie. I became convinced that she was somewhere ahead of us, with another group, searching for us. The Kwana would never have let her stay with Mamie, would they? So she *must* have come past us. My eyes and ears played tricks on me, giving me a flash of orange to one side that vanished as I turned my head; a giggle suddenly cut off as I listened. I desperately wanted water, and my feet throbbed. There was a strange buzzing in my head – and as the hours went by, I fell into a kind of walking stupor, unable to think of anything any more.

'Watch where you're going!' a woman snapped at me.

'Sorry.'

She had two small children with her who dragged their feet with exhaustion, their eyes blank. As I glanced across at her, I registered the sound of an engine and pulled Jenna out of the way just as a battered-looking car came sputtering past. She fell against me, muttering her thanks. 'I didn't hear it.' Her voice was thick and I knew her tongue must be as swollen as mine.

If I had not felt so wretched, I would have been interested in the other people on the road. There was a baby that cried incessantly, and an old woman who marched as fast as anyone, muttering constantly, a stream of nonsense rippling from her cracked lips. There were three young boys holding hands tightly, fear in their faces. I would have wondered where their parents were if I'd had energy to wonder. I'd have made up a whole story about their past if my imagination hadn't been exhausted. Presumably everyone was heading to the camp at Altiers. Where else would they be going? Did anyone actually know where it was, or were they just following the people in front, as we were? Would there be room for all of us when we arrived?

Every now and then there were people sitting by the roadside, hollow-eyed with despair, holding out their hands for water, money – I don't know what. Some lay still. Were they sleeping? Or were they dead and no one knew? I turned my face away. They reminded me of Potta.

'How much further, do you think?' whispered Jenna.

She had to repeat it before I heard her. It had been so long since we last spoke, I had become locked into my own mind. 'I don't know,' I said, and tried to swallow, but my mouth was too dry.

'My feet hurt.'

Mine did too. Our sandals had never been of the highest quality, and they were already worn from our daily chores. I glanced at Jenna's feet. They were cut and bleeding like mine from all the sharp little stones that got stuck in our sandals and dug into our toes. 'Should we stop and rest?' I croaked.

She shook her head. 'Vivie . . .'

I knew what she meant. If Vivie were up ahead, then stopping now would mean she drew further away from us. And if we stopped, would we be able to start again?

'Jenna?' said a voice. I looked up to see a woman bent double under the weight of a basket crammed with belongings. I hadn't given her a second glance as we passed her, but now I peered into the headscarf, trying to see who it was. Surely it was Davir's wife from the market?

'Lakma?'

The woman eyes brightened in a smile. 'Amina! It is good to see a familiar face. Have you had a birthday?'

'A birthday?' I stared, but then I realized. I was still wearing Jenna's headscarf. 'Oh – no. We swapped.'

Lakma looked from me to Jenna in some confusion. 'I see.'

I didn't have the energy to explain. 'Are you on your own? Where is Davir?'

Lakma's face creased. 'Taken into custody. He told me I should get out of Talas – it would be safer.'

'Why was he taken?' I had not forgiven Davir for

his treatment of us at the market, but I had seen enough people get on the wrong side of the Kwana recently.

Lakma shrugged. 'Trading, not trading, dealing with the wrong people – how do I know? It could have been anything. They said it was because he had not declared his earnings correctly, but I know that was a lie.' She put down her basket and rummaged around in it, finally extracting a half-full water bottle. 'Here. You both look like you could do with this.'

I reached for it eagerly. 'Only a little,' Jenna warned me as I lifted the bottle to my lips and drank. 'Not too much, Mini – it isn't ours.'

Never had water tasted so good, even warm, dusty water such as this. 'Thank you so much,' I said, passing the bottle to my sister. Jenna sipped carefully, though I could tell she wanted to gulp it all down. Then she held the bottle out to Lakma.

Lakma shook her head. 'Keep it,' she said. 'I have three more in my basket.'

I felt a rush of gratitude sweep over me. 'Are you going to the camp at Altiers too?' I asked.

'Camp?' said Lakma. 'No, I am going to stay with my sister. She lives in a village several miles from here and I've heard that it is safer than Talas. I'm hoping that they'll take me in, seeing as I'm family.' It was only now that she seemed to realize there were people missing from our group. 'Aren't your parents with you?'

'No,' I said. 'Potta is . . . is . . . they killed him.'

Lakma stared at me, shocked. 'Who did?'

'The Kwana. In the street.' I was determined not to let my voice tremble. 'And Mamie is a Q, so they arrested her at the checkpoint.'

Lakma bowed her head. 'I did wonder. She had the gypsy colouring.'

'We didn't know,' Jenna said.

'That must have come as a shock to you,' said Lakma gently.

I nodded, blinking back tears.

'Have you seen our sister?' Jenna asked.

'Sister?' Lakma raised her eyebrows. 'Little Vivie? No, I don't think so. What happened to her?'

'We lost her,' said Jenna, and her gaze was sweeping the road and I knew she wanted to get going again. But Lakma was standing still, her basket at her feet. 'We think she may have gone on ahead.'

'On her own?' Lakma made a clicking noise with her tongue. 'Oh dear.'

Somehow those two little words, *oh dear*, made me anxious all over again. 'You haven't seen her?'

'No,' said Lakma, and her eyes were filled with pity. 'You have all been split up, then? You poor things – didn't you have a brother? Can't he take care of you?'

I opened my mouth to explain about Ruman, but then I hesitated. Should we tell Lakma that our brother had gone to join the rebellion? Was it safe to tell people, even those we considered friends? What if they told the Kwana? My heart sank at the thought.

'We've lost him too,' said Jenna. Then she burst into tears.

I stared at her helplessly, trying to fight the rising tide of panic inside me.

Lakma made the clicking noise again and patted Jenna on the shoulder. 'You two are exhausted,' she said. 'Come with me to my sister's house. I don't suppose she could take you in, but we could at least find food and water for the rest of your journey.'

'We must . . . find . . . Vivie,' sobbed Jenna. 'Keep . . . going.'

'But you can't keep going without something to eat and drink,' said Lakma gently. 'You will stand a better chance of finding her if you keep your strength up.'

It was so exactly what Mamie would have said that I felt a lump come to my throat.

Jenna still resisted. 'If she's looking for us . . .'

Lakma nodded. 'I do understand. It's up to you.' She hoisted her basket back onto her head.

'Jenna,' I said, 'we should take Lakma's offer. We don't know where Vivie is, and we've overtaken a lot of people on this road already. Vivie will be heading to the camp like us, won't she? So if we take an hour or so to get food and drink, we won't drop that far behind.'

'Is this a refugee camp?' asked Lakma.

I nodded. 'One of the soldiers at the checkpoint told us.'

We began to walk again, side by side. 'Well,' she said, 'you've got until I turn off the road to decide whether you're coming with me or not.' She smiled. 'It will be good to have the company in the meantime.'

129

I made the effort to smile back. 'I expect it will be nice for you to stay with your sister.'

'I am not so sure,' Lakma admitted. 'My husband and her husband quarrelled a long time ago, and I haven't seen her for several years. I'm hoping they haven't moved away – she doesn't know I'm coming. I would have written, but there wasn't time. Davir was arrested before we had time to think.' She cast me a regretful look. 'I'm sorry about the way he treated you at the market. There were so many rumours about different letters of heritage – which ones could be trusted and which ones would get you into trouble. He didn't want to risk offending the Kwana – but it happened anyway. No matter what you do, it seems, you still get into trouble.'

We nodded, and again I thought of Potta and my stomach clenched in pain. I looked away.

There had been some scrubby trees alongside the path, but now there was nothing but dirt and sky and the occasional shack. It was hard to tell how far we had come. Everything looked so similar. Every now and then we came to a cluster of dwellings, some built strongly of brick and stone, others made of hastily tied-up iron and plastic sheeting. The people there ignored us as we passed; I guessed they had seen so many go by that we were no longer interesting. Again, I wondered how many would be at the camp and if there would be room for us all. What would happen if we were turned away? Where would we go?

Jenna sniffed, and for a moment I thought she was still crying, but then a delicious smell reached my nose and I sniffed too. 'What is that?'

'That' was a stall set up on the roadside, though we couldn't see what was on it because it was surrounded by people. My mouth watered as we drew closer. We hadn't eaten anything since rice porridge the night before. 'Smells like bread cakes,' murmured Jenna, and I nodded. Mamie used to make little cakes out of flour and eggs and spices, fried in butter – delicious straight from the pan.

Having almost forgotten my hunger, I now felt it return in full force. 'Do you think . . . ?' I began, but Jenna shook her head.

'We haven't got any money.'

It was true. Mamie had been carrying what little money we had, so Jenna and I had no way of buying anything.

'I have money,' said Lakma, hesitating.

'No,' said Jenna instantly. 'Don't buy it for us. You need the money for your sister.'

I opened my mouth to argue, but Jenna shot me a look. Lakma might want to contribute to her sister's household costs, maybe as a thank you for taking her in . . . Still, wouldn't there be a *bit* left over for a few bread cakes? I lingered on the outskirts of the huddle of people, sniffing the delicious air and wishing I had just a few coins to purchase something.

A short woman with a round face and tired eyes pushed her way out of the crowd and murmured something to another woman. The second woman's voice rose in a sharp, '*How* much?'

Her friend shrugged. 'He said take it or leave it.'

'But that's extortion!' The two of them stared at a couple of coins in the first woman's hand. 'It's not enough.'

The taller of the two glanced towards the stall again. 'It's not right,' she said loudly, 'taking advantage of people like that.'

The round-faced woman shrugged again sadly. 'They can do what they like. They know people are desperate.'

'Well, not us,' said the tall woman. She put her hand over her friend's, covering the small amount of money they had left. 'Come on, we'll eat the bit of cheese I've got left.' They turned away.

'Did you hear that?' asked Jenna. 'It sounds like we couldn't afford the food even if we did have our money.'

Lakma looked at me. 'Sorry, girls.'

'It's all right,' I forced myself to say as we turned away from the stall. My stomach growled in response and I squeezed my hands into fists to try to block out the head-swimmingly delicious scent. I could have cried. Instead, I tried not to breathe as we walked away, in case I could still smell the cakes.

As the day wore on, the water levels in the bottles sank lower and lower. We tried not to take much, but it was hard when we were so hot and thirsty. Conversation dries up too when your mouth is parched, and we walked several miles in complete silence before Lakma finally announced, 'Here we are!' as the road forked in front of us.

I could not see anything within sight that looked like a village, but beside the track leading off to the right, someone had helpfully added a little handwritten sign saying, *Gas and Water*, with an arrow.

'Does your sister run a garage?' I asked.

Lakma laughed. 'No, she runs the bakery next door.' Her face sobered. 'This is where I leave the main road. Are you coming?'

I looked at Jenna. Her eyes were tired. 'I don't know,' she said weakly. 'What do you think?'

'I think we're in need of food and drink,' I said, 'and we're not going to get them before the camp. Who knows how much further it is?'

'What about Vivie?'

For the first time, I felt a flutter of impatience at that argument. 'What *about* her?' I said. 'What can we do right now? We need to eat, Jenna, and re-fill our water, otherwise we can't go on. We're no good to her dead, are we?'

I regretted the words as soon as I'd spoken them, and Lakma's intake of breath told me I'd spoken out of turn. Jenna's face crumpled. 'I'm sorry,' I said quickly. 'I shouldn't have said that.'

'You're right,' Jenna said, though tears were springing to her eyes again. 'We should go with Lakma.'

Lakma smiled. 'I am sure my sister will help two girls in need.'

It was only a short walk down the dusty track before a cluster of homes came into view. The garage was a run-down affair that smelled strongly of petrol and had only one pump. The bakery was tucked away behind it, one faded sign forlornly promising HOT FRESH BREAD EVERY DAY. My stomach ached at the sight.

The shop door was closed, and Lakma turned to us, suddenly hesitant. 'Perhaps it would be better if you waited here for the moment.'

Jenna and I sat on a broken pavement opposite, glad to rest our swollen feet. Lakma took a breath, placed her hand on the door, and went into the shop.

'I wish we had some family we could stay with,' said Jenna, staring wistfully at the sign in the window.

'Perhaps we do somewhere,' I said. 'After all, we didn't know about Mamie's background, did we? Maybe there are other things about our family they didn't tell us.'

'Our grandparents are dead,' said Jenna.

'How do we know?' I said wonderingly. 'Maybe they weren't telling the truth . . .'

We sat side by side as the shadows lengthened. A car pulled into the garage and an old man came out of the shack to fill it up. There was an argument about payment, but money finally changed hands and the car departed in a haze of dust. I tried to imagine what it would be like to ride in a car, to cover the land so quickly. Mile after mile of dust and dirt and trees and mountains and . . . then what? Something different? My imagination came up with no other pictures. We had walked a long way today and it was all the same – maybe that's what it was like for ever, all the way round the world. Maybe the jungles and oceans I'd seen in Ruman's school books were just fantasy.

A few people came down the road and glanced at us before looking away again. I wondered if we were becoming invisible. The air temperature dropped and I shivered. 'Do you think Lakma's forgotten about us?'

Jenna rubbed her hands over her arms. 'I'm sure she hasn't. She's probably having to complete the family traditions and all that. She'll come out soon.'

But more time passed and the sky darkened completely. 'Where are we going to sleep?' I said quietly.

'Wait,' Jenna told me. 'Be patient. Lakma said she would help.'

I bit my lip. What would we do if Lakma never came back? The street was empty now and the mosquitoes were biting. It would get colder than this too, and we still had no water or food. I began to wish I hadn't persuaded Jenna to come here – maybe if we'd stayed on the road, we'd have reached the camp already?

Suddenly the door of the bakery opened and light spilled out onto the road. Jenna and I both looked up hopefully.

# 10

It wasn't Lakma but another woman of similar age. She looked across at us and gave a slight sigh before hurrying over. 'Are you Jenna and Amina?'

We scrambled to our feet, bowing our heads in acknowledgement of an older woman.

She tutted. 'Typical, just typical. She doesn't contact me for years and then shows up with two orphans, not even any relation.'

'Orphans!' I said, horrified. 'We're not orphans, we're— Our mother is still alive.'

'But where is she, eh?' said the woman, giving me a sharp look. 'Under arrest, that's where.'

'She didn't do anything wrong,' I said.

'Then why was she arrested? You tell me that. Officials don't just go around arresting whoever they like.'

I stared at her. Didn't she know what was going on? Weren't the Kwana doing the same thing here as they were in Talas?

'That's what I told Lakma too,' she went on. 'I said, if they arrested Davir, then they must have had good reason. You can't go around behaving how you like – there's the greater good to think of. Rules are there to be kept, not flouted. This stupid revolution will blow over and things will be under control again. Ranami is only doing what's best for the people, as he has always done.'

My heart sank. She was a Ranami supporter. We would get no sympathy from her. I marvelled that she could be Lakma's sister. There was a slight facial resemblance, but this woman had a harder expression and eyes that didn't look like they knew kindness.

'I suppose you think you have a right to food and shelter here? That we'll just take you in out of the kindness of our hearts and share our hard-earned goods with you?'

'We don't think we have a right to anything,' said Jenna, her voice trembling. 'We're sorry to have troubled you.'

I closed my mouth, thankful that for once my sister had spoken for us. I could only think of harsh things to say. And Jenna's response worked too. Lakma's sister looked at us and her gaze softened. 'Never let it be said that Leilah wouldn't help a defenceless child.' She sighed. 'We don't have room for you in the house, but there's a shed at the back of the garage you can use for the night if you want.' From under her tunic, she produced a loaf of bread and a lump of whitish cheese, discoloured at the edges. 'This is all we can spare, and if your story is true, then I'm sorry for you.'

'Thank you very much,' I mumbled, my eyes fixed on the food. I heard Jenna say the same.

Leilah nodded, handed the bread and cheese to Jenna, and took one final look at us before turning on her heel and going back into her shop.

There were no thoughts in my head except desire for the food. I held out my hands.

Jenna hesitated. 'We should find that shed first. Then we can sit down and eat. We shouldn't eat in the street. We could get into trouble.'

'What kind of tr—?' I started to say, but bit my tongue. Jenna was right – eating in the street, at night time, would get us noticed by someone at some point. It would be safer to be out of sight.

The shed wasn't hard to find, although it was hardly a shed – a sheet of corrugated iron stood on some rickety bricks, balanced by the back roof of the garage building. We nearly knocked off the sheet as we struggled to squeeze inside. It was hard to see anything, but luckily the moon was rising so there was a bit of light. 'Look,' said Jenna with relief, 'there's a water tap here.'

I suppose it must have been for filling up the cars, but any water was better than none, and we fastened our mouths greedily over the spout. It tasted foul, but then, my mouth was so swollen, I suspect anything would have tasted bad.

Jenna carefully broke the bread exactly in half and then did the same with the cheese. The bread wasn't too stale, but the cheese smelled distinctly suspicious, and Jenna peered at the brown discolouration. 'Do you think it's meant to look like that?'

'I don't know. Maybe we could pick those bits off.' But once we started eating, our hunger returned, and in the end we ate the whole lot, brown patches and all. I just hoped that it was all right – I couldn't have stopped myself from eating it if I'd tried.

The bread and cheese wasn't nearly enough to fill our stomachs, but it was better than nothing. It was too dark to find any stray crumbs, so we huddled together and I dug the sheet out of my bundle and wrapped it around us. Then we sat and looked at the stars through the gap at the end of our roof.

Jenna sighed, and I knew she was thinking about Potta and Mamie and Vivie. In another moment she would be crying, and then I would be too, and then neither of us would get any rest. I looked around in desperation. What could I say to take her mind off things? The night sky glittered overhead. 'Did you know,' I began, without any real plan, 'that those are not actually stars?'

'What?' said Jenna, momentarily distracted from her sadness. She looked up. 'What are you talking about?'

'They're not stars,' I said again.

'Mini . . .' Jenna sounded tired. 'This is another one of your silly stories, isn't it?'

'Stories aren't silly,' I said obstinately. 'And how do

you know they're stars? Have you ever actually *seen* one up close? Have you *been* to a star?'

Jenna rolled her eyes. 'All right, then, have it your own way. What are they if they're not stars?'

'They're . . .' I cast around for a suitable answer. The events of the past few weeks swam into my mind. 'They're soldiers.'

'Mini, not more soldiers,' said Jenna. 'Please, let's just go to sleep.'

'Oh, not the sort of soldiers we've seen,' I went on hurriedly. 'These are a noble race of warriors.' Warriors sounded much better than soldiers, didn't they? 'They're from an ancient time. Thousands of years ago.'

Jenna yawned. 'Then what are they doing up there in the sky?'

'I'm about to tell you,' I said. 'Give me a minute.' I could tell she was smiling. 'It's the best story you'll have ever heard,' I went on.

'Well, that's a big promise.' Jenna was silent for a moment. 'But maybe a story *would* be nice for once. I keep thinking about everything – Mamie, Potta, Vivie . . .'

*And Ruman*, I added in my head. I felt a pang that

Jenna had missed him out. Mamie had declared she didn't have a son any more – but I still missed my brother.

'I keep seeing Potta,' added Jenna, and her voice shook. 'On the ground . . . and Mamie, at the checkpoint, and . . .' I heard her sniff, and I swallowed hard to stop myself bursting into tears too.

'Well, that's why this is going to be the best story ever,' I said firmly. 'Because it has to be, to stop us thinking about all the bad stuff.' I looked up at the sky again. 'So, these warriors, they were great empire-builders, but they were kind too. The lands they conquered – they didn't kill the people who lived there, or make them into slaves. They sorted out all the problems and ruled wisely and kindly.'

Jenna stopped sniffing. 'That doesn't sound very likely.'

'This is my story, all right?' I said, annoyed. 'So I say what happens.'

She gave a snort. 'All right.'

'The leader of these warriors,' I went on, 'was the greatest of them all. Even though he could be fierce in battle . . .' I suddenly realized that this didn't make much sense. How could these warriors be so kind if they had to kill people in battles? Never mind. I had started now, and I'd promised Jenna that it was going to be a fantastic story, so I had to carry on. 'His name was Alham,' I said. 'And he was very ambitious. He wanted to conquer all the lands there were, and bring running water and electricity to everyone.'

'Electricity? I thought you said this was ancient times.'

'All right, not electricity. Running water, and food. Making sure everyone was properly fed and looked after, so there were no poor people and no one was homeless.'

Jenna sighed but said nothing.

'So this Alham, he wanted to conquer every land there was. And he had wise men too, as advisers, and they had maps and plans, and they told him which lands to invade next and things like that. But what Alham didn't know was that the wise men were in league with his evil brother, Null, who was plotting to overthrow him and become emperor in his place.'

'Null? That's a silly name.'

I scowled. I had just been getting into the story myself. 'It's not a silly name. I saw it in a school book once. Null means nothing – it's another word for nothing. And in the story Null is an evil man and therefore he is worth nothing. So Null is the perfect name for him.'

'All right.' Jenna paused. 'What happened next?'

'You have to promise not to interrupt.'

'Sorry, Mini.'

'Anyway, where was I? Oh yes – Null. He was evil because he wanted to rule the empire without doing any of the work. In fact, he wanted to become a god. And he paid the advisers to work for him. So when Alham came to them next to consult their charts and plans, they showed him a new map that they had just created: a map of a land in the sky. At that time there weren't any stars in the sky, only clouds. And the advisers said they were the city walls of the sky land. Alham wasn't sure about it to start with, but they kept telling him that there was a whole land up there waiting to be governed and ruled, and that if he could only cross the cloud walls, he would find it all waiting for him.

'Alham was a bit worried about the risk, but he was a great leader and he didn't want anyone to think he was scared, so he agreed – and he asked Null to look after the empire while he was gone, because he didn't know that Null was really evil. And then he gathered up fifty thousand of his strongest and bravest soldiers, and twenty thousand horses, and all the weapons he could carry.' I had a sudden image of the infinite line of vehicles bringing soldiers to our country. 'Along with building materials,' I added hastily, 'and pipes for the running water, and books for the schools and other useful things.

'And then Alham took one last look at his empire and his people, and he called to his brave warriors – and with one gigantic leap they jumped up into the air and away to conquer the sky. And the people waved and cheered them on, none louder than Null. But when the soldiers had all vanished behind the clouds, Null rubbed his hands with happiness because he knew that his brother would never return.'

'This is a *happy* story, isn't it, Mini?' Jenna asked quietly.

I blinked. Even my imagination was being influenced by real-life events. 'Of course it is,' I reassured her. 'Very happy. I haven't got to the happy bit yet.'

'So Alham came back?'

'N-no,' I said. 'No, he didn't. When he'd been gone for a year with no word from him or his warriors, Null declared himself proper emperor and said that Alham must have died. But he wasn't as good a ruler as his brother, and gradually things began to go wrong in the kingdom. And as another bit of the empire crumbled away, the people started to notice bright shining lights in the sky. Every time a piece of the empire was lost, another star appeared. And after a while the people said it was Alham, trying to return to save his empire, but unable to cross the barrier between earth and sky.'

Jenna gazed up. 'That's still sad, Mini.'

'Wait. I'm just getting to the happy bit. One day, Null was murdered by the very same advisers he'd been paying—'

'That's not happy!'

'*And* the empire got a new ruler, who was much kinder. In fact, she was a girl – I mean a woman.'

'Oh, now you're making it all impossible.'

'No, I'm not. She was Alham's younger sister, and the people loved her. And more and more stars appeared in the sky, and people said that it was Alham and his army smiling down on the new ruler and bringing peace to the country again.'

'But earlier they were saying he was trying to get home,' argued Jenna.

'They were wrong,' I said simply, ignoring the fact that I'd just contradicted myself again. 'And the reason I know this is because one evening, a group of people counted the stars in the sky, and there were fifty thousand and one exactly – the same number as Alham and his army. One of them burns brighter than all the rest.' I pointed up at the sky. 'Look – that one. That's Alham, looking down on his empire and watching over his sister for ever.'

'I thought he didn't have any empire left?'

I lost my temper. 'I'm doing my best, Jenna, all right? He had a bit of empire left – enough to rule over wisely and kindly – and his sister was a brilliant leader and she didn't bother to go out conquering lands for the sake of it because she was happy with what she had. All right?'

Jenna breathed out. 'All right. Sorry, Mini.' She reached for my hand and squeezed it. 'It was a wonderful story.'

I still felt annoyed with her for pointing out all the parts that didn't make sense. 'I'm out of practice,' I said. 'I've always been told off for making up stories.'

149

'I know.' Jenna kept hold of my hand. 'But thanks for telling me a story tonight. It did help.' She looked out at the sky. 'Maybe we should count them? See if there really are fifty thousand?'

I was about to make a retort. She knew it wasn't real, didn't she? But then I looked up, and the stars shimmered at me. Did it matter if a story was real or not? For a few minutes we had forgotten the pain and grief. They were such heavy feelings; it was good to be released for a short time. 'Yes, let's count,' I said.

So we began. 'One, two, three . . .'

And we got quite a long way before our eyes closed and we slept.

# 11

I woke early, and for a moment I couldn't remember where we were. Jenna's head rested heavily on my shoulder, and my neck was so stiff that I had trouble looking over to my right. The sun was only just up, but already there were noises of life around us. Somewhere a cockerel was crowing, and there was a pair of birds quarrelling on a nearby roof. Nearer still, a faint scratching sound indicated that we weren't exactly alone in the little shed. I scrunched up my toes and tried not to think about rats.

My stomach growled, and that heavy feeling of grief had returned. But at the same time, I was anxious to get back on the road to see if we could find Vivie. Where there were people, there would be news. I shook Jenna. 'Come on. We should get going.'

Jenna stirred. 'I'm thirsty,' she said sleepily.

We drank some more water from the tap, but this morning it tasted worse than ever. 'I hope we don't get ill.'

'We'd already be ill, wouldn't we, if it was bad?'

I didn't know. I got to my feet and nearly cried out with the pain from the blisters and the other injuries from the stones. It wasn't as though we weren't used to walking long distances, but the hours on the rough road had taken their toll. Jenna too winced as she stood up, but she didn't say anything.

As we emerged from the shelter, the door to the bakery opened, and a woman came out. My stomach growled in anticipation. 'Look! Leilah is bringing us breakfast.'

But it wasn't Leilah – it was Lakma. She looked furtively around before coming over. 'I can't stay,' she said. Her eyes were nervous, and there was an odd shadow on her cheek.

'Lakma, what happened to your face?' I asked, reaching out to touch it.

She jerked backwards, pulling at her headscarf to cover it. 'Nothing,' she said. 'I fell over.'

Fell over? I had a sudden memory of the black eye

Ruman had got at school. Had someone punched Lakma?

'I've brought you some breakfast,' she said hurriedly. 'I'm sorry I couldn't come out to you last night. My sister's husband was a bit surprised to see me.' She hesitated. 'And he wanted to know all about Davir and – and everything.'

Had her brother-in-law been the one to hurt her? I had a cold, sick feeling. 'Are you all right?' I asked.

Lakma's expression became blank. 'I'm fine, thank you, Amina. I am with family now.'

I didn't know what else to say so I said nothing. But it struck me that Lakma's family hadn't given her the welcome she had hoped for.

Lakma thrust her bundle at us. 'There's bread and cheese there, and some dried meat. I took what I could – I didn't dare take more. I mean,' she amended, 'it wouldn't have been fair to take more. Leilah and Beklam have their own needs.'

'Thank you,' I said, taking the wrapped bundle. Lakma reached beneath her tunic.

'I re-filled my water bottles too,' she said. 'From the tap in their garden. I didn't know if there would be water here.' For the first time, her eyes travelled over the little shed. 'You slept in here?'

We nodded.

Lakma's shoulders sagged. 'I am sorry. I wish I could do more.'

'It's fine,' said Jenna gently. 'We understand.' I knew she had the same suspicions as I did about Lakma's poor face.

Should we try to persuade Lakma to come with us? But it wasn't our place to do so, was it? Surely she was better off with her family than travelling with us on the road . . . I felt helpless.

Lakma handed over the two water bottles. 'I hope you find your sister,' she said, and there was a whisper of a smile across her face. 'Good luck.'

'Thank you,' said Jenna. Impulsively, she reached out to touch Lakma on the shoulder. 'I hope – I hope you will be happy here.'

Lakma nodded, though her mouth trembled. She gave us one last quick glance before heading back into the shop. A movement at a window above caught my eye and I looked up to see a man glaring down at us. Instantly, I dropped my gaze and, without a word to each other, Jenna and I turned away.

'We should have done something,' I said after we had hungrily eaten the bread and cheese.

'Done something?'

'About Lakma. She's scared of that man. Her sister's husband. Do you think he hit her?'

'I know how you feel, Mini, but there's nothing we can do about it.'

I bit my lip. Those were some of Jenna's favourite words – *there's nothing we can do about it* – and, as ever, they made me boil inside. She might be right, but shouldn't we have tried? I wished I'd asked Lakma to come with us instead of staying with a family who obviously didn't want her. How could things ever change for the better if no one risked trying?

'There's the main road,' Jenna said, and I heard the energy return to her voice. 'Maybe we can find someone to ask about Vivie.'

There were certainly enough people coming along. It felt like there were more than yesterday, and it made me nervous. Where were they all coming from? Were they all going to the camp? I pictured a friendly village-type place, with white tents and food wagons. Would we all fit in?

I was still wearing Jenna's headscarf. It seemed more sensible, as we both knew I was more confident about speaking to people. But as the day went on, even conventional Jenna abandoned tradition and begged people to tell us if they had seen a little girl with dark eyes and hair. Most were polite but unhelpful; those who had seen a girl fitting Vivie's description could never remember where it was or who she was with, and as one woman pointed out to us, that description applied to hundreds of little girls.

'We'll never find her on the road,' Jenna said in despair. The sun had crossed the highest part of the sky and we had drunk over half the water Lakma had given us. Nevertheless, I still felt desperately thirsty, and if Jenna hadn't been carrying the bottles, I think I would have drunk the lot.

'We'll just have to look for her at the camp,' I said. 'This is pointless, trying to find her on the road. There are too many people and they're too spread out. At least at the camp, everyone will be in one place.'

'We shouldn't have left the road last night. Maybe she came past—'

'Jenna, if we hadn't left the road we wouldn't have

had anything to eat or drink. We couldn't just go on like that. It's not our fault.'

'Mamie wouldn't have left the road,' said Jenna.

*Mamie's not here*, I wanted to say, but didn't.

I'd like to say that looking for Vivie kept us going; gave us a purpose. But actually I think we kept going because we couldn't stop. The road stretched for miles and miles, sometimes bending around hills, sometimes unrolling in front of us so that the furthest point disappeared into the sky. There were people all along it, some walking faster than us, some crawling along so slowly that you could hardly tell they were moving. I saw children without parents; old people sitting quietly at the side of the road, so still that you could never be sure they were still breathing; birds and wild dogs that chewed at rags and other things I didn't want to see.

'Where are all the men?' murmured Jenna. Most of the people we saw were women and children. I wondered whether all the other men had been arrested or killed, and then I made myself stop wondering.

We ate the dried meat and drank the last of the water that evening, and eventually it became too dark to walk safely. 'There.' I pointed at a tree, spindly and with a scattering of leaves. Two other people were already lying under it, huddled together, but there was room for us on the other side. It wouldn't provide any real shelter, but it felt better, somehow, than just lying down at the edge of the road. I pulled out the sheet from my bundle and we tried to wrap ourselves as tightly as possible. The air temperature was dropping quickly, and now that we weren't walking, it felt even colder.

'I can't see the stars tonight,' said Jenna, shivering.

'There's one.' I pointed. 'Low on the horizon – look.'

She gazed at it for a moment, and then said unexpectedly, 'Is that Alham, do you think?'

'Who?'

'The leader of those warriors.'

I stared at her. The story I had told the night before seemed like a distant dream. 'I thought you said it was silly.'

'I said bits of it didn't make sense. But that doesn't matter. Can we pretend it's all true again?'

'What for?' I felt tired. 'It won't help anything.'

'It will help *me*,' she said. 'Please, Mini. Every day we spend away from Mamie and Vivie and – and

Potta, and Ruman – makes me feel less real. Like I don't belong anywhere. I don't have your imagination; I can't pretend I'm really at home or in a bath or flying.'

Her words made me smile. 'All right. But that's not Alham. Alham is up there, see? The one you were pointing at is someone else.'

'Who?'

'One of the warriors.'

'What's his name?'

I took a breath and stared at the sky. 'Brekel. His name's Brekel and he's one of Alham's commanders.'

'What's he like?'

'Tall,' I said. 'Very tall – the tallest man in the whole army. And with white-blond hair, like an angel. But he had a very sad childhood. When he was born, his mother died, and his father was devastated.'

'Mini,' said Jenna in a warning tone, 'this needs to be a happy story, remember?'

I felt annoyed with myself. Why did I have to keep adding in sad bits? 'Sorry,' I said. 'I'll explain. Brekel was born with no hair at all. And when it finally started to grow, it was white. Completely white.'

'Like Old Lina, from Talas,' breathed Jenna.

'Yes, just like Old Lina. And people in Brekel's

village said it was a sign of death, his white hair. They said it meant that the child had aged before his time because he had caused the death of his mother. So everyone said that Brekel's life would be tragically cut short.

'Because of this, Brekel's father, who was called . . .' I cast about in my mind for a suitable name, suddenly remembering the father of a girl I had known at school. 'He was called Sol – well, he wasn't very affectionate towards his son. He believed what everyone said – that the white hair meant that Brekel would die soon – and so he didn't want to love his son because then the pain would be twice as bad when he died. So he refused to cuddle his son, or tell him stories, or play with him. He wouldn't even smile at Brekel. And so Brekel grew up thinking that his father hated him, whereas actually Sol was just trying to protect himself from being hurt again.'

'Poor Brekel,' murmured Jenna, and her eyelids started to droop.

'Of course, as Brekel grew up, he learned about his father's strange belief and he did everything he could to reassure him. "I'm not going to die, Father," he would say. "Look at my muscles! Look how healthy I am! Why should I die?" But Sol turned his head away and wouldn't listen.'

I gazed up at the stars. They seemed to have a direct connection with my imagination, putting thoughts and words into my head. I could see Brekel so clearly in my mind's eye. 'Brekel became very lonely. He made friends with a boy who lived next door, and they went climbing together – trees, hills, everywhere. If it was tall, they climbed it. Until one day the other boy slipped and fell, and was badly injured. Brekel carried his friend all the way home, crying for help. But a few days later, the boy died of his injuries.

'And then people started to look at Brekel oddly – they didn't say anything to his face, but behind his back the rumours grew. The idea was that Brekel, being the cursed one, had somehow escaped his fate only for another to die. "It should have been you," Sol told his son sadly. "You were the one who should have died, not him." And the boy's mother, desperate with grief, began to shout at Brekel whenever she saw him. "You killed my son!" she yelled through her tears. "How can you live with yourself, knowing that your curse has taken my child from me?"'

My confidence in the story grew. 'There is only so long that a person can live surrounded by hatred, and in the end Brekel knew he had to leave. He bundled up everything he owned, which wasn't much, and he left early one morning. When Sol got up, he found a note from Brekel which said that he had gone to join the army, where he would surely find death and therefore not be a burden to anyone any more.

'And as soon as Sol read the note, he was over-taken by a terrible grief, and he knew that despite everything, he had come to love Brekel. He hadn't saved himself any pain at all – the years he had spent pushing Brekel away had all been for nothing because now he was alone. And it was too late to tell Brekel that he loved him.' I swallowed. Sol and Brekel were as real to me now as Jenna, sitting silently beside me.

'Sol tried to contact Brekel, but the army trained many miles away and there was no way of sending messages that far. So he waited, sitting in a chair out-side his home, for his son to return. But Brekel never came, and when Sol heard that Alham had taken his army into the sky, he also heard about the brave com-mander, Brekel, who had faced death in so many battles and never flinched. And he knew that Brekel wasn't going to come back.

'But one evening, as he looked up at the night sky, he saw a new star. It hadn't been there the night before, Sol was sure of it. And it seemed to be directly over Sol's house, shining down with a bright white light. The next night it was there again – and the next. And Sol told anyone who would listen that this star was his son Brekel – the boy with the white hair who would never die now that he was immortalized in the stars. One night, sitting out on his chair and looking up at Brekel's star, Sol simply passed from this life to the next. Maybe, in death, he could finally tell his son how much he loved him.'

I fell silent. My throat felt thick with sadness. I had done it again. In trying to create something that would make us forget our grief and sadness, I had made up a story full of tragedy. 'I'm sorry,' I said to Jenna. 'It wasn't meant to end like that. I was going to have Brekel come home, but the story went on by itself.'

I expected her to retort that stories couldn't do things by themselves, but she didn't. When I looked at her, I realized she was asleep, her face tilted towards me and her dark hair creeping out from the edges of her headscarf to lie in tendrils across her cheek.

I was relieved. Next time, I vowed, my story would have a happier message.

The next morning I was woken by Jenna's sudden jolt of alarm. 'Get off!' she shrieked.

A large black bird flapped lazily into the sky. 'It was pecking me!' she said, shivering all over in the early morning chill. 'Look!' Blood seeped from her little toe.

I shuddered. 'That's disgusting. Why was it pecking you? Did it think you were dead?' I spoke the words without thinking, and Jenna gasped sharply.

'Dead? What – because we were lying down?'

I looked around. The couple who had been on the other side of the tree were gone, and I couldn't see anyone else for the moment. 'Maybe it just thought you were an animal,' I said.

'You're not making it any better, Mini,' said Jenna in an unusually hostile tone. She felt her little toe gingerly. 'Ouch.'

'Can you walk?' I asked.

'Yes. But I feel sick.'

It was hard to pick ourselves up. The night had been cold and we hadn't slept well. Our muscles were stiff and our feet hurt from all the blisters, not to mention the extra wound to Jenna's toe. 'I wish we'd saved some food and water,' I said, tying the empty bottles into the sheet again.

'So do I. Maybe it's not far now. To Altiers.'

Our eyes met, and I knew mine reflected the same thought I saw in hers. If we didn't reach the camp soon, would we be too weak to walk any further? What would happen to Vivie if we didn't find her? My stomach twisted painfully at the thought that Jenna and I might die and not one member of our family would ever know what had happened to us. Now I felt sick too.

It's funny how quickly you get used to something. Walking, trudging, putting one foot in front of the other, I found myself losing track of time. Minutes could feel like hours, and yet at other moments it was as though I had lost time completely: the sun was just coming up, and then it was high above our heads – how had that happened?

Yesterday we had walked with purpose, asking

everyone we met about Vivie. Today, I found myself staring at the stones in the path. I knew that I should still be asking; should still be looking around; but the lack of food and water was making me dizzy and it was hard enough to walk without becoming disorientated. Thumping at the back of my head was a series of images – flashbacks. Kwana at the door of our house . . . Potta on the ground . . . Mamie screaming, her head turned to the sky . . . Vivie silent and appalled . . . Ruman walking away . . . the soldier at the checkpoint looking sympathetic . . . Lakma's frightened eyes . . .

I tripped on a stone and tried to block out the memories. Left . . . right . . . left . . . right . . .

And then, just as I was drifting into a semi-conscious haze – just as I was trying to swallow for the umpteenth time with a dry mouth – just as Jenna twisted her ankle again and let out a small cry – there was a breath of wind that brought something new.

It wasn't a pleasant smell – it was the smell of decay and desperation – but it was mixed with a new sound. The sound was faint to start with, but with each step it grew more recognizable.

It was the sound of people. *Lots* of people.

# 12

Along the road from Talas we had seen many people, but we had either overtaken them or lost sight of them in other ways, so to see the numbers suddenly increase took me by surprise. Almost out of nowhere, there were dozens, hundreds, maybe more, sitting or lying by the road, gathering in small groups, staring at the ground or arguing with each other.

My steps couldn't really have quickened, because I was so exhausted, but it felt as though I had a new sense of urgency. Jenna reached for my hand again, and I was glad of it because I felt overwhelmed. Were we finally at Altiers? The further we walked, the more people there seemed to be, until they were so densely packed that we were forced to a halt. 'Can you see what's up ahead?' I whispered to Jenna.

She was slightly taller, so she might have more of a chance of seeing.

She leaned on me as she tried to go up on tiptoe, biting her lip at the obvious pain it was causing her. 'No. Just a bunch of people, as far as I can tell. But there's a sign. I can't read what it says – it's too far away. It must be the entrance to the camp, mustn't it?'

A woman in front of us turned round and swept unfriendly eyes over us. 'Yes, it's the camp,' she said. 'But you have to have the right papers.' Her eyes fastened on the letters of heritage that we still wore. 'And the right letters.'

'Which are the right letters?' I asked, trying to prevent my voice from wobbling.

The woman cast another look at me, one side of her nose wrinkling as if we smelled bad. 'Who knows?' she said, and spat on the ground before turning away from us again.

Jenna squeezed my hand and we exchanged uneasy looks. What if we were carrying the wrong papers? What if they wanted to know where our parents were? What if they said we were too scruffy and unwashed? 'I thought they'd let everyone in,' I whispered.

'So did I. Why wouldn't they?'

Panic gripped me. 'Maybe they haven't got enough room.'

'Or enough food for everyone.'

My mouth watered, and my stomach ached with hunger. What would we do if we couldn't get in? What if Vivie were already inside and we were prevented from joining her? Maybe we should never have stopped at Lakma's sister's place. Maybe we should have just kept walking, right through the nights, to make sure we got in before they closed the camp. If we'd known . . . I wanted to shout with the unfairness of it all, but I was terrified too. What if we'd come all this way for nothing?

We stood in that queue for the rest of the day, occasionally moving forward an inch or two. To begin with, I took an interest in the people around us, exchanging a few words with a woman nearby or smiling at a small child. But as the day wore on, I had no energy to spare for other people and simply stared at the ground. Somehow, standing still was worse than walking, and in the heat of the day, the world around me began to take on a strange dreamlike quality. People's voices; the colours of the headscarves;

the dust – all became mixed and swirled together, and it was as though I were surrounded by plants or trees rather than people, swaying in a non-existent breeze.

'Mini.' Jenna shook my arm. 'Careful, you're falling asleep.'

'Am I?' I hadn't noticed my head nodding forward, but now it snapped up again.

'We're nearly there – look.'

I looked up and was amazed by how far we had come, even though it felt like just a few steps.

In front of me, just a few metres now, was a check-point of sorts: a couple of makeshift huts housed military-looking men in beige and brown, the colours of the invading army. They looked tired and fed up as they took papers from people at the head of the queue and examined them closely, asking questions. Sometimes they searched the refugees, squeezing the baggy tunics as though they thought they might find something interesting inside. Those who were allowed through passed under an archway, and I could see there were high-wired gates, which at the moment stood open. To either side of the gates ran a fence, at least three times my height, with barbed wire at the top and an inner fence a few metres further in. My stomach lurched.

'Is this how you thought it would be?' Jenna whispered.

I remembered my idea of white tents in a row, all neat and tidy and clean and friendly. 'I didn't think there'd be all these fences. But I suppose they have to keep people safe. So that's good, isn't it?'

The fence ran as far as we could see, to left and right; and all the way round the outside people were camped right up against it. They looked sad and ill, and the children were hollow-eyed and silent like their parents. 'Why are they outside the fence?' I wondered.

The woman in front, who had not spoken to us for several hours now, tossed 'Rejected' over her shoulder, and despite the hot weather I felt a shiver pass through me. It was clear which side of the fence was preferable.

'I suppose if you're this side of the fence you don't get aid,' said Jenna.

'Which people are being rejected?' The woman in front had said those with the wrong letters. But surely the soldiers didn't care about the letters, did they? It was the Kwana who cared about the letters . . . In my exhausted state, I began to wonder whether the soldiers were really the Kwana in disguise, and that the camp was all an illusion, designed to lure people in to their deaths . . . Maybe we shouldn't have come at all!

'We're nearly there,' said Jenna as we took another step forward.

I swallowed convulsively, steeling myself to face the checkpoint. But just then, the worst thing happened. The soldiers started to consult amongst themselves, glancing at their watches and looking up at the sky, which was turning a dusky peach. Then the gates closed!

A moan went up from the crowd. I was unable to repress making the same sound. 'They're closing the gates!'

'Vivie!' cried Jenna suddenly. 'Vivie, are you there?'

But there was no chance of hearing a reply amongst the protests from the people outside the gates. 'Let us in!' I cried hopelessly.

'Closed for the night,' said the guard as he fastened

the huge padlock from the other side. 'Sorry. We'll open again in the morning.'

'But we've no water and no food,' whispered Jenna, but only I heard her. For a moment we stood dumbstruck. What were we going to do? Then, all around us, people started to sit down – sit down exactly where they were in the queue. The woman in front of us scowled and grumbled as she sat, but then she pulled a water bottle from her tunic and sipped at the contents, and I felt my knees buckle. Jenna and I sank to the ground.

'I can't believe it, I can't believe it,' Jenna was whispering, but my thoughts were numb.

The sky darkened, and the talk gradually subsided as people slipped into sleep. 'Tell me another story,' said Jenna, looking up at the sky.

But I couldn't.

I've never felt as thirsty as I did that night. The thirst did strange things to my mind. I was convinced that I was still awake, but then I would realize that I was leaning sideways on some stranger's shoulder with my mouth open. At one point I opened my eyes to see a man urinating by the fence. A baby cried. A fight broke out just behind us over a water bottle. The woman in front hastily stowed hers out of sight, and I found my gaze fixed on her tunic, wishing I could burn a hole through it with my eyes and take the water.

There was a sudden urgent exchange of voices up ahead, and I strained through the darkness to see what was happening. Someone rattled the chain links of the fence – a woman cried out, 'But my child is dying!' – and there was a sharp retort from the guard on duty. The cocking of his gun echoed through the night, and from then on there were no more disturbances.

People around me took on a strangely monochromatic appearance. I couldn't see colours any more – everyone was dressed in shades of grey. Even their faces and eyes were grey. I looked down at my own grey hands curiously, and it was as though they multiplied in front of my eyes, giving me eight fingers and two thumbs on each hand. I laughed, and the sound was peculiar, like bubbles being blown through water. The thought made me even thirstier.

The gates didn't open until the sun was fully up, and by then I had convinced myself they never would. A new group of soldiers appeared to relieve the ones who had stood guard over the gate, and they laughed and joked with each other. They smelled of food and good health, and my stomach turned over.

People struggled to their feet, and Jenna and I did the same. I felt dizzy at the movement and we clutched each other for support. 'One at a time,' called one of the soldiers. 'Just remain calm.'

That was easier said than done, and I clutched my papers convulsively, filled with an unreasonable terror that someone would try to steal them from me.

It took nearly an hour before it was our turn. The woman in front of us was waved through the gate with no questions asked, and she turned to give us a triumphant look before disappearing into the camp.

Then a man was stopped. The soldier looked very carefully at his identity paper and began shaking his head. 'Please,' said the man.

'Sorry,' said the soldier.

I felt cold. Why was the man being refused entry? He took back his paper and his shoulders slumped. As he turned away, I could see tears in his eyes. I had never seen a man cry before. Forgetting my place, I put a hand on his arm. 'Why won't they let you in?' I asked.

He stared at me, defeated. 'My brother works for the Kwana,' he said simply, and held out his hand. A crumpled badge with the letter A stared up at me from his palm.

My hand fell from his arm as I remembered the boy at school who had punched Ruman and not been punished because his father worked for the Kwana. The man in front of me made a resigned face, as if he knew he would be hated by everyone, and walked slowly away. People hissed at him as he went. I didn't know how to feel. He was just a man, just a person, like us. But . . . The Kwana were responsible for so much tragedy. They'd killed Potta. How could I feel sorry for this man and at the same time hate what his family stood for? If he didn't work for the Kwana himself, was he bad?

A small part of me felt a rush of relief. Presumably the soldiers were refusing entry to those with Kwana connections, then, which meant that we should be allowed in.

All of a sudden it was our turn.

'Papers,' said the soldier, holding out his hand. I gave them to him.

'We are sisters,' I told him, my throat hoarse, but he waved his hand to indicate that I should stay quiet. He read our papers very carefully and examined the badges on our tunics. 'Where are your parents?' he asked. He spoke our language clearly but with a foreign accent.

I swallowed. 'Our father is dead, and our mother – got lost.'

Jenna nodded.

The soldier looked at me and then at Jenna. His gaze swept over us from head to toe, and I felt suddenly very alone and nervous. The corner of his mouth twitched up and he made a comment in another language to a soldier standing next to him, who turned to look at us and then laughed. 'You can go through,' said our soldier, handing back our papers with a smile.

'Oh, thank you!' I said fervently.

Jenna babbled, 'Thank you, thank you,' as we hastily squeezed through the narrow gap between soldiers and on under the archway and through the gate.

Once inside, I felt vaguely surprised. On the other side of the gates was a row of wooden huts, and some army jeeps. Soldiers were sitting in the sunshine, passing round bottles of water, playing cards, polishing boots. It all looked so normal. And yet, at the same time, there was something not quite comfortable. Guns were tossed casually over tent pegs, the banter sounded loud and unfamiliar in my ears, and every now and then some of the men would look over at us. After I accidentally met the frank gaze of a young soldier, I blushed and kept my eyes down. But I knew that the laughing comments were directed at us, even if I didn't understand the language.

Jenna had reached for my hand again, and we kept each other moving forward. There was a soldier on the other side of the huts who was calling out instructions, his foreign accent making it difficult to decipher his words. 'One bottle perpers. One bottle perpers.'

'Perpers?' said Jenna in bewilderment, but I had seen the truck filled with water bottles, and in an instant I had run over, my hands held out. 'Amina!' I heard Jenna say in admonishment, but then the soldier handed over the precious bottle, and I ripped apart the plastic seal and guzzled down the contents.

'Hey!' said the soldier. 'One bottle perpers. Last all day.'

Jenna caught up with me and wrenched my arm down. 'Don't drink it all! It sounds like that's all you've got for the day.'

'For the *day?*' I said in alarm. I had already drunk over half the bottle. My throat was burning for more, but I reluctantly put the cap back on while Jenna received her bottle.

'Don't lose,' said the soldier, pointing at the bottles. 'Refill.'

We nodded. 'Where do we go now?' asked Jenna, but the soldier didn't understand and simply waved us away, reaching for another bottle for the people coming in behind us.

We took a few steps back. 'It must be that way,' said Jenna. 'That's where everyone else is going.'

I screwed up my nose. 'What's that smell?'

As we passed the remaining trucks, an astonishing sight met our eyes. As far as the eye could see, there were tents. But not the neat, rectangular white tents of my imaginings. These were makeshift affairs of sheet and stick, held together by string and wire;

flimsily constructed sheds of corrugated iron and bricks; blankets simply spread out on the dusty ground.

And people. People everywhere – old, young, male, female, shouting, silent, busy, unconscious . . . Person upon person, skin upon skin, crammed together.

Jenna gripped my arm. 'Oh, Mini,' she whispered. 'Look at them all. I never thought there were this many people – I mean, I didn't think . . .'

I nodded in silent agreement.

'Hey, you!' A soldier called to us. 'Pretty girls! You need tent?'

I blushed again, and I knew Jenna was blushing too. We weren't used to being called 'pretty girls', and Potta would have been furious if he'd heard those words. I glanced at the soldier and then quickly away. But we did need a tent, didn't we? I looked at him again, and he smiled back at me and headed straight over. Instantly I felt nervous.

He was blond, with dark glasses and a lopsided grin. 'I can get you tent,' he said.

Jenna wouldn't speak, so I had to respond in some way. 'Where?' I looked around, but there was no truck full of tents, like there had been with the water.

The soldier leaned towards me – too close. 'What you give me?'

'What?' I stepped back.

'What you give me?' He reached out and touched my arm. 'For tent?'

'Nothing! I haven't got anything. What do you mean?'

Jenna pulled me away. 'Come on, Mini.'

I could hear the soldier laughing as we hurried away. I felt humiliated. Was this how men behaved in other countries? How did the girls cope with it? Weren't they embarrassed?

There were paths of a sort, but nothing formal, so it was a question of zigzagging our way through the tents, blankets, cooking pots and people. We had been walking for about ten minutes when Jenna suddenly stopped. 'Where are we going?'

The encounter with the soldier had been churning around in my head and I hadn't even noticed where we'd walked. Now I dragged my attention back to the present moment. 'I don't know. I suppose we need a bit of space for us. To, you know, make our own home.'

'With what? We don't have a tent, or food, or anything.'

We stared at each other in despair.

'I wish Mamie was here,' said Jenna in a small voice.

I swallowed the lump in my throat. 'And we need to look for Vivie.'

'You two all right?' A woman with a kindly face was looking up at us from a nearby blanket. Her black hair was braided with once-bright threads, and on her lap she held a young child, who was playing listlessly with a bit of rag.

I couldn't help myself. 'Not exactly,' I said. 'We don't know where to go or what to do. We haven't got any food, or a tent.' I gulped. 'And I've drunk nearly all my water already.'

'Just arrived?' said the woman sympathetically. We nodded. 'No parents?' she asked, her gaze flicking from Jenna to me.

I shook my head, not trusting myself to speak any more. My throat ached.

'Sit down with me for a bit,' said the woman. 'Lemo and I could do with the company, couldn't we?' The child looked blankly at her. He was small and thin, with dark eyes that looked as though they saw things that weren't there.

'Are you sure?' I said.

'We really ought to be finding a place for ourselves,' said Jenna hesitantly.

'No hurry,' said the woman. 'There'll still be just as little space by the end of the day as there is now.'

'I didn't expect to see so many people,' I said.

'No one does. It's funny – you think that things are only bad in your own little village, and then you come here and realize that it's everywhere. Everyone is hurting.'

My vision blurred as tears fell from my eyes. My knees shook.

'Sit down,' said the woman softly. 'You look like you've come a long way, and you could do with a rest. I might even be able to find a bit of bread for you.'

Such kindness, when we'd been so scared, made me want to sob my heart out. And the mention of food was too much to bear. Without even consulting Jenna, I folded myself into as small a shape as possible so as not to take up too much room on the grubby blanket. Jenna hesitated for another moment but then sat down too. It was a relief to take the weight off my feet again, and I wiped my eyes, determined to stay strong.

'I'm Cosima,' said the woman. 'And this is Lemo, and he's four. Say hello, Lemo.'

Lemo picked up his bit of rag again. Cosima sighed.

'I'm Amina,' I said, 'and this is my sister Jenna.'

'Pleased to meet you,' said Cosima, giving us a smile. She fumbled in a bag by her side and produced a grubby flatbread. 'I was saving this for my son,' she said, 'but I'm sure he'll be able to find something else.'

'Oh, we wouldn't want to take food away from Lemo,' said Jenna quickly.

Cosima smiled again. 'My other son. Aron. He's off doing what he does – you know. Collecting water and suchlike. He'll be back sometime.' She nodded towards our water bottles. 'Keep those by you at all times, even when they're empty. You go to refill once a day, and if you've lost your bottle, they won't give you another one. Likewise, if you find one lying around, it's yours to keep, and that means you get twice the rations because they don't check. But you won't find one lying around.' She chuckled. 'They're worth more than gold in here. So make sure they're safe at all times, even when you're sleeping. People are desperate.'

I took the bread and tore it in half as carefully as I could, although my hands were shaking. I tried to eat it as slowly as possible, nibbling away like a mouse, savouring each bite. It tasted wonderful, and I felt calmness sweep through me with each bite. Maybe I could keep going a bit longer now.

Cosima watched us eat. 'Not eaten for a while?' she said. 'Have you come far?'

Jenna nodded. 'Several days' walk.'

Cosima raised her eyebrows. 'Only days? You were lucky. It took us three weeks to get here.'

'Three weeks?' I stared at her. 'Wasn't there a camp closer to you?'

Cosima laughed. The sound was almost shocking after our miserable few days. 'There aren't any other camps,' she said. 'Not official ones, anyway. This is it.'

'For the whole country?'

She nodded. 'That's why there are so many people here. Altiers is the only place you can get help.'

I looked across the heads of the people I could see around me, sitting, talking, bustling between tents and sheds. Just from where I sat, I must have been able to see at least a hundred. A hundred people within a few metres – and many more beyond. They were, almost without exception, grubby, smelly and exhausted. They didn't look like they were getting much help to me.

# 13

Cosima told us about herself and her two sons. 'I had
a husband,' she said sadly. 'But things went bad
in our village.' She paused, and I wondered if the
same thing that happened to Potta had happened to
her husband. 'It was those letters. Set neighbour
against neighbour, that's what they did. Suddenly
people you thought were your friends didn't want to
know you.'

I nodded, thinking of Davir at the market.

Cosima sighed. 'Never mind. We don't talk of it
because it upsets Lemo.' She stroked the child's head
affectionately. He stared blankly at the bit of rag, rubbing it over and over between his thumb and finger. It
unnerved me slightly – it was as though he wasn't
really taking in what was happening around him.
There'd been a boy in our village who had looked like

that. There was something wrong with his brain, his parents said. He wasn't very good at understanding things. One day he simply wasn't around any more and I never asked where he'd gone. His parents hadn't mentioned him again and after a while we'd all forgotten he existed. It was funny how one thing could remind you of something you'd forgotten a long time ago.

Now I leaned forward. 'Hello, Lemo.'

He showed no sign of having heard me, and I didn't know what to say next.

'What was your village like?' Jenna asked into the silence. 'Was it nice?'

A smile brightened Cosima's face, and I could see the laughter lines at the corners of her eyes. 'Oh yes. Lots of nice neighbours and never any trouble. I used to go to market twice a week, and my husband' – she swallowed – 'my husband ran a successful business. We had a lovely little house, with brick walls. My husband built it for us when we were married. It had five rooms and running water.'

'Five rooms and running water!' It sounded like luxury.

'Two bedrooms, a kitchen, a washroom and an

188

entertaining room,' said Cosima proudly. 'I decorated it myself with things I made.'

'Like what?' asked Jenna.

'Oh, anything. I like making things. I found a broken mirror one day and made it into a mosaic set with pebbles. You could see fifty different versions of yourself in it.' She laughed. 'And I hung scarves and fabric from the ceilings, to brighten the place up. It's amazing what you can do with a little imagination.'

I glanced at the tent behind her. It was worn and patched with bits of rag. Cosima followed my gaze and sighed. 'I know. Not much imagination to be found here.'

'Amina has too much imagination,' Jenna said unexpectedly. 'That's what our parents used to say.'

Cosima turned to me, interested. 'Really? I don't think there's such a thing as too much imagination. Do you make things too?'

'No,' I said. My face reddened. 'I tell stories.' It sounded silly.

'How lovely. We love stories, don't we, Lemo?' She stroked his head gently. 'Stories can help when nothing else works.'

Jenna nodded. 'That's what I think too.'

Cosima gave me a very kind look. 'You're lucky – and to be able to tell stories to your younger sister too: that's a great gift.'

'Younger? Oh – the headscarf.' I touched the navy fabric around my head. 'This is Jenna's. We swapped because I'm better at talking to people.'

'Ah!' Cosima smiled again. 'You needn't worry about that in here. Everyone talks to everyone. You could even take them off – some women have.'

'Take them off?' Jenna sounded appalled, and even I hesitated. We'd worn them for such a long time, it would feel very strange not to.

'I think we'll keep them on for the moment,' I said, 'but maybe we should swap back again, Jenna.'

She unwound the green scarf quickly and handed it over. My head felt bare for a moment until I put my own back on. It was odd how comforting it was – and yet I could have cheerfully burned it only a week ago! Maybe it was because it was one of the few things we had brought from home.

Home. My eyes filled again at the thought. Was Ruman still in Talas? Was he still a rebel? Would we ever see him again? I missed my brother dreadfully as it struck me that he would be the perfect companion to have in this camp. He had always been the person in the family with whom I felt I had most in common.

'Can you tell us a story now, Amina?' asked Cosima. 'I'd love to hear one.'

I shook my head.

She saw my sadness. 'I'm sorry. It's hard to find that imagination sometimes, when you're surrounded by this. I know how you feel.'

'How long have you been here?' Jenna asked.

'Ten days, three hours,' said a voice behind me. I twisted round, blinking, to see a tall boy about Jenna's age, with a shock of black hair and a dusty face. He didn't look friendly. 'Who are you?'

'Oh, Aron,' said Cosima. 'This is Jenna and Amina. They're sisters – only just arrived. I asked them to sit with me for a while to keep me company.'

Aron frowned, and I dropped my gaze out of habit. Inside, my heart sank. It had been a relief to sit and chat with Cosima. She was a comforting presence. But now that Aron had arrived, the atmosphere changed.

'Mother . . .' he said.

'What?' Cosima replied, challenging. 'It's lonely here, and these girls have nowhere to go.'

'We have little enough as it is,' said Aron. 'You can't go around taking in charity cases.'

Something in me twisted. 'We're not charity cases,' I said sharply, forgetting myself and glaring at him. 'We don't want anything from you.'

'Really?' Aron met my gaze squarely with deep black eyes. 'Are you trying to tell me my mother hasn't already given you something?'

I flushed, remembering the flatbread – Aron's flatbread, the one Cosima had been saving for him. I looked down again, hating the way boys always had the upper hand.

'I thought so . . .' Aron shook his head in disgust.

'We didn't ask for it,' said Jenna in a small voice. When he didn't answer, she started to get to her feet. 'I'm sorry. We didn't mean to cause any harm. We've just been walking a long time, and we're all alone.' Her voice caught and she swallowed. 'Your mother was kind to us. But don't worry, we'll find somewhere else.' She reached a hand down to me. 'Come on, Amina.'

I felt small and young and tired all over again. And I envied Aron and Lemo: they still had their mother.

'Now, wait a minute!' Cosima was on her feet too

now, Lemo tumbling to the ground without a whimper of protest. She was taller than I had imagined, and her dark eyes flashed at her son. 'How dare you speak to our guests like that, Aron! I have invited them into our home – our space – and you treat them with contempt. I am ashamed of you! I didn't bring you up to speak to young ladies like that. Living in this godforsaken place has clearly robbed you of your manners. And let me remind you that while you may now be the man of the family, I am your *mother* and you will respect my wishes and my actions.'

To my astonishment, Aron looked very uncomfortable and started scuffing at the ground with his foot. It was almost as though his mother's words had reduced him to a child again – this tall boy who was nearly a man. 'I'm only thinking of you and Lemo,' he said in a voice that had more than a tinge of complaint to it.

'No you're not,' said Cosima sharply. 'You're thinking of yourself and your own needs. What about the needs of other people? You are not the only one to suffer – look around you. Why should your suffering outweigh the suffering of others?'

I felt almost as ashamed as Aron looked. Cosima was right, of course – what made one person's suffering worse than another's? So we hadn't eaten for a few days – so we had lost some members of our family. We weren't the only ones in that position. At least Jenna and I still had each other, and were able to walk, talk, see, hear. We had hope that we might even find Vivie! I had started to feel too sorry for myself.

'Please,' I said, 'don't blame him. I would feel the same way in his situation. We've taken advantage of your kindness. We're not really in that much need: we can work – I'm sure we can find ways of feeding ourselves. And we have family somewhere – I don't know where, but we hope to find them again.' I turned to smile at Aron. 'You have a very kind mother. I'm sorry we ate your flatbread; we were hungry, but we didn't have to take it from you. Maybe we'll see you around the camp.' I reached out a hand to Jenna. 'Come on. Cosima, thank you so much, but we don't need to add to your worries. I wish you well.'

Cosima nodded at us, speechless. Aron too seemed lost for words, his dark eyes unreadable. Jenna and I began picking our way through the blankets and tents again, but we had gone hardly twenty steps before Aron caught up with us.

'Stop,' he said. 'Come back. I was rude – my mother was right.'

'It's fine,' I said, 'really. You don't have to do this.'

'You don't understand,' said Aron. 'Mother would be glad of the company. And I . . .' He swallowed. 'I would be glad if you stayed with us. I have to spend most of the time getting food and other things. It would set my mind at rest if there was someone else there to watch over them.'

I felt a bit nervous. Aron hadn't been friendly. If we stayed, would he start to order us about, like boys and men always did back home? Would it not be better for us to concentrate on looking for our own family, rather than joining another? But a big part of me was drawn to Cosima. It would be so nice to have someone looking after us again . . . 'Do you have room?' I asked, glancing at Jenna, who looked as undecided as I felt.

Aron shrugged. 'We have enough – we can make room. And, like you said, you can be useful too. Maybe we could share the work.'

I looked into his dark eyes and felt a jolt of

kinship. We were all in this together, after all. Maybe we could help each other. 'Jenna?' I asked.

'I think we could all benefit,' she said quietly.

Aron nodded, still looking at me. 'Come on, then.'

Cosima beamed at us when we arrived back at her patch. 'Right,' she said practically, 'let's get you sorted, shall we?'

I was glad that Cosima had given us the bread because I quickly realized that being in the camp wouldn't involve a lot of sitting around – not for us, anyway. Aron took me and Jenna on a tour, pointing out the important places, and I felt my jaw drop lower and lower at the scale of it all. 'I never thought it would be so big,' I murmured to Jenna after we had picked our way through rows and rows of people.

Aron heard me. 'It wasn't this crowded when we arrived,' he said. 'More people come every day. They're going to run out of room before too long.' He pointed to a long line of people. 'That's the queue for food.'

I tried to see the beginning of the queue but it wound round a corner.

'It stretches almost all the way round the camp,'

Aron informed me. 'It takes hours to feed everyone, and sometimes they run out of food before the end of the queue, so you have to make sure you get a good place.'

'How do we do that?' I wondered.

'We have to start queuing as soon as it gets light. They serve food from midday onwards. We must get you your tins.'

Jenna and I glanced at each other. This felt like another world, full of new rules and ways of doing things that we had no knowledge of. I wished again that Mamie was with us. I felt too young for all this. 'Tins?'

'Over here.'

Within an hour, Aron had secured our food tins from the administration hut, with the use of our identity papers. 'Don't lose them,' he said sternly. 'You won't be given another – see they've put a mark on your papers? That shows you've already been given your tin. It's to stop people taking more than they're entitled to.'

We nodded. I was glad to get away from the administration hut; it was staffed by soldiers who stared at me and Jenna in the same way as the others had. 'What are we going to do about food today?' I asked. 'We're too late, aren't we?'

'I have a system,' said Aron. He pointed. 'See that boy there? The one with the scar on his face? That's Ghion. He's representing several people.'

'How do you mean?'

'Well, later in the day, when the food is about to arrive, I'll take our tins and go and join him.'

Jenna frowned. 'Isn't that cheating?'

Aron glanced at her. 'Everyone cheats. You have to, otherwise you don't get anything. That's just how it is.'

I nodded. It made perfect sense to me, but I could see why Jenna didn't like it. It wasn't fair, exactly, was it?

'We take it in turns,' said Aron, 'to stand in the queue.'

'We who?'

'There's four of us. You can't really form a bigger group than that or people kick up a fuss and the soldiers start getting involved. And you don't want that, believe me.' He laughed.

I shivered. I wanted as little to do with the soldiers as possible. Seeing them on the dusty track outside

Talas, taking off my headscarf to wave and cheer – all that felt like a very distant memory. Besides, seeing soldiers passing in cars and trucks was quite different to standing in front of one, smelling his aftershave as he examined your identity papers. 'What sort of food is it?' I asked, to try to think about something else.

'Stew, mostly. Bit watery, but it's better than nothing. Sometimes meat, though it's full of gristle, sometimes maize, usually beans.'

It showed how hungry I was that the description made me salivate. Stew! With meat and beans! I didn't care if it was mostly gristle and water, it was food. 'When will we get it?'

Aron grinned. 'Not for ages. Sorry.'

His frank look made me blush. I wasn't used to boys poking fun at me in a friendly way. Only Ruman had ever spoken to me that way before and it made me feel embarrassed. But it was also nice. Aron had obviously got over his initial hostility and was treating us more like family.

Or was it simply that here in the camp, there were fewer boundaries? Everywhere we went, we saw men, women and children sitting together, eating together, talking, playing . . . Back home, you could hardly move without tripping over family traditions and Kwana rules. Maybe, because there were no Kwana here in the camp, people didn't feel they had to behave the same way any more?

Thinking of the Kwana made me wonder what had happened to the sad man outside the camp, the one whose brother was a member of the Kwana. Was he sitting outside the gates, hoping for a change of heart from the soldiers? Or had he turned round and gone home, wherever that might be? For the first time, I wondered why he had left his home and where the rest of his family were. How many people had been torn apart from their loved ones in the past few months?

'Amina?' Jenna pulled at my arm. 'Are you all right?'

'What?' I blinked. 'Oh, sorry. I was miles away.'

'Come on,' said Aron, 'I'll show you the latrines.' He said it naturally, as though there were no shame in the word. I blushed again and was angry with myself for doing so. We were going to have to adapt very quickly if we wanted to live here.

'I haven't seen Vivie,' Jenna said in a low voice.

I was startled. I hadn't been looking for my sister,

and Jenna's words made me gulp with guilt. 'Neither have I.'

'There are so many people . . .'

I was going to reply, but a terrible smell reached my nostrils and made me gag. As we rounded a corner, my eyes grew wide in horror. 'This is it?'

There was a little row of ten huts, with broken doors. People were queuing outside them, taking turns to go in and pull the door closed as much as they could. The smell was horrific. 'We have to go . . . in *there?*' I said, appalled, my voice muffled through my sleeve.

Aron nodded. 'The soldiers get angry if you go anywhere else. It's disgusting, but at least it's cleaned out once a day.'

I stared at the line of people, trying not to breathe. 'How many latrines are there for the camp?'

'There's another ten at the far end. That's it.'

The thought of using the stinking latrines filled me with horror. I turned away to see Jenna wiping her eyes. 'What kind of a place *is* this?' she said, her voice shaking.

'You get used to it,' said Aron, and his voice was

surprisingly kind. 'And at least we don't have to clean them out.'

I was thankful that his family's tent was a good distance from the rancid stench. We had gone over a hundred metres before I was brave enough to take my arm away from my nose and mouth.

By the time we got back to Cosima and Lemo, it was nearly time for the daily food rations, so Aron collected up all our tins and went off to join Ghion. 'I'll tell the others about you two,' he said.

'Won't they mind?' I asked.

He shrugged. 'Why would they?'

*You did*, I thought, but kept it to myself.

'Thank you,' said Jenna.

'Yes,' I agreed, inwardly scolding myself for lack of manners, 'thank you.'

Cosima, who had been gazing up at us from her position on the blanket, gestured to the ground. 'Sit down with me. You look like you need a rest. It's a shock, isn't it?'

'The latrines . . .' said Jenna in a horrified voice.

'I know. Back home, I would never go somewhere like that. But here, we live in filth.' She sighed. 'This is the best we can hope for at the moment.'

I stayed silent. The latrines were bad, but they weren't the worst thing about the camp. With every step, I had seen people lying on the ground, discarded, as others walked by and kicked dust in their faces. Or children whose arms and legs were thin as reeds but whose stomachs were as round as the moon. And everywhere, that blank stare from people who had lost everything, including their hope.

Jenna must have seen the same things as I did, but neither of us spoke of it. Words had never normally deserted me, but faced with this . . . There were no words big enough or sad enough or scared enough to describe how we felt.

That night we huddled together on Cosima's blanket and cried. Neither of us spoke, and we made no sound, but we cried all the same.

# 14

'We have to search for Vivie,' Jenna said the next morning.

I nodded. Lemo looked at me with his big eyes.

'Now?' asked Aron, but Cosima shushed him.

'Of course now. She's family.'

Aron shrugged. 'All right. Do you want me to come with you?'

I was surprised, and touched by his offer. 'Are you – don't you have to fetch water or food or something? I mean, can you spare the time?' Aron knew the camp like the back of his hand, and what was more, he was a boy and— No. I must stop thinking like that. It wasn't his job to protect us and speak for us. I straightened my shoulders. I didn't have to be subservient any more. The idea was quietly thrilling.

'I will go and speak to the others,' Aron told us,

'about the food queue. Maybe one of them will go for water for us too.' He disappeared.

'How will you look for her?' Cosima asked. 'Does she have anything particularly unusual about her? People here don't look quite as they did back home . . .'

'We'll know her when we see her,' Jenna said firmly, and I agreed. In my mind, Vivie's face was as clear as the blue sky. Though when I thought about her, I always pictured her standing next to Mamie, and that made me ache with sadness. Where was Mamie now? How was she being treated? Would she ever be able to come and find us?

By the time Aron came back, I was fidgeting impatiently. 'It's all right,' he said. 'Everything is sorted for today, but I owe a few favours.'

'Thank you so much,' Jenna said gratefully.

'Are you going to ask people, or what?' Aron said.

'I thought we could just look at them,' said Jenna hopefully. 'As we go past. I don't want to cause any trouble.'

'What about the people who are in tents?' I wondered. 'I mean, Vivie might be in one of them and we'd walk right past her without realizing.'

Jenna bit her lip. Then she shook her head. 'No. Vivie will be looking for us too. She won't be hiding away. We will just walk up and down, looking at as many people as we can.'

It was slow work, and the more people I saw, the fewer I wanted to see. Some glared back at us, and I looked away in embarrassment. Others didn't even notice us staring, and that was almost worse because they didn't seem to notice anything. It was hard too, trying to find ways between tents and blankets without stepping on people. There were a few main paths marked out, but in between those the people were tightly packed. Noises and smells overwhelmed me.

There were a lot of children in the camp – many of them Vivie's age. Jenna and I stared and peered at the grubby, grey and scruffy; at the crying, wailing and moaning; at the running, tripping and playing. Many of the girls no longer had headscarves, which made it easier and harder to recognize our sister. We knew her face so well, but we had hoped that her orange scarf would make her easy to pick out in a crowd. I never thought that I would wish for those scarves!

We picked our way through family after family, trying to look everywhere at once. Sometimes a face flashed past me, and I turned, convinced it was Vivie and trying to see where she had gone. Once a girl with flying dark hair came running towards me, and for one heart-stopping moment I thought, *It's her!* and held out my arms to embrace her.

But the girl veered to one side, glancing at me in confusion, and I realized it wasn't Vivie at all. My heart sank again.

By the time the sun was high in the sky, we were exhausted and thirsty, and I could tell Aron was starting to become impatient. 'We need to get back to Cosima,' I said to Jenna, while my eyes scanned the surrounding people for any glimpse of familiarity.

'All right,' she said unwillingly, 'but after a rest we should come out again.'

'I can't believe we haven't seen anyone from Talas.'

A young woman sitting nearby looked up at us. 'Talas?' she repeated. 'Did you say Talas?'

'Yes,' I replied, hope clutching at me. 'Why? Are you from Talas too?'

'Yes, but' – her forehead creased – 'you don't look familiar. Which side of the market were you?'

Jenna and I eagerly explained, our words tripping over each other's. The woman, who couldn't have been much older than Jenna but seemed to be in charge of two small children, nodded. 'I know where you mean. Near the Strame family.'

'They lived next door!' I felt a rush of excitement at finding someone who knew Talas. 'My name is Amina – Amina Ambrose. This is my sister Jenna.'

'I'm Clea,' said the young woman. 'Do sit down, please.'

There was only a tiny amount of space on their rug and it was encrusted in mud, but it seemed rude to refuse. I glanced up at Aron. 'Do you want to go? We can find our own way back.'

I could tell he was glad of the offer. 'Are you sure?'

I nodded. 'It's fine.'

'All right, then. See you later.'

Clea and her two young daughters had lived closer to the market than we had, but she knew many of the same people. Her husband had been a teacher at Ruman's school, she said.

Jenna and I exchanged glances. Ruman's teacher? Then was he perhaps . . .

Clea's eyes filled with tears. 'They killed him,' she said quietly. 'Outside the school, in front of everyone.'

I didn't know what to say.

'We know,' said Jenna softly. 'He taught our brother.'

Clea shook her head angrily, though her cheeks were wet. 'He was stupid and too outspoken; I told him so, many times. I knew it wouldn't be long before something happened, but *that* . . .' She wiped her eyes and took a breath. 'My girls and I were lucky to escape.'

The girls were playing with a bit of rag, passing it backwards and forwards and occasionally pushing each other. They couldn't have been more than two or three.

'We're looking for our sister,' I told Clea. 'She tried to go back when our mother was stopped at the checkpoint.'

'When was this?' she asked.

I tried to remember. 'A week ago? Less?' How many days had it been since we left Talas? I could no longer tell.

'We must have come through at about the same

time,' said Clea. 'We only arrived yesterday afternoon. We would have been here sooner but I kept having to carry the girls and it slowed me down.'

I couldn't imagine walking all that way carrying two children, and I looked at Clea with respect. She must be very strong.

'What was your sister like?' asked Clea.

We told her about Mamie and her forged papers and how Vivie had started screaming that she wouldn't be parted from her.

Clea's face cleared. 'I remember that!'

'You do!' Jenna reached for my hand impulsively. 'Did you see what happened?'

'We were further back. I didn't see the event, but I heard the yelling, and I saw the Kwana holding a woman. The little girl was trying to get to her.'

'That's right, that's right! Did you see where they went?'

'The little girl pushed her way right back to her mother, I think, and clung onto her waist. I saw the Kwana trying to peel her off, and heard them telling her to let go. But she didn't – and then I think someone said it wasn't worth the fight. But I don't know whether they were talking about the woman or the little girl – and then we were at the checkpoint and I didn't see any more.'

'So maybe Vivie *did* go with Mamie after all!' I breathed.

'I don't know, I'm afraid.'

'But she did get back to Mamie after we left,' said Jenna. 'That's more than we thought.'

We looked at each other again. I didn't know whether to feel happy or sad. If Vivie had gone with Mamie, then at least they would be together. But that meant . . . that meant we were here on our own. Just the two of us.

'Is that good news?' asked Clea hesitantly. 'There was a woman on the road whose husband was in the Kwana in Talas. He'd told her to get out of the village and go to the camp to be safe, but of course I don't know if they let her in. She said her husband worked on the checkpoint. Maybe she'd know more about your sister and your mother?' One of the little girls climbed onto her lap and banged her head against Clea's chest. She sighed and stroked the little girl's cheek. 'There's nothing there, sweetest. It's all dried up.' The girl was suddenly and violently sick.

Jenna and I jumped to our feet in alarm.

'I'm so sorry, I'm so sorry,' said Clea, trying to clear it up.

'No, no, it's not your fault,' said Jenna. 'Can we – can we help?'

I screwed up my nose. I didn't want to help; it smelled awful.

'No – you go,' said Clea, not really looking at us as she soothed her daughter, who was now wailing. 'It's fine, we'll be all right. Come and see me tomorrow, though. It's so nice to find someone who knows Talas.'

We promised we would and then hurried away.


'So what are you going to do now?' asked Cosima when we had told her everything that Clea had said.

What could we do? Nothing had changed, had it? We couldn't go home. Neither Jenna nor I knew how to answer.

'Please stay with us,' said Cosima. Her eyes were kind. 'Until you find your family. Stay with us.'

I was glad she said 'until'. It suggested that one day we would all find each other again.

'All right,' Jenna said, and I nodded. 'Thank you. We will.'

*

We settled into a routine. Each day was very like the one before, in terms of structure. Every four days it was our turn to wait in line for food, which meant standing there nearly all day. Since it was the most tedious thing we had to do, Aron, Jenna and I took turns so that at least I only had to do it once every twelve days. Aron had been right that it was usually stew, and to my surprise it was tasty and not watered down. It was our only proper meal of the day, so I was grateful that it was of good quality.

As for the latrines, the least said about them the better. I learned to go quickly, breathing through my mouth to reduce the smell, and not to look too closely at anything on the ground. Even my imagination couldn't erase the appalling stench, though I tried valiantly to tell myself stories of beautiful things while I waited in line.

First thing in the morning, two of us would go to the water tap with our bottles in a tightly wrapped sheet. It was safer for two to go, since people sometimes tried to steal bottles away from you as you were filling them up. Most often, it was Aron and me who went, and Aron would stand guard with a big piece of wood while I carefully filled up our five bottles. Then we would carry them back to the others.

I had to learn how to make my water last all day. The first few days we were there, I drank too quickly, and by sundown my throat burned with thirst. Jenna offered me some of hers, but I refused all but a tiny sip because I was angry with myself for not being more careful. She, of course, rationed her water much more efficiently than I did. It never felt like enough to drink, but re-joining the water queue would have taken several more hours and wasn't worth the effort.

On the third day, Aron and I were walking away from the tap when we heard an anguished cry behind us. I turned to see a woman distraught over the bottle she had accidentally dropped. The plastic had split, spilling the water onto the dry ground and leaving the bottle unusable. 'But my baby is ill!' cried the woman. 'Please, please, someone – I need a new bottle.'

The soldiers guarding the tap looked sympathetic but did nothing. She ran up to one of them and tugged on his jacket. 'Please,' she begged. 'My baby will die without the water. He's only two months old and he's ill.'

He spread his hands in a helpless gesture, and the woman turned to the other people in the queue. 'Please!' she begged again. 'Please someone – surely someone will be kind enough?'

I turned away quickly, hot with shame. *I should help her, shouldn't I?* But the water . . . it was so precious. I clutched my bottle. I couldn't live without it.

But neither could her baby.

Someone else would help, wouldn't they? Of course they would. But tears pricked my eyes as Aron and I walked away.

'You did the right thing,' Aron said to me in a low voice as we headed back to our patch. I jumped. Had he read my mind? 'Don't feel bad.'

'She said her baby will die . . .' I didn't know how to go on. 'How could we all stand there and not do anything?'

'Maybe the baby will die anyway,' suggested Aron. 'You can't be sure that giving her water would save its life. And we're all desperate.'

'I don't know . . .' *Mamie would have given the woman a bottle*, I thought. Or would she? If it meant all of us going with less, would she still sacrifice it? 'The soldiers should give her another one!' The thought relieved me and I stopped. 'I should go back and tell them to give her another.'

'Are you mad?' Aron grabbed my arm as I turned to go back. He looked alarmed. 'You can't go getting involved with things like that.'

'But I'm sure they've got spare bottles,' I argued. 'Someone should explain to them – someone should stand up for that woman.'

'It doesn't have to be you,' said Aron. 'I've seen people get in trouble for confronting the soldiers. I've been in trouble myself. Believe me, you don't want to make them angry.'

I stood, hesitating. Aron seemed to sense that his argument hadn't quite won me over. He gave an exasperated sigh and lowered his voice. 'Look, by the time you get back she'll have gone anyway. It's not your problem, Amina. In here, it's every person for himself.'

My shoulders sagged. 'I know. I just – we're all in the same situation, aren't we? Shouldn't people help each other out?'

'They do,' Aron pointed out. 'Like the food queue. And if people have got a bit extra, they do share it with others. But we haven't got any extra, have we?'

'No . . .' I sighed. 'It's just not fair. That's what I don't like.'

'You have to get used to it,' Aron said, and his voice hardened again. 'You have to get used to a lot in here.'

I glanced at him curiously, but he had turned away.

'I would have felt like you,' Jenna said, after I had told her what happened. 'There's too much death here already. And a baby . . .'

That was the difference, wasn't it? Even on that first tour round the camp, we had seen people lying so still that I was sure they could no longer be breathing. Since that first day, I had seen more bodies and heard more cries. Death was common, from starvation and sickness. You only had to listen for the wails and the sobs to know that death was never far away. But somehow it was so much worse when it was a baby.

I looked out for the woman when I next went to the water tap, but I didn't see her. I wondered every day whether her little boy had survived or not. People came and went, and sometimes you never knew why. Jenna and I had gone back the next day to talk to

Clea again about Talas, but she had gone, and so had her little girls.

I hoped very much that something good had happened to make them leave so quickly. And I wished that I had asked her the name of the woman she'd met on the road – the one who might know more about the Kwana checkpoint and what had happened to Mamie and Vivie. We stood no chance of finding her now.

After a few days Jenna started teaching Cosima to weave – since we didn't have reeds, she made use of all the bits of blanket and rag that were lying about. We took to having a small tin of water for washing in, and Jenna would rinse the rags in this tin and hang them out to dry on the tent. Then she and Cosima tore them into suitable strips and started to weave them together.

To start with, it just seemed like something to do, but after a while people noticed what they were making and started bringing them bits of rag, along with requests, such as: 'I'd love a blue mat for our tent,' or 'Can you weave pictures into the rug?' Jenna's mats were hard-wearing and offered some protection against the hard ground. She soon found herself inundated with orders for handmade mats and bags, and people paid with whatever they could find – more bits of rag, a tin pot or two, a small piece of soap, a pair of shoes – even, sometimes, loaves of bread or sweetmeats. 'Best not to ask . . .' A woman winked at an astonished Jenna as she handed over a bar of chocolate. 'You don't want to know where I got it.'

I helped with the weaving and found it far more satisfying than the sharp reeds we had woven at home, but I still didn't have the patience necessary to do a really good job. Still, it was nice to feel that others valued our skills, and the bartering of goods went some way to making me feel better about not giving up a water bottle. People *did* help each other – Aron was right – but in their own individual ways. Soon we had a thriving little business going, and that helped pass the days

Sometimes I awoke in the night and the awful crushing grief was too much to hold inside. At those times, Jenna would usually wake too and we would press ourselves together and rock in silent sobbing. We had a new life here, but it was nothing compared with memories of the old one, and I knew that both of us would give almost anything to return to the past. But we couldn't let ourselves become swamped by sadness. And besides, people around us were in the same situation; we could see what happened to those who gave in to despair. They were the ones who sat staring into nothing, gradually wasting away until they were gone. Those who fought, who showed strength – they were the ones I looked up to.

Kindness too was sometimes found in the most unexpected places. I was walking back from the water tap one day and dropped one of the precious bottles without realizing. When I got back to our patch, I was distraught. 'You idiot!' exclaimed Aron. 'How could you have let go of it? You know we'll never get another one!'

His sharp tone hurt me. 'I'm so sorry,' I said, looking at the worried faces around me. 'I'll go back and look for it.'

'Don't be stupid,' he said. 'It won't be there any more.'

I bit my lip as my eyes filled. He'd never spoken to me like that before. And then, from behind me, I heard: 'Is this yours?' A woman, with long hair let loose by the loss of her headscarf, held out the bottle, still full. In the other hand she had a small girl by the ear. The girl was squirming and grumbling.

I was speechless for a moment. 'Thank you, oh, thank you,' I said, gratefully taking the bottle from her. 'How very kind of you – I can't begin to thank you enough.'

'We have enough suffering in this camp without stealing from each other,' said the woman, giving the girl's ear another twist. She yelped. 'I keep telling her – the only way we can survive is to work together. Each of us must play our part. The minute we stand alone, we fall alone.' She nodded at me, and then walked away, releasing the girl, who stuck out her tongue at us before dashing off.

'Well!' said Aron, clearly as speechless as I. 'Well!' I felt so relieved that he wasn't going to shout at me any more.

The woman's kindness was all we talked about for the rest of the day. The only person who wasn't surprised by it was Jenna. 'It wasn't her water bottle,' she said, shrugging. 'She had no right to keep it, and she knew who it belonged to. I would have done the same.'

I stared at her. 'Would you really?' Since the day we'd seen the woman with the broken water bottle, I had wrestled with this. As time went on, I felt more and more possessive about the few things we had: they were never enough. I felt hungry and thirsty so much of the time. If I'd found a water bottle lying on the ground – even if I'd seen someone drop it – I knew now that I would have kept it.

A strange feeling made me glance to one side, and I realized that Aron was watching me. It gave me a nasty jolt to think that I had now come round to his way of thinking; that neither of us would have returned the water bottle.

Did that make us bad people?

# 15

'I don't *do* anything,' I moaned to Jenna one day soon after the mishap with the water bottle. 'You're always weaving things – being useful. Mine are no good, you know that. What can I do?'

'What's brought this on?' she asked.

I shrugged. 'Nothing in particular.' But in my head, I could still hear the young woman who brought back the water bottle. *Each of us must play our part,* she had said. *We must work together – each person should bring something to the whole.* My guilty conscience over the woman with the baby, and the knowledge that I wouldn't have returned the stolen water bottle, made me anxious to do something good. But what could I do? My imagination was the only thing that had ever been remarkable, but it had almost completely deserted me since we arrived in the camp – and what use would it be here anyway?

That night, Lemo started to scream. He had done it before, but usually only in his sleep. Once awakened, he would quieten again, but not tonight. Cosima held him and rocked him, but Lemo continued to scream, his eyes wide with unseen terrors.

The rest of us stared blearily as Cosima looked helplessly at Jenna. 'What should I do? He'll wake everyone up.' And indeed, there were already mutterings from the nearby tents.

'Maybe he needs fresh air,' suggested Jenna. So they took him outside, but if anything Lemo's screams grew louder. Aron and I looked at each other.

'Why does he do this?' I asked.

Aron hesitated. 'He saw bad things.' His mouth closed, and it was as though his expression closed too. I wondered what he meant – what kind of bad things? Had Aron been there too? But there was no sense in asking him now.

I got up and followed Jenna outside. 'Ssh, ssh, there there, it's all right,' Cosima was whispering to Lemo. 'My poor boy, don't upset yourself. Look how peaceful it is here. Everyone is asleep.' She looked upwards in despair. 'Even the stars are sleeping peacefully – see them?'

Lemo screamed.

'Some of them aren't sleeping,' Jenna said hurriedly. 'In fact, some of them are fighting great battles. They're warriors, you know.'

Lemo's scream stopped abruptly and he stared at her.

'Amina knows all about it,' she went on in desperation. 'Tell him, Mini.'

'What . . . but *here*? Now?'

Lemo took a breath and let out another scream.

'Mini,' said Jenna in an angry tone, '*tell him the story right now!*'

I blinked. I'd never heard my sister sound so commanding! But Lemo's scream was the kind that drilled through your head and made your eyes water. So I said hurriedly, 'Jenna's completely right, Lemo. They're not stars, they're warriors – fifty thousand of them. They went into the sky to fight a great battle.' And I repeated the story of Alham and his army – the tale I had told Jenna when we were on the road to the camp. I remembered most of it without too much trouble. By the time I had got to the bit about

Null and the wicked advisers, Lemo had quietened completely, and was sitting cross-legged next to me, one hand resting gently on my knee. Cosima, astonished, was sitting behind him, and although she had begun by stroking his shoulders, her hands stilled as my story went on.

'And that's why the stars twinkle so brightly,' I told Lemo. 'Because they're all warriors, each and every one of them – trying to get home, but too far away to make it now. So they watch over their loved ones instead, sending light in the darkest times.' I stopped, surprised by the last line. I hadn't consciously meant to say that, but it sounded right.

There was a silence, and I suddenly realized that Lemo wasn't the only one sitting listening. Several people from nearby tents had come out too.

'That's a beautiful story, Amina,' said Cosima quietly. 'Really beautiful.'

'More,' said Lemo, and we all gasped.

'Oh, my boy,' said Cosima, and her voice wobbled. It was the first time he'd spoken since they arrived.

'Amazing,' breathed Aron. His gaze flicked from his brother to me, and there was something like awe in it.

'More tomorrow,' I told Lemo. 'If you choose a star, I will tell you which warrior it is. But now it's time to sleep.'

Lemo nodded, and his eyelid drooped in response.

Cosima gathered him into her arms. Her eyes were bright with tears. 'Thank you,' she whispered to me. 'Thank you so much, Amina. He spoke!'

'It's like you hypnotized him or something,' Aron said. 'Just by using words.' He shook his head, as though he couldn't think of anything else to say.

Cosima smiled at me. 'You have an extraordinary gift, Amina. Extraordinary. You should treasure it.' There were answering murmurs of agreement from a couple of people sitting nearby.

I was quite glad it was dark so no one could see me blush. Cosima and Aron went into the tent with Lemo, who was fast asleep. Jenna squeezed my arm and said, 'Come on. We must rest too.'

I felt slightly embarrassed as I lay down to sleep. Who would have thought that my silly made-up story would have such an effect? But there was a warm glow inside me too. My imagination hadn't disappeared after all. And here, maybe, it would be valued.

\*

The next evening, Lemo came and sat next to me, looking up hopefully. 'He wants another story,' said Cosima, smiling. 'I haven't seen him this excited for ages.' She had a new air of happiness about her too, as though Lemo's animation had sparked something in her.

'All right,' I said, encouraged. 'We should wait a bit longer though, so that we can see the stars properly. Then you can choose a star, Lemo, and I'll tell you the story of that warrior.'

Lemo nodded and settled himself on the ground, gazing upwards.

An old man called Maklam came out of the tent next to us. 'You are going to tell another story?' he asked.

I was a little taken aback. 'Yes.'

'May I listen?'

'Of course,' I said, feeling embarrassed again.

Maklam put his head back into the tent and murmured something. Two women came out after him, glancing at me shyly. They were his sisters, but they usually stayed in the tent, and I had heard them sobbing many a night. 'My sisters will join me,' he said. 'We will all listen.' The women nodded.

'Oh – all right.' I couldn't help smiling. 'I used to get told off for telling stories,' I admitted.

'Amina!' Jenna frowned.

The old man's face cracked into a wide smile, revealing four or five teeth. 'Things are different now,' he said. 'Stories are all we have.'

Cosima had told me that Maklam's family had been split apart by fighting and that somewhere he had three children and five grandchildren. Maybe that was why the women cried at night. Tonight's story had better be a happy one, I told myself sternly.

I turned to Lemo. 'Have you decided on a star?'

He pointed. I leaned across, trying to follow the line of his arm. 'That bright one?' I asked. He nodded. I couldn't be sure I was looking at the same star he was, but it didn't matter. 'Good choice,' I told him. 'This one's a lovely story. That warrior is called Clemus, and he grew up in the countryside. His father made wine and his mother washed and boiled the bottles, along with crushing the flowers and fruit.' I was pleased. Already this story sounded nice and positive.

Lemo placed a hand on my knee and I put mine over it. What would appeal to him? I wondered.

'Clemus was a bit of a naughty boy,' I went on. Lemo's eyes brightened. 'He liked to play silly jokes on people. Once, he hid a frog in the bucket of fruit that his mother was due to crush. When she put her hands in, the frog jumped up her arm and into her shirt. She screamed so loudly that everyone thought she was having some kind of fit.' Was that a glimpse of a smile from Lemo? Certainly, there were chuckles from other people, including Aron. I felt warm inside. Aron was so serious all the time, a laugh from him was a rare thing.

'Everyone came running,' I continued, 'and when they discovered the frog, Clemus was in so much trouble! His father was so angry he locked Clemus in a cupboard for three days. He wasn't just angry because Clemus had upset his mother and shown disrespect – he was also angry because the frog had contaminated the fruit in the bucket, and so the whole lot had to be thrown out.

'Clemus was very upset. He hadn't meant to make everyone angry. He thought it was funny. He liked playing jokes on other people, but he wasn't very good at thinking about how they might react. He was cross with his father for locking him in a cupboard.

He thought it meant that his father had no sense of humour, but he didn't realize how much trouble his father's business was in.'

Tonight's story was flowing so easily! It was almost as though, having not been used for so long, my imagination was bursting to be heard. It was no trouble at all to think of what might happen next.

'Clemus's father was a very proud man, and he didn't like to admit that he was losing money. So for a long time he hid his worries from everyone. But day by day he grew more anxious, and in the end it was impossible to hide any longer. Besides, Clemus was not stupid, and one day he said to his father, "Father, what are you keeping from us?" And the father broke down and cried, and told him that the business was failing and he wasn't even sure he had enough money to keep the vineyard and orchard any more. "The seasons have been unkind," he said. "First there was not enough rain, then too much. The flowers have not blossomed as they should and the fruit has been of poor quality. Nobody is buying wine from me any more."

'Clemus was shocked. His father had always been such a stern, proud man, and here he was, looking broken and old. Clemus was still only thirteen, but he felt very strongly that he should do something to help.' Help – that's what we all needed, wasn't it? And helping each other was something that was so important in the camp.

'Clemus said, "Don't worry, Father. I will help. I am old enough to go out to work, and I will make sure that you and mother never have to worry again."

'His father looked at him and said, "You? But you are just a boy. How can you help?"

'Clemus said, "I am not just a boy. I am nearly a man, and this is my chance to prove it. I will go to the city and make my fortune." And he went straight to his room and started to pack the items he would need for his journey.

'When his mother heard, she came rushing to him, begging him not to go. "The city is full of evil people," she said. "Whatever has happened here, we can mend it ourselves. Don't leave!" Clemus felt sorry for her, but gave her a kiss and said he would be back before she knew it, with the money to save the business. His mother cried and cried at the loss of her only son, but Clemus took one last look at his home and started on his journey.'

I swallowed. All this storytelling had made my mouth go dry but, as usual, I had drunk all my water before sundown. Then Jenna passed me her bottle. I took a grateful sip – not too much – and looked around. It felt as though there were just us few – Aron, Lemo, Cosima, Jenna, Maklam and his sisters – existing in a special little world. It made me feel warm and safe; something I hadn't felt in a long time.

I took a breath and went on with the story. 'Clemus set out on the main road, and on the way, he met a merchant who was taking carpets to market, but his wagon had broken down. Clemus was anxious to get to the city, but he thought he could spare a few minutes. So he helped the merchant to mend his wagon, and in return, the man let him ride all the way into town, which took two days. "Lucky for me that you came along," said the merchant. "You've mended my wagon and kept me company too."

'When they got to market, Clemus helped the merchant to unload his carpets. "I tell you what," the man said. "If you help me sell my carpets today, I'll give you some of the money I make." Clemus thought for a moment and then agreed. He was so good at selling carpets that the merchant sold twice as many as he did normally. "You bring me such good luck," he told Clemus. "Why don't you come and work for me?"

'"No thank you," said Clemus. "I'm off to seek my fortune." But before he set off again, he put the money he had made into a parcel and determined to send it to his family just as soon as he could find a messenger to take it.

'The next person Clemus met was a young woman who had been abandoned by her family. "They didn't want me," she said tearfully, "because of this." And she showed Clemus the side of her face, where a large growth spoiled her beauty. "I can sing," she said, "and play the guitar, but people won't listen to me because of how I look."

'Clemus felt sorry for her. "Can't something be done?" he asked.

'"Yes," said the girl. "I could have an operation. It's not a difficult one, but I don't have the money to pay for it." And she started to cry again.

'Clemus hesitated for a moment, thinking of the money he had planned to send to his family. His mother had always said he should be kind and helpful. What would she want him to do? He offered the money to the girl. She was so grateful she asked him to come along with her while she had the operation.

"'Look at me now!" she cried afterwards. "See how happy you have made me!" Clemus thought she looked very beautiful, but he felt awful that he had no money to send home to his family.

"'Now I will repay you," said the girl, and she took her guitar and set herself up by the side of the road, and began to sing and play. And everyone who went past said how beautifully she sang and gave her lots of money. At the end of the day she gave it all to Clemus.

"'But you earned it!" he said.

"'Yes," she replied, "but if it hadn't been for you I couldn't have. And besides, I can earn more tomorrow."

'Now Clemus had even more money than he had earned selling carpets. He felt so happy that he could send it home to his parents. But as he sat eating supper, he met a man who was so poor he hadn't eaten for five days. Clemus shared his food with the stranger and then decided to give him all his money.'

There were gasps from those around me. 'All his

money?' echoed Cosima faintly. 'What about his parents?'

I smiled. I had already worked out the ending to this story. 'Wait and see,' I told her.

'The stranger thanked him and took the money, and that night Clemus slept in the street, because he had no way to pay for shelter. And although he was pleased that he had helped the stranger, he felt sad that again he had nothing to send home.'

'I should think so too,' muttered Cosima.

'But the next morning, the most amazing thing happened,' I went on, excited to be able to reveal the end of the story. 'Clemus awoke to find the stranger standing in front of him in the street, now wearing grand robes. The man smiled and revealed his true identity. It was none other than Prince Alham himself! "I thought my father's kingdom was full of selfish people," he told Clemus, "but you have restored my faith in humanity. In return, I am offering you a job in my palace."

'Clemus was astonished, but of course he wasn't going to turn down an opportunity like that. So he went happily along to the palace with the prince. Not only was he given an important job there, he also received a generous wage. And every week, when he got paid, Clemus put the money into a parcel and sent it home.

'Back home, his parents were amazed to receive money so quickly from their son, and before very long they had enough to put the business back on its feet. And once it was all right again, they built it up so that in the end they were one of the wealthiest families in the country.'

Cosima sighed. 'What a relief.'

'Ssh,' I said with a smile. 'There's a bit more. One day, the father said to the mother, "You know, I'm so grateful to Clemus for all this. If it hadn't been for him, we would probably have died from starvation years ago. Why don't we go and visit him?"

'The mother thought this was a brilliant idea, so one day they packed up their things and set off for the palace. But when they got there, they discovered it was the day that Alham and his army were due to set off to fight the country in the sky, and Clemus was going too. All the fifty thousand warriors were dressed in their shiny armour and riding their fine horses, and Clemus's parents couldn't tell which one he was. In despair at the thought that he might leave without them saying goodbye, they painted a huge banner with the words WE'RE PROUD OF YOU, CLEMUS on it, and spread it out over the ground, so that when Clemus and his horse leaped into the sky, he would see it.

'And Clemus did indeed see the banner as he jumped into the blue sky, and it made his heart sing with happiness. And every night now, his star shines very brightly in the sky, glowing with happiness that he had saved his family and they were proud of him.'

I looked down at Lemo. His eyes were no longer blank – instead they looked as though they were seeing the warriors in the sky as he gazed upwards. His whole body seemed more alive, somehow. I felt proud of myself. It was a strange feeling; one that I wasn't used to. But I had made a difference to him, just by telling my stories.

Then, quietly at first, there was a little pattering sound. People were clapping – and not just the people who had started off listening, but others who had joined us during the story without me noticing.

They were clapping my story.

# 16

After that night, Lemo seemed to take it for granted that I would tell him a story every evening before bed. Not only that, but other people took to dropping by to listen too, so that by the end of the week there were at least forty or fifty who turned up as dusk fell, and squashed into what little space there was. Maklam and his sisters beamed and made more room on their shabby blanket.

'This is amazing,' said Jenna, looking around. 'Who would have thought people would want to come and listen to stories?'

I felt defensive, the way I used to when my family questioned the use of my imagination. 'They make them happier,' I said. 'They make them forget the bad things.'

'Oh, I know,' said Jenna hastily. 'I just meant that

when people have so little, you wouldn't think they'd want to sit around and listen to stories.'

Stung, I retorted, 'Stories are just as important as rugs, but in a different way.' Then I felt bad as Jenna flushed.

Aron broke in. 'What I can't understand is how you constantly come up with new stories every evening. How do you think of them?'

'Oh,' I said, diverted, 'I don't really know. They just come to me.'

'But do you spend the day thinking what you're going to say that evening?'

'No, not really. I just start talking, and the story sort of tells itself.' I realized how strange that sounded, but I didn't have any other way to describe it. Now that I was telling stories regularly, it was becoming easier and easier. I just started off, and the story unrolled like a long carpet. All I had to do was keep walking along it. Sometimes I was aware that I was remembering people or things that had happened in my own life; sometimes not. It didn't matter. The story told itself.

People started to come up to me after each story, to press my hands or murmur thanks. The first time it happened, I felt horribly embarrassed. A woman I'd never seen before came towards me through the darkness, her cheeks shiny with tears, her arms outstretched. I automatically took a step backwards, but she grabbed my hands and squeezed them between her own. 'Thank you, thank you,' she said, her voice shaking with emotion.

'Um . . .' I said. 'You're welcome?'

'Thank you,' she said once more, and then turned and vanished into the gloom, still sobbing.

I didn't know what to say, and neither did Jenna. Aron was less surprised. 'Look at the effect the stories have on Lemo,' he said with a shrug. 'They're like magic.'

The next night, someone else came up to thank me, and that seemed to prompt a veritable flood of people. I found it all a bit overwhelming, but Cosima urged me not to be ungracious. 'They need to say thank you,' she told me. 'You have given them something.'

'It's not a *thing*, though,' I said uncomfortably. 'Not like food or water.'

'It's just as important,' she said.

I had to admit that a small part of me was buoyed

up by the enthusiasm of my listeners. It was as though I had finally found a place for me: something I was good at was something other people liked and wanted me to do.

One evening, a woman who must have been in her forties came to listen. She came the next night, and the next, scuttling away as soon as the story was over. On the sixth night she approached me, weeping. She didn't seem to know what to do, though – she made as if to hug me and then did a sort of bow, which embarrassed me. Then she started mumbling some words I didn't catch. 'I'm sorry?' I said. 'What did you say?'

Another woman standing close by said, 'That's gypsy language,' and gave the older woman an uneasy look.

Gypsy language, just like Mamie had been able to speak all her life but had kept a secret! My breath caught in my throat. 'Are you from Talas?' I said impulsively.

She shook her head and my heart sank. 'Calabash,' she said, or something like that. Her accent was unfamiliar to me, but she did add, 'Beautiful story,' before dissolving into tears again.

That evening it had been about a mother and son who had loved each other so much that she had made all kinds of trinkets and talismans to keep him safe in the battle for the sky. 'My son,' said the woman. 'Love my son.' And then she began to cry again before shuffling away.

The next day she brought me the most beautiful ornament to hang on the tent, made out of string, wire and shiny pieces of glass. 'To keep away evil,' she told me as she passed it to me.

'I can't take this,' I said, amazed. 'It's too precious.'

But the woman had already turned away, nodding in satisfaction. We hung the decoration on the tent, where it twinkled in the sunlight, and people stopped to say how pretty it was. Every time I saw it, it made my heart thump with pride. It wasn't the same as selling baskets at market for real money, but someone had thought my story good enough to be rewarded. That was worth a lot to me. And I couldn't stop thinking about the woman and her gypsy heritage. 'We should look for Mamie,' I told Jenna.

'For Mamie?' She stared. 'What are you talking about? Mamie is in prison, back in Talas.'

'We don't know that,' I said. 'It's ages since we

arrived and there are a lot of people here now. Some of them must be from Talas. They may have news; be able to tell us what has happened there since we left. We should look for Ruman too.'

'Mini—'

'Maybe there are relatives here, Jenna! Mamie's family, the ones she never really talked about? Maybe some of them are here – maybe the woman we saw is actually *related* to Mamie?' I was fired up with enthusiasm now.

'Amina! Stop getting carried away!'

'What's the matter?' I stared at her. She was pale. A suspicion crossed my mind. 'Have you given up on them, Jenna?'

'*No!* No – how can you even say that? No, of course not! But Mini . . .' Jenna looked around helplessly. 'Where do we start? You remember what it was like, that day we looked for Vivie. And every day since, when I've seen a girl who looks a bit like her – I keep thinking she's here, and then she's not, and it makes me sad all over again . . . It's just that, if we're going to look for them again, we need to do it slowly. Carefully. I can't have my heart broken twenty times a day.'

I took a breath. 'All right. I'll slow down. But you *do* think we should look for them? All of them?'

'I think,' Jenna said hesitantly, 'that we should look for whatever might give us a clue.'

'A clue. Yes!' I liked that. It made it sound fun and more like a mystery that we had to solve, rather than what it really was: a search for the other pieces of our hearts.

# 17

Once, when I was little, I had a story book. A real book, with pages and pictures, and it was all mine. It was about a mouse who was a detective, and he went everywhere looking for clues. I loved that book so much that I read it every day, sometimes three or four times. It was old and battered before I had it – Potta had found it on a rubbish dump – and after so many readings, it fell apart completely. Then, one day, Vivie got hold of one of the pages and tried to eat it. She was only a baby at the time, but I was so upset I cried for a week. I treasured that book – not just because it was a thing that belonged to me, but also because it gave me a glimpse of another world.

Now, setting off the next day with Jenna, I felt like I was in a story too. Amina the detective! Surely, in a camp this size, there must be one person at least who could give us a clue to the whereabouts of the rest of our family? We just had to find that person; and if it meant asking every single individual in the camp, then that's what we had to do.

Curiously, the person I longed to see most at that moment was Ruman. He would have understood what I felt about clues and mysteries. He'd have been turning the camp upside-down to find us, I was sure.

'Can I come?'

For a moment I didn't realize who had spoken. Lemo was on his feet, looking up at me with his big brown eyes. 'What?' I said, astonished. He hadn't spoken since that evening when he had said the single word 'More' at the end of my first story.

'Can I come?' he said again. His voice sounded weak but it was there.

Cosima's jaw dropped. 'He spoke!' She shook her head, as though unable to believe it. Then she put her hands on his shoulders and turned him to face her. 'Keep going, darling. Try again.'

Lemo frowned and wriggled out of her grasp. He looked up at me again. 'Please. I want to come too.'

I looked from Jenna to Cosima, not knowing what

to say. Lemo didn't know his way around the camp. What if he ran off? 'Um . . .'

Jenna too was baffled. 'I suppose . . .' she said slowly.

'Lemo,' said Cosima, recovering herself, 'why don't you stay here with me? Jenna and Amina will tell us everything when they get back.'

Lemo was obstinate. 'I want to go with Amina.' It was as though the Lemo we had met when we arrived had been replaced by a completely different boy. What had happened?

'It's not safe,' Cosima tried. Then she took a breath. 'All right. If Amina and Jenna say you can.'

Lemo gazed on me with imploring eyes. He ignored Jenna completely. I felt touched that he wanted to be with me.

'But,' went on Cosima, 'you must stay by their sides all the time – you understand me? No running off. In fact, you should hold Amina's hand so that she can make sure you're safe.'

Immediately, Lemo slipped his hand into mine. It was small and warm, and holding it reminded me suddenly of Vivie. 'Now, no running off,' I said gruffly, trying to swallow down the lump that had appeared in my throat. 'You stick by me all the time.'

Lemo nodded enthusiastically, a beaming smile breaking across his face. He straightened himself, as though going into battle.

I could see that Cosima didn't want him to go at all. She was biting her lip and taking deep breaths. 'I'll look after him,' I assured her.

'Just you make sure you do,' she said – so fiercely that I blinked. 'Don't you let him come to any harm. I'm relying on you, Amina.'

Relying on me! I didn't think anyone had ever said that to me before. I wasn't sure whether to feel proud or terrified. 'I will,' I said, hoping that nothing would go wrong.

Jenna, Lemo and I set off through the camp. 'We should work systematically,' said Jenna. 'Start at one particular place and then work in a straight line. That way we can make sure we don't miss anyone.'

We started at the edge of the camp nearest the water tap, but I thought privately that working in a straight line would be near impossible. Straight lines weren't common in Altiers!

Jenna took the lead, which surprised me, as she'd never liked talking to strangers or putting herself forward. But since our conversation the day before it was as though she had a new determination about her. 'Hello,' she would begin, 'my name is Jenna and I'm looking for my family. Can I ask where you're from?'

People liked her polite way of speaking, and were polite in return. I wouldn't have started that way, but I was impressed by my sister. After watching her for a few minutes, I suggested that Lemo and I could target other people so that we could cover more ground in the time. 'Do you think it's a good idea to split up?' Jenna asked, looking a little nervous.

'I'm just hanging around at the moment,' I pointed out, 'while you do the talking.'

She smiled. 'Seems like we've changed places.'

'I know!' It made me laugh. Who would have thought that talkative Amina and good-girl Jenna could swap roles?

'All right. But stay in sight, yes? As much as you can anyway.'

So I took Lemo along and started asking people questions in the same way Jenna had. 'Hello, my name's Amina. I'm looking for my family. We lived in Talas – do you know it?'

An elderly woman with cracked lips and chipped

teeth beamed at me. 'Talas,' she said nodding sagely.

'Yes!' I said. 'Talas! Are you from Talas too?'

'Talas,' she repeated. 'Talas.'

'Did you live there? Whereabouts? Did you go to the market?'

She smiled at me, and then at Lemo. 'Talas,' she said again, and kept nodding.

My heart sank. 'Thank you,' I said politely, and moved on, tugging at Lemo, who was staring at the woman with fascination. Her mind was somewhere else, that was clear, and she couldn't help us.

'We'll try someone else,' I told Lemo.

He nodded. 'Talas,' he said. 'Talas? Talas. Talas!' It was as though he were trying out a new word, or maybe mimicking the old woman.

I felt a bit embarrassed. People were staring at Lemo; if they thought he was out of his mind, they wouldn't want to talk to me. 'Oh, look!' I said, trying to distract him. 'That tent has a flag flying over it.'

Lemo blinked. 'England,' he said abruptly.

I stared at him, and then back at the striped blue and red flag. 'Really? How do you know?'

'Books,' said Lemo, losing interest. He tugged on my hand. 'This way.'

Books! Did Lemo love books too? All of a sudden I wanted to know what kind of books Lemo had had back at home. Was this why he loved stories as much as I did? Then he and I were kindred spirits! 'Tell me about your books,' I started to say, but Lemo had stopped still in front of a small group of people, and they were staring at us. With an effort, I dragged my mind back to the present task. 'Hello, my name's Amina. I was wondering if you could help me?'

After a while I lost count of the number of people I spoke to. One of them had heard of Talas, but most hadn't. Then it occurred to me to mention Gharsad, since that was where Potta had taught at the university. More people had heard of Gharsad, but still no one knew anything about Talas or our family.

One woman with a thin face and kind eyes smiled sadly at me. 'Seeing you gives me hope,' she said, after admitting that she didn't know Gharsad or Talas. 'I have lost my daughter too. I pray that she is looking for me – that way I can hope that one day we will be reunited. At least you have your brother with you.'

I glanced down at Lemo. I liked the idea that people might think he was my brother. 'That's true,'

I said. Lemo squeezed my hand and smiled at me.

'Aren't you the girl who tells stories?' came a sudden voice.

I turned to see a boy, younger than me, staring from his position on a nearby blanket. 'Well,' I said, hesitating, 'which stories do you mean?' Did he mean telling lies?

'The stories about the stars,' said the boy.

'Yes,' said Lemo, before I could answer. 'This is her.'

The boy jumped to his feet, delighted. 'I knew it! Heard you the other night. It was a really good story.'

'Oh – thank you.'

'Do you tell stories every night?' he asked.

'Mostly,' I replied. 'I've sort of got into the habit of it.'

'My mother used to tell me bedtime stories,' said the boy. He blinked rapidly and raised his chin defiantly. 'She's gone now. I miss her.'

'Oh. I'm so sorry.' I didn't know what to say. 'My mother's gone too.'

'Bad, isn't it?'

'Yes. Yes, it is.' *Bad* wasn't a big enough word to describe it, but I knew what he meant. 'Why don't you come and listen again tonight? I'll do a special story just for you.' An idea struck me. 'You can choose the star.'

His face broke into the biggest smile I'd ever seen. 'Really? Can I?'

'Of course.'

'I'll be there! Thank you – can I tell my friends?'

'Why not?' I said, shrugging. 'Bring them all if you like.'

'My name is Tiger,' said the boy, grinning from ear to ear.

'Really?'

'It is in here,' said Tiger, grinning even more widely.

Lemo suddenly detached his hand from mine and threw his arms around the boy in a quick hug. Tiger didn't have a chance to react before Lemo let go and put his hand back in mine, looking shy. 'Right,' I said, trying not to giggle, 'let's go.'

That morning, Jenna and I made more contacts than we had in the three weeks since we arrived. No one knew anything helpful, but many of them said they would keep their ears to the ground and come and find us if they heard anything about Mamie, Ruman and Vivie.

'We should have done this before,' said Jenna.

'We did,' I pointed out. 'Sort of.'

'We didn't speak to people, though. Not properly. We didn't ask them about themselves – we were only interested in finding Vivie.'

'People are interesting,' said Lemo in his little voice.

'You're right,' I agreed, 'they are.' And maybe this was another way for us to be helpful in the camp. By talking to people. It would help us, if anyone knew anything about our family, but it might help them too. More than one person had asked me to come back to talk to them again. They seemed grateful that we had come by. Some of them, of course, were ill or old, and they weren't able to walk about much. The older ones especially wanted to talk to us – in fact, it was hard for me to get away from one old woman! You'd have thought, with so many crammed into such a small space, that they'd all have plenty of people to talk to. 'But maybe they've got bored with talking to their neighbours,' I mused out loud.

Jenna heard me. 'Mamie never did.'

It made me wonder if the Strames were still in Talas – and what had happened to Noori's family.

A peculiar thought occurred to me: perhaps before too long, every single person in the country would end up in this camp.

No, they couldn't. It wasn't big enough, and we already knew they turned people away.

Tiger turned up that evening with at least ten other children. 'Do your parents know where you are?' asked Cosima sternly.

I nudged her. 'Tiger doesn't have a mother,' I whispered.

Instantly, she softened. 'I suppose you can all stay to listen. But then you must go straight back.'

There were some muttered scufflings, and two of the boys shoved each other.

'And if you've come to listen, then you mustn't disturb everyone,' added Jenna.

I glanced at her in surprise. What had happened to my meek, never-speak-up-for-yourself sister? She sounded more like a mother now . . . My heart gave a sudden twinge of pain. In just over a year, Jenna would be old enough to marry and have children. If we never found the rest of our family, what would happen to me?

'Are you ready to begin, Amina?' asked Cosima.

I gave a start, blinking. I had been standing staring at nothing for several seconds, it seemed. Now I looked around. As well as Tiger and the children, there was our usual small crowd, squashed into the tiny spaces between the tents and blankets. Our neighbours were used to it by now and didn't seem to mind, though they were starting to look a little more concerned as the newcomers took up more and more space.

It might have been intimidating if they were all strangers, but I recognized so many of them that it was like talking to old friends.

'Right,' I said. 'Well, then. We need to choose a star.'

Everyone looked up to the sky. 'Tiger,' said Lemo.

'That's right, Lemo.' I was pleased he'd remembered. 'I did promise Tiger that he could choose.'

Tiger's chest expanded with pride. He stared up at the sky, twisting this way and that. Then he pointed. 'That one.'

I tried to look in the same direction. 'That one that flickers? The pinky-red one?'

'No, a bit further over. The one with another little star right next to it.'

'I see it. Ah, so that warrior has a younger brother.'

'No,' Tiger contradicted me. 'A twin.'

I was taken aback. No one had told me how to tell my stories before! 'All right,' I said. 'A twin.'

Tiger nodded in satisfaction, and I began.

'Once, in a high mountain village, a woman gave birth to twin boys. She and her husband had never had any children before, and at first they were as happy as could be. But then the woman took sick and died, and the father was left to bring up the two sons on his own.'

My audience was already quiet, and I slipped easily into my 'storytelling voice'.

'The boys were called Claudio and Diurm, and from the beginning it was obvious to everyone that Claudio was the bigger, stronger twin. He had been born first, and even though he was the older by only a few minutes, he did everything faster and better than Diurm. He walked, talked, ran and killed his first pig before Diurm, and soon people forgot that the brothers were actually twins because there was such a difference between them. Claudio was strong, healthy and brave. He was always the leader when the boys played games; he was always the brave and heroic warrior who won the battle or rescued the maiden.

'Diurm was a pale boy, skinny and with a tendency to catch illnesses. If both boys ate unripe plums, it would be Diurm who was sick. If both boys climbed a tree, it would be Diurm who fell out of it. If both boys went swimming in the glacier lake, it would be Diurm who caught a chill. But despite all this, the boys were devoted to each other. Diurm looked up to Claudio with hero-worship. In his eyes Claudio could do no wrong. In his turn, Claudio did his best to prevent Diurm from coming to harm, although even he could get exasperated sometimes. "It's just a log," he said one day to Diurm as they were crossing a deep ravine. "You only have to walk across it."

'Diurm was quaking and shivering because he was afraid of heights. "I can't do it," he said. "It's too high. What if I fall?"

'Claudio, already on the other side, stretched out his hand. "You won't," he said, and he sounded so confident that Diurm believed him. "I won't let you fall."

'So Diurm started across the ravine, trying to place one foot in front of the other and not look down.

And he was nearly across – his hand was within touching distance of Claudio's – when he suddenly slipped on a piece of moss, and fell sideways off the log.

'But Claudio leaped forward and grabbed Diurm by the wrist. Diurm let out a yell, and there they were for a moment, Diurm dangling from Claudio's hand; the only thing keeping him from plunging to certain death.

'And slowly, slowly, Claudio hauled Diurm over the edge of the ravine, until both boys lay panting on the grass. "You saved my life," said Diurm. "And not for the first time."

'Claudio grinned. "I'll go on saving it, as long as you can't look after yourself. Come on, loser." He playfully punched Diurm in the shoulder, but was very alarmed when Diurm cried out in pain. "What's the matter?"

'"It's my shoulder," said Diurm, trying not to cry. "I think I hurt it when you grabbed me."

'When the boys reached home, their father made Diurm see the local doctor, who said that Diurm had pulled his shoulder out of its joint. He re-set it (which made Diurm yell even louder), but the shoulder was never as good as it had been before, and from that day onwards, Diurm had a weakness on the left side.'

'Just like Livia back home,' I heard one little girl whisper to her friend. 'She had one arm that didn't work properly.'

'Ssh!' said her friend. 'I want to know what happens.'

I smiled to myself. 'When the boys grew up, they both wanted to join the army. Well, Claudio wanted to join the army, and of course Diurm wanted to go wherever Claudio went. But there was a problem – Diurm's weak shoulder. The army rejected him, saying he would not be any good in a battle.

'Diurm was devastated. Claudio had passed the requirements easily, and was very excited about going off to train with swords and horses. But the two brothers would be separated at last. "Don't worry," said Claudio. "I'll come back and visit you." But that wasn't what Diurm wanted to hear. As the day approached when Claudio was due to leave, Diurm went into a terrible sulk. "You are not my brother," he told Claudio. "A real brother wouldn't go off and leave me behind."

'Claudio hated to see his brother upset, and even

though Diurm was being a pain, he understood that it was because he was bitterly disappointed. "What can I do?" he said.

'Diurm shrugged. "Oh, I don't care. Go on, then. Go away. Leave me behind. I know that's what you've been trying to do for years anyway."

'Claudio was very hurt by this. "That's not true!" he said. "You know that's not true. I would take you with me if I could." And then, suddenly, an idea occurred to him. Maybe they didn't have to be parted after all? "Listen," he said. "Maybe there's a way . . ."

'And that is how Claudio and his cousin Dram joined the army. Claudio smuggled Diurm in, saying he was his cousin from overseas and didn't speak their language. However, he was a good fighter – and Claudio demonstrated to the officers that Dram could win a fight against him. Of course, it was all faked – Claudio pretended to be beaten by Diurm – but the officers were taken in and agreed to give Dram a place in Prince Alham's army.

'And so the brothers were never separated. No one knew they weren't cousins but twins – no one would have guessed anyway because they weren't identical. And since they joined the army just before Alham decided to take the battle into the sky, neither of them had seen fighting at first hand. Both of them were very excited about fighting in the sky, and when they leaped up into the blue air, Diurm was at Claudio's right hand, as always. And that is where he remained, doing his best to glow next to his brightly burning brother, who had always and would always outshine him, even in the sky.'

There was silence for a moment when I stopped speaking, and then a sort of sighing noise, as though everyone listening had breathed out at the same moment. I liked that moment the best. It was as though we were all – the audience and me – in some distant place together. Then the clapping began.

'That was wicked!' said Tiger enthusiastically. The children with him were all wide-eyed and glowing too.

I smiled at them. 'I'm really glad you liked it.'

'We're coming back tomorrow,' declared Tiger.

The little girl who had whispered to her friend earlier chimed in, 'And I'm bringing my sister.'

'I'm bringing my aunt.'

'I'm going to tell my cousins and they'll all come too.'

I felt a little nervous. 'Um . . . let's see how much room we've got, all right?'

Maklam beamed, hearing this. 'We will all have to sit on each other soon.' He seemed delighted by the idea.

As the people gradually drifted away into the gloom, Aron grinned at me. 'Looks like you're becoming a local celebrity. Maybe I should build you a stage.'

'Oh, very funny,' I said. 'Aren't you worried, though? I mean, if people keep coming and there isn't room for them . . . Maybe I should stop telling stories to everyone.'

'No,' said Jenna – so sharply that I jumped. 'You can't stop. If more and more people hear about Amina who tells stories, then there's more of a chance that Mamie or Vivie or Ruman will get to hear – and then one evening they might find us. You can't stop. You mustn't.'

# 18

'Radio!'

I turned from helping Jenna tie a strong piece of sacking onto our tent. 'What?'

Lemo ran full tilt into my legs, making me wobble. I dropped the corner. 'Radio!' he said again.

'Who's got a radio?' I demanded.

Lemo pointed. 'Man! New man!'

Jenna and I exchanged excited glances. 'You go,' she said. 'Someone has to stay here and guard the bottles.'

'Cosima's inside,' I said. 'She can look after them.'

'She's lying down. She's got her pains – you know.'

'Oh. Are you sure?'

'You go.' Jenna smiled at me. 'Go and find out what's happening.'

Lemo took my hand and led me in and out of the

tents and shacks to a little broken-down shed. A small crowd of people gathered around it, calling and shushing to each other. A man balanced unsteadily on the roof, a wire aerial held above his head, while a loud crackle came from a battered black radio below.

I felt a surge of excitement. Everything we heard here in the camp was second-hand. People told us things that had happened two weeks ago. We never heard anything up-to-date, unless it was a scrap of conversation between two soldiers, and even then it was almost always about something happening in Bremir or another major city. But this was a radio! There might be news of things happening right now – maybe even in little places like Talas! It was now over three months since we had left. Were things still the same there?

The radio crackle grew louder and there was a sudden burst of language. The gathered group fell silent, craning forward to hear. The man on the roof froze, his arm at an uncomfortable angle.

Lemo looked up at me as I tried to catch the words. There was a lot of hiss and crackle on the radio still, but suddenly it died away and the words came through crystal clear.

'. . . since the letters were removed. Fighting continues on the streets of Hasuf and we know that a curfew has been imposed. We urge all citizens to stay strong. It is only by strength that we will overcome our oppressors . . .'

The crackle burst out again, along with a high-pitched whine that made the listeners clap their hands to their ears and protest loudly. 'I haven't moved!' cried the man on the roof indignantly. 'It wasn't my fault!'

Lemo whispered to me, 'Where is Hasuf?'

'I don't know,' I told him, my mind buzzing. The letters of heritage had been removed? Did that mean people didn't have to wear them any more? Perhaps Mamie was no longer in prison!

'Is it a city?' persisted Lemo.

'I don't know.'

'What's a curfew?'

'Be quiet, Lemo!' I snapped. 'I'm listening!'

He subsided, injured. We waited some more as the radio whined and rustled, occasionally spewing out a couple of words. I fidgeted impatiently. 'Can't you get a better signal?' asked an elderly man at the front in frustration.

The man on the roof shrugged, sending a fresh

crackle through the radio. 'I'm doing my best.'

Lemo tugged at my arm, trying to pull me away. 'I can't leave,' I said. 'What if we get some more news in a minute?'

He pulled a face. 'Boring.'

'You go,' I said. 'Tell Jenna I'm staying for as long as I can. If you need anything, come and get me.'

He nodded before scampering off. I turned back to the little crowd, wishing I could push my way through to the front and thus be nearer the radio. But many of them were men and so I didn't feel comfortable making myself conspicuous. Instead, I hung around at the back and stood on tiptoe in the hope that it might help me hear better.

'That's not an official station, is it?' I heard someone say. 'He said "we" when talking about the people.'

The elderly man at the front shook his head. 'The official ones are still saying the Kwana have control. Propaganda. This must be a pirate station.'

'That's dangerous,' said the first man, though there was respect in his voice. As he turned, I realized he was blind. His milky eyes stared sightlessly past me. 'If he's discovered . . .'

The greying man shrugged. 'The military have other things to worry about. I heard the Kwana were running low on resources. They can't hold out much longer.'

'Do you think that's true?'

'Who knows?'

They turned to face the radio as the words became clear again: '. . . must continue to fight, to stand up for the rights of ourselves, our children. How many of you . . .' The voice died again.

I wondered if I would hear anything useful at all, but somehow I couldn't leave. This radio was a link with the outside world. This was a possible chance to find one of those elusive clues we'd been searching for.

'You've been gone hours.' Jenna was hopeful. 'Did you hear anything?'

'I'm sorry.' They had sent Lemo to fetch me, to tell me that Aron had arrived with the food. I agonized over leaving the radio, but I had heard nothing of any use in the time I had been standing there, and my stomach clenched with hunger. 'It's so hard to work out what's going on. They do sometimes mention places, but I've never heard of any of them. And just when you think they're getting to an important bit, the signal cuts out. It's so frustrating; it makes me want to hit something!'

'You're not the only one,' said Aron irritably.

I glanced at him and my jaw dropped. 'You've got a black eye! What happened?'

'Everyone's going crazy,' he said, touching it and wincing. 'The woman behind me thought I'd taken her tin, and she got her friend involved, and then all of a sudden people were ganging up on me.'

'Did you take her tin?' I asked.

'Of course I didn't!' He sounded hurt that I could even ask such a question. 'I'm not a thief. But no one would listen, and then someone hit me. And when I got to the front of the queue, the soldier on duty said I was a troublemaker and only filled half our tins. He said it was to teach me a lesson.'

I was outraged. 'That's so unfair! We should go back and complain.'

'Complain to who?' asked Aron bitterly. 'You know they wouldn't take any notice.'

I peered at his eye, which was swelling by the minute. I had a sudden urge to try to make it better. 'That looks really sore. Are you all right?'

'I'm fine. Don't fuss.'

'But—'

'I'm fine,' he repeated, shooting a look at the tent. 'Don't make my mother worry.'

'Oh. All right.' I wondered what I could do to help instead. 'I'll go for food tomorrow, in case they remember you.'

'Who would remember me?' Aron gave a short laugh. 'We all look alike to them.'

'I'd remember you,' said Jenna unexpectedly.

Aron glanced at her and she reddened slightly, turning to call for Cosima and Lemo. 'You might,' he said, although it was so quiet she couldn't have heard him.

There was a funny feeling in my chest, like dust in my lungs. Had I just imagined that? The way Aron had looked at Jenna . . . was there something going on between them? She had blushed! The funny feeling intensified and made me cough. 'You all right?' Aron asked me.

I recovered myself. I must have been imagining things. 'I'm fine,' I said shortly, then couldn't resist adding, 'But I'd better go tomorrow because, with your black eye, *everyone* will remember you.' Then I bit my lip. Had I been too bold in poking fun at him? Would he think I was being rude?

To my relief, Aron grinned. 'You could be right. Thanks, Amina.'

I was pleased that he didn't mind sharing a joke with me. But the funny dusty feeling in my chest stayed around for quite a long time.

That evening, the stars weren't as clear as usual. 'There are storms coming,' Cosima said, looking up at the sky. 'That explains the mood.'

'And why the radio stopped working,' said Aron. He had come with me after we'd eaten, to listen again. But the radio had let out a few stuttering squawks and then died completely. 'All that electricity in the air.'

'Storms?' I looked up. If that meant rain, then I would be only too happy to see a storm. Rain meant more water to drink. 'That's good.'

'Is it?' Cosima looked troubled. 'Nature is stronger than we are, Amina.'

I wasn't sure what she meant by that, but for the first time I found myself struggling for a story. There was a restlessness about the audience; they were fidgety and grumpy, and when I faltered in the middle of the tale, some woman made a tutting noise, got up and walked away. A quiet muttering started. I looked helplessly at Jenna, who sat on my left, and Lemo, who leaned on my right knee. Lemo looked up with the same expectation as ever, but Jenna gave me a smile, and suddenly I found the courage to go on with the story. My voice rose. 'And so Camilla cut off all her hair and dressed herself in boy's clothes, and she went along to the training ground where she had worked as a maid all those years.'

It was a tale about a girl who was determined to be as good as any boy, and who disguised herself as a soldier in order to fight for her country and the prince she loved. Alham discovered her identity in the end, but he was so impressed by her dedication and her fighting skills that he fell in love with her too and took her with him on his last great battle. By the time I had finished the story, the audience was listening as intently as ever, but when I looked up to the stars, as I always did at the end, I could hardly see them for the clouds that had swirled into being during the last hour. Others looked up too, and the murmuring began again. I wriggled my shoulders as the last of them melted into the night. 'I feel all icky.'

Aron nodded. 'There's definitely a storm in the air. We should get under cover before the rain comes.' He turned to me. 'That was a very romantic story this evening.'

I coughed. Was there dust in the air? 'Oh, really?' I replied.

'Yes . . . I wondered . . .'

'What?' I wasn't sure I wanted him to go on. I had a strange feeling that he might be going to talk about Jenna and it made me uncomfortable. My gaze flicked sideways to where she, Cosima and Lemo were yawning and getting ready to go into the tent.

'I wondered if you'd been talking to your sister . . .'

Something gave a twang inside my gut, something painful. Maybe the meal we'd had today was disagreeing with me. 'What do you mean?' I started to say, but with a crack that sounded like the sky was ripping in half, a bolt of jagged lightning speared the clouds, and we flinched, instinctively ducking. Lemo gave a short yell and then took off, running wildly into the darkness.

'Lemo!' shouted Cosima. 'Lemo, come back!'

'I'll have to go after him,' said Aron. 'He's frightened.'

He vanished into the gloom. I pulled my scarf over my head, my heart thumping wildly, and ducked into the tent. I felt terrified and relieved in equal measure – I didn't want to know what Aron had been about to say.

Jenna was tugging on Cosima's skirt. 'Cosima, come in. You should get under cover.'

Cosima was staring out into the darkness. 'I should have had a tighter hold on him, Jenna. I should have seen this coming. Why didn't I get him inside earlier?'

'It's not your fault,' Jenna told her. 'And Aron's gone after him. He'll be fine.'

Cosima turned to look at us, her face creased with worry. 'I know he's more like his old self, but he's still such a little boy. And he's terrified of the dark. It was during the night that – that they came. When my husband died. And' – she swallowed – 'and Lemo was there, holding onto my husband's tunic, when they shot him.'

Jenna and I exchanged glances. Cosima had never spoken about this before. I felt a twinge of painful sympathy for Lemo. Aron had said he'd seen bad things. Now I realized we had even more in common – our fathers had both been killed in front of us. Poor

Lemo – so little to have been through that. I hoped that Aron would find him quickly. Lemo had become like a brother to me. It would be terrible if he went back to not speaking to anyone. Jenna reached for Cosima's hand and squeezed it. 'He'll be all right,' she said firmly. 'Aron will find him and bring him back.' Then she managed to pull Cosima into the tent.

The sky seemed full of sound and light – great crashing waves of noise that rolled from one end of the camp to the other, and spiky beams that lit everything with a light brighter than the sun. And then the rain started to fall, big, fat drops of liquid that kicked up dust from the ground and splattered the opening of the tent with mud. Jenna's mats soon darkened with dirt and our legs and feet turned grey. We tried to close the tent flap, but Cosima wouldn't have it. She sat in the opening and stared into the thundering darkness, willing her two sons to come back.

It seemed like an age that we sat and waited. There was no conversation – indeed, it was difficult to hear each other over the noise of the thunder – and Jenna and I only looked at each other in order to exchange agonized glances. I thought that if Aron had any sense, he'd get Lemo under the nearest shelter rather than try to bring him back to our tent, but I didn't like to suggest this to Cosima.

I had seen storms before, but then we had always been safe in our little home, looking out between the cracks of the walls and doors and marvelling at the sight. Storms had been something of wonder, of beauty, but this was altogether different. Our little tent was not built to withstand this kind of onslaught, and patches of damp were already appearing inside the ceiling and walls. Puddles were seeping underneath the edges too, and it wouldn't be long before we were simply sitting in wet mud. Jenna and I did what we could to shore up the edges, but if this rain kept up for several hours, then there would be nothing we could do. I hoped the ground would be thirsty enough to swallow most of it. And of course, there was the extraordinary opportunity to collect our own water for once, so we lined up our tins outside the tent flap and watched as they rapidly filled. Never one to turn down an opportunity to drink, I gulped the water from the tins until I felt sick. And still they filled with rain.

Finally Cosima let out a cry of recognition, and the

next moment Aron had staggered into the tent with a bundle in his arms. Both the boys were soaked to the skin, and Lemo's eyes were closed as Aron lowered him to the ground. 'He's gone funny again,' Aron said, gasping for breath. 'He won't talk or move. I had to carry him all the way like that.'

My heart squeezed to see Lemo so silent, and tears pricked at my eyes. But Cosima was more practical. 'What took you so long?' she cried, quickly stripping Lemo's clothes from his motionless body.

'He was hiding. It was difficult to find him.'

There was nothing I could do for Lemo at the moment: Jenna was helping Cosima. I suddenly realized that Aron was shivering, although whether from cold or exhaustion it was hard to tell. I said to him, 'You should get out of your wet clothes too.' I pulled at his tunic. Water cascaded to the floor. 'Here . . .' I held up a blanket which had so far escaped a complete soaking, and rubbed his hair unceremoniously. Aron winced as I brushed against his eye. 'Sorry. But you've got to get warm. We won't look, promise.'

I held up the blanket so that he could strip off behind it, and then wrapped it round him. 'Thank you,' he said, through chattering teeth. And then his legs gave way, and he stumbled against me.

'Lie down,' I ordered him. 'You need to rest now.' He did so, and I felt a strange throb of power in my chest. At that moment, in that place, I knew I had a purpose, and that I absolutely and completely *belonged*. It took me by surprise.

Cosima and Jenna settled down on either side of Lemo, wrapping their arms around him. 'He's so cold,' whispered Cosima.

'Don't worry,' said Jenna. 'He'll soon warm up.'

'But will he ever speak again?' Cosima brushed a lock of hair out of Lemo's eyes. 'Just when he was doing so well . . .'

*I can tell more stories*, I thought to myself. *I made Lemo better before; I can do it again.* The powerful feeling was spreading through my whole body. For a moment I felt almost invincible. I sat next to Aron, and rubbed his back through the blanket. I didn't know why, but if Jenna had come over to help, I would have fought her off. He was *mine* to look after; it was right that I should be doing it. But he was still shivering and shuddering. How to get him warmer . . . ?

I gave a quick glance at the others, but they were preoccupied with Lemo. This was no time for tradition. I lay down behind Aron and folded myself into his back, wrapping my arm round his shoulders and pressing myself up against him as closely as I could. I had never been this close to a boy before. The contact made me feel quite strange, as though my insides were trying to climb out of my throat. I couldn't decide if it was horrible or nice. But I did know that I couldn't pull away. His shivering went right through me and I could feel the chill from his body spreading into mine. I pressed myself closer and hoped that some of my warmth and power was going the other way too.

Some time later, I awoke to find the skies quiet and the only sound that of regular breathing in the tent. Jenna and Cosima had fallen asleep, Lemo's little body huddled between them. Aron had definitely stopped shivering, and his back now felt warm. I lay gazing at the back of his head, acutely aware of every single part of my body that was touching his, and I wondered whether I could move without disturbing him. It wouldn't do for him to wake and find me pressed up against him – what would he think? The exhilarating rush of energy I'd had earlier was gone, but I was surprised to find myself very reluctant to move. Somehow, this was cosy and comforting, and the strange insides-climbing-out-of-my-throat feeling had subsided, leaving a warm glow in my stomach like honey in the sun.

My arm was resting heavily over his side, and my hand dangled somewhere in front of him. I carefully flexed my fingers, checking that they hadn't gone numb, and almost jumped out of my skin when his hand grasped mine. 'Shh,' he said.

'I thought you were asleep!' I whispered.

'I just woke up.'

'Me too. I was going to . . .' I started to pull away slightly, but his hand closed firmly, lacing his fingers with mine. It felt warm and strong.

'Don't.' It was barely a whisper. 'Just – just stay how you were.'

I hesitated. 'Are you sure?' I tried to twist round to make sure the others were still sleeping. Lying this close to a boy was completely unacceptable. We weren't married! Mamie would be horrified.

'I'm sure,' Aron whispered. He tucked my hand

into his chest, where I could feel his heart beating steadily. It made my heart race and trip in response, and my face started to heat up from my neck to the top of my head. 'Just for a bit longer.'

I bit my lip. 'All right. But only for another minute.' He mustn't think— What *was* he thinking? For the first time in my life I would have dearly loved to know what was going on in someone else's head! Did he think – an awful idea gripped me – did he think *I was Jenna*? I nearly jerked away, but my hand was held too firmly. No, he must know it was me. In which case . . . in which case he was grateful for the warmth I was giving him and he was holding my hand like a sister, I told myself sternly, trying to ignore the stab of disappointment. Yes, that must be it.

Within a few minutes Aron's hand relaxed in mine; his breathing deepened and I knew he was asleep again. I didn't sleep a wink for the rest of the night. Instead, I lay awake, listening to his breathing, feeling his back gently expand and contract against my chest, and tingling all over, as though tiny fireworks were exploding in my body.

# 19

When I heard the others stirring the next morning, I pulled my hand away from Aron's and wriggled around so that we were back to back. It was still closer than we would normally be, but at least no one would think there was anything suspicious going on.

Aron himself slept heavily for another hour, so I was actually away from the tent by the time he awoke, joining the water queue on my own. Somehow I didn't think there would be such a demand for water this morning, and I had even expressed a suggestion to Cosima that we might give it a miss today.

She shook her head. 'There may be water everywhere, but you can't be too careful when it comes to drinking it. My cousin's family all caught an illness from drinking rainwater that had stood on the ground for a day. Straight from the sky is all right, but otherwise you stick to drinking water from the tap, Amina.'

So I had set off to the water tap, casting a reluctant look back at Aron and at Lemo, who was also still sleeping heavily.

The camp smelled different – everything was somehow sharper; more pungent. It looked different too – there was a lot of water around and some people's tents had collapsed under the onslaught. Women were wringing rags onto the ground outside their patches and having arguments about who was the wettest.

The sky wasn't clearing, either. Although it had stopped raining, the clouds were still covering the blue, and they didn't look white and fluffy but grey and threatening. There wouldn't be any sun today to dry the puddles, and I felt a strange foreboding about the day and night to come.

The oppressive feeling before the storm had dispersed, and people looked less tense but more depressed. Despite my expectations, there was already a long line of people waiting for water. Cosima wasn't the only one to be suspicious about drinking the rainwater, although on my walk I saw plenty of small children lapping happily from the puddles, faces smeared with mud.

It took a couple of hours to get the water, and when I struggled back with the five bottles, I discovered that Aron had already gone out. 'He's fetching some plastic,' Cosima told me. 'We need to make this place as weatherproof as we can. There's more rain on the way.'

Lemo was still lying on the rug in the tent, though his eyes were open. I went to sit next to him. 'Hello, Lemo,' I said, and patted his shoulder. He made no sign that he had seen or heard me. 'You looking forward to our story tonight?' I went on, as though nothing had changed. I sort of expected him to sit up, smile at me and say, 'Joke!' but he didn't. 'Which has been your favourite story so far?' I asked. Normally when I asked this, Lemo would think very hard and then choose whichever story I had told most recently. But this time he didn't even blink.

For the next few minutes I tried to get a response, but it was like talking to a wall. The shock of the storm had brought all the bad memories back, I guessed, and now it was as though that happy, friendly Lemo had never existed. I felt sad.

'It's awful, isn't it?' said Jenna in a low voice as I joined her outside.

'Back where he started,' I agreed. 'That night his father died – it must have been so scary for him.'

'For them all,' said Jenna. 'Aron's never mentioned it, but he must have been there too.'

'Of course.' I stared out at the camp. Aron must have seen the same 'bad things'. Had he tried to protect his father? What had happened that night? I wondered if I had the courage to ask him.

Jenna was sorting through the rags we had prepared for her weaving. They were all completely sodden with mud. In fact there was barely anything in the tent that wasn't soggy. 'There's no point washing them again, is there? They won't dry anyway.'

'Probably not.'

Maklam too was surveying his tent, shaking his head. 'No good,' he said. It was in an even worse state than ours, one corner of it collapsed completely. 'Lots of work to do today.' Then he beamed at me. 'It will be like a story, yes?'

I couldn't help smiling back at him. Maklam had changed since I started telling stories. Now he smiled at everything and never seemed to be sad. 'That's right,' I said. 'You are a star warrior fighting the elements of the sky.'

He laughed. 'Water from the sky! True!' And he set to work.

Jenna and I looked at each other. 'What should we do?' Jenna wondered. 'Should we be helping Maklam?'

'We could go out looking for plastic too,' I suggested. 'Aron can't cover the whole camp on his own.' My face flushed as I said his name, and I was doubly glad that no one had seen us in the night. Since the realization that Aron had been through the same terrifying experience as Lemo, I wanted to see him even more urgently – though what I would say to him when we met I had no idea.

Jenna glanced at Lemo, who was sitting in a corner staring blankly at nothing. 'Do you think we should leave him?'

'I'll be here,' said Cosima. 'You two go. The more plastic you can find, the better. Bags, sheets, wrappers, anything. You can collect for Maklam too.'

So we headed out, my heart thumping oddly at the anticipation of seeing Aron again.

'What's the matter with you?' Jenna asked me several times over the next couple of hours. 'Your mind is somewhere else completely.'

We hadn't bumped into Aron once yet, which wasn't really surprising given the size of the camp, but I kept thinking I saw him, which was very distracting. 'I'm fine.'

Jenna tugged a bag out of my hands. 'You're not. You've practically pulled this to pieces, and you keep dropping things. What is going on?'

I hesitated. But what could I say? There *wasn't* anything going on, apart from the fact that I'd spent all night huddled up to Aron. What would Jenna say if she knew? And – worse – what if she had feelings for Aron, as I half suspected? I shook my head. 'Nothing's going on, I told you.'

There were a lot of other people out looking for plastic, and more than once I had to give up the piece I had found to someone bigger and faster. Jenna's sharp eyes spotted even small pieces tucked under bricks and rubbish, but I soon became fed up. A couple of girls bumped into me as I pulled at some-thing, and I felt a tugging around my waist, where a plastic bag was tied.

'Hey!' I turned, but one of the girls had her hands firmly on the bag and was pulling hard. 'Get off me!'

The other girl joined in, and I felt the bag tighten and stretch against my tunic. Fingernails scratched my hands, and I let go with an exclamation of pain. The bag ripped, and with a cry of triumph the two girls ran off with their prize. I gave chase, but soon lost them amongst the crowds.

Furious, I returned to Jenna. 'I should have hidden it in my underclothes,' I said. 'Now I've lost it, and it was the biggest bag I'd found.'

We went back to the tent when it seemed clear we wouldn't find anything more for the moment. My stomach was growling, and I hoped that one of Aron's friends had remembered to queue up for food. It wasn't our turn.

Aron was tying a battered piece of plastic to the inside of our roof. He looked so completely normal that my anxiety over feeling weird evaporated. 'Why are you putting it on the inside?' I asked. 'Shouldn't it go on the outside, so the water can't get through?'

He turned to look at me. He was covered in mud, and I guessed he'd been fighting and digging for plastic too. There was a dark smudge across one cheek and his black eye was still visible under the smears. 'No,' he said, and there was a sharpness to his tone, 'because then people could steal it.'

'Oh.' I felt hurt. 'I suppose so.' Was he angry with me?

He turned back to the ceiling, grunting in frustration as the knot came undone.

'Let me do it,' offered Jenna, and he thanked her, heading out of the tent without even glancing at me.

Had I imagined everything last night? Had he not grabbed my hand in the dark and asked me to stay close to him after all? Had my imagination finally taken me over so that I couldn't tell reality from fantasy?

'Are you all right, Amina?' asked Cosima.

I blinked. 'I'm fine. Fine.'

She was anxious. 'You're not feeling ill or anything?'

'No, why?'

'There's sickness in the camp,' she told me. 'Just like I feared.'

'Already?'

'The filth on the ground mixes with the water. It doesn't take long to have an effect.'

I thought of the children I'd seen drinking from puddles and my stomach lurched. Now I *did* feel ill!

I heard Aron's voice and couldn't help myself. Pulling the tent flap aside, I saw Ghion, one of Aron's friends who shared the food run with us. Ghion looked dreadful, pale and filthy, like all of us. But his eyes were frightened. 'What is it?' I asked.

'Ghion's tent was washed away,' Aron told me, 'along with all their tins.'

My jaw dropped. 'All your tins? Oh no, Ghion, that's awful. What . . . what are you going to do?'

Ghion shrugged, though his hands were shaking. 'What can we do? We've been to see the soldiers, but they say they haven't got any spare tins for another week. The floods have washed away parts of the road and their trucks can't get through.'

I looked at Aron, and he caught my gaze. I knew what he was thinking. Should we offer Ghion one of our tins? More than one? Ghion had five people in his family – that was a lot of mouths to feed . . . It was the old question again, wasn't it? Them or us?

'You must have two of our tins,' said Cosima firmly, emerging from our tent and holding them out.

'Mother . . .' said Aron hesitantly.

'No, I can't,' said Ghion, though his eyes were fixed on her hands and I knew he was desperate to take them. 'You won't have enough.'

'You must take them,' Jenna agreed, coming to stand next to Cosima. 'Of course you must. And when you get new tins, we'll have ours back.'

I pressed my lips together to prevent myself saying anything. Jenna and Cosima were right, I knew they were – but I wouldn't have given up two of our precious tins, even though Ghion was a friend. Once I would have been ashamed of my feelings, but the thought of being even hungrier than we were already was terrible.

I caught Aron's eye and it was like looking in a mirror. He wouldn't have given Ghion the tins either. All the tiny hairs on the back of my neck and shoulders seemed to stand up at once, and I shivered.

'Go inside,' Cosima said. 'You're cold. Go in and keep warm.'

I dropped my gaze and went into the tent, my heart thudding in my chest.

Lemo was lying curled up on a soggy blanket.

He hadn't moved at all today. His eyes were open and staring. 'Hello, Lemo,' I said conversationally. 'Aren't you wet?'

Behind me, the tent flaps rustled. 'I don't think he should lie on this blanket,' I said over my shoulder. 'It's all wet.'

'It's the driest we have,' said Aron, and I jumped slightly.

'Oh,' I said. 'Oh – well, then I guess . . .' I trailed off. All of a sudden I felt that funny feeling in my chest again. It made me stare at the ground instead of at Aron.

He didn't seem to notice anything was different. Instead, he crouched down on the blanket next to me. 'You all right?'

'Yes,' I said to the ground. 'You?'

'Yes . . .' he said, but it sounded like he wanted to say more. 'I just – the tins . . .'

I looked at him then. 'You didn't want to give them to Ghion.'

He looked right back. 'Nor did you.'

'No.'

We stared at each other for a long moment.

'It's not because we're unkind,' I said.

293

'No,' he said savagely. 'We're survivors. You and me, Amina, we're the same.'

I flushed at the way he said 'you and me'. 'Survivors,' I echoed, to cover my reaction. 'Yes, that's it.'

Jenna stuck her head into the tent. 'Shall I go for food?' she asked. 'It's getting late.'

'I'll go,' Aron and I said at the same time. I laughed.

'Maybe we should go together,' he said. 'It would be safer, especially if people have lost tins in the floods. We can't risk someone taking the three that we have.' I knew when he said 'three' that he was thinking that it should have been 'five'.

'All right,' I agreed, hoping my voice sounded normal.

Jenna came properly in. 'How's Lemo?'

I glanced at him. 'The same.'

She sighed. 'I'll sit here for a while. Cosima says there's a rumour going round that a new medical tent is setting up. She's gone to see if there's anyone there who could help Lemo.'

'I'm sure he'll snap out of it again,' I said. 'Maybe I should tell a story tonight.'

Jenna gave me a slight smile. 'But you can't see the stars.'

'Doesn't mean they're not there,' Aron put in.

I smiled. 'That's right.'

'We should go.'

'Yes – see you later, Jenna.'

As we threaded our way through the tents and blankets to the food line, Aron said, 'Your sister's always thinking about other people, isn't she? I mean, she never thinks about herself.'

I wasn't sure what to say. 'Mmm.'

He nodded. 'It's kind of amazing.'

I opened my mouth and then closed it again. Aron had sounded admiring. Did he wish we weren't the survivors he'd just talked about? Did he wish I were more like my sister?

I felt a stab of jealousy. So much for thinking that he and I were developing some kind of special bond. The rain began again.

By the time we reached the front of the queue, my teeth were chattering from cold, and I was wetter than I could ever have believed. The food was running low, and the stew was more like soup from all the extra rainwater. 'Hardly worth it,' commented Aron as we walked away, carefully carrying our three tins, which were filling further with rainwater.

'We need to cover these,' I said, blinking the water out of my eyes. 'Otherwise there'll be no stew left at all by the time we get back.'

'Cover them with what?' asked Aron snappily. I saw his hands were shaking as much as mine.

I glanced around but there was nothing suitable within sight. So I unwound my headscarf and wrapped it as carefully as I could around the tins. 'It might make a bit of difference,' I said doubtfully. 'We should get back as soon as we can though.'

'Yes,' said Aron, but he was staring at me.

'What?' My dark hair was plastered to my head, water streaming off the long tendrils. I hadn't brushed it since we left home, let alone washed it. I couldn't imagine how it must look.

'Nothing,' he said. 'Come on.'

The ground was slippery, and everything had taken on the same mud colour. Thinking about washing my hair reminded me of home. Jenna and I hadn't tried to look for our family since the rains started, and now there was less chance than ever of finding any clues. But right now, that mattered less than getting the tins back to the tent intact.

'Mini!' Jenna was watching anxiously for us. 'You're wet through!'

'It's raining,' I said unnecessarily.

'Come in quickly. We're wet in here too, but the plastic is keeping out the worst of it. Just mind the back corner; the water is seeping underneath the blankets.'

We struggled in gratefully. Cosima was back, sitting with Lemo on her lap. She made a noise of sympathy as she saw the state we were in. Jenna took the tins from Aron and unwound my scarf. I gave a groan as I saw a couple of drops spill from the over-flowing container. Jenna exclaimed, 'Goodness, what is this meant to be?'

'Wasn't much l-left,' I said. 'Rain in everything. Tried to cover them up.'

'Better than nothing,' said Cosima robustly. 'Sit down and eat, and then we'll get you both warm.'

We ate – or perhaps drank would be a better word – the stew from the three tins, which was stone cold and greasy. Cosima had to tip the contents into Lemo's mouth for him, since he wouldn't grasp the tin himself. It tasted disgusting but we all knew better than to refuse. Any nourishment, however small, was better than none.

'Well,' said Aron, taking the last gulp from his tin, 'that'll make all the difference.'

I couldn't help myself. A bubble of hysteria formed somewhere in my guts, and pushed its way upwards. I choked, coughed, spluttered, and then my shoulders were shaking and I was laughing so hard I thought I might split in two.

'Amina!' said Jenna in alarm.

'Sorry,' I spluttered, 'it's just so – so funny . . .'

And then Aron started laughing too, and Jenna's mouth twitched, and soon we were all giggling and chuckling, while tears ran from our eyes and the rain thundered on the roof.

# 20

It rained, and it carried on raining. At first I thought it would be like the first shower and there would be a break, but every time I woke up, it was still raining, and I was lying in a puddle of mud.

Aron stole a large wooden pallet from the back of an army jeep and used it to raise our tent up off the wet ground. The difference was considerable, though after a few days the combined weight of all of us bowed the wood back down into the mud. Days were spent in a constant battle to find new ways of getting and staying dry. Falling in the mud was a common occurrence and my knees were covered in bruises and scratches, some deeper than others.

Cosima's sharp eyes missed nothing, and she examined a scrape one day and proclaimed it 'deep'. 'Keep it clean, Amina. It's important.'

'I'm fine,' I said, trying to ignore the throbbing.

'I wish this rain would stop.' Jenna looked at her hands. 'I'm filthy.'

'All this water, and we can't get clean,' I said. 'Funny.'

'Not really.'

'No, not really.'

It had been ten days now, and the mud and filth covered everything. We had so little, but even those things were taken by the water. The beautiful glass ornament hanging from our tent disappeared one day – by accident or design, we didn't know. I grieved when I discovered it gone.

'It was just a trinket,' said Jenna, trying to comfort me.

'No it wasn't,' I said. 'It was beautiful.' And it had been given to me because of my imagination. It was a kind of validation that I was important – that my imagination was important. I couldn't say that to Jenna because I didn't think she'd understand.

My stories had been affected by the rain too. I couldn't see the stars at night, and somehow that made it harder to find inspiration. How could I feel as though we were part of some huge universe when we spent our days confined to a soggy tent? I tried every now and then, urged by Cosima, who was still hoping that Lemo would come out of his stupor – but any stories that I started lost their way and felt unsatisfying. They had no visible effect on Lemo, and I hated seeing Cosima's disappointed face. No one else came to listen, of course, since it would have meant sitting in the rain. Maklam tried to squeeze into our tent one evening, but he accidentally leaned on a pole and snapped it, and we had to stop the story to repair it. He was so apologetic, he didn't come again. I missed my audience; the familiar faces looking at me so intently. And I missed the applause; the feeling that I had achieved something amazing. For a while I had been someone special, and now I was back to being un-amazing Amina. It made me grumpy.

We were all getting on each other's nerves, and my knee wasn't healing properly either. Cosima saw me screw up my face when I tried to sit down. 'Show me,' she said sharply. When I did, she sucked in her breath. My knee was swollen and puffy, and the scratch was red and inflamed. Cosima poked it gently, and a yellowish liquid seeped out. 'It's infected,' she said.

'Infected?'

'It should have been kept clean.'

'How could I do that?' I said, frustrated. 'Everything is so dirty.'

'Why didn't you show it to me before?' Cosima tutted. 'It must have been hurting for days.'

It had, but I didn't want to complain. I shrugged. 'Didn't think it was that bad.'

'Then you are a fool,' she snapped, with no hint of her usual comforting tone.

'It's just a cut.' I was tired and cold and wet and miserable, so I was ruder than I might otherwise have been. 'I don't see why you're making such a fuss.'

Cosima's eyes flashed with anger. 'Because you could get blood poisoning and *die*, you ignorant child.'

I felt my face go white. 'What?'

'Blood poisoning spreads quickly,' she said. 'All it needs is some dirt and a way into the body. Both of which you've provided.' She paused for a moment. 'You will have to go to the hospital tent.'

I had seen the queues of people waiting to be seen

there and my heart sank. 'There's no point. There are hundreds of people there.'

But Cosima was insistent, so Jenna and I set off together, me limping all the way. The rain wasn't so hard today, but it was still drizzling steadily, and my bad temper, combined with fright at Cosima's words, made me almost impossible. When we saw the line of people at the tent, I scowled. 'This is stupid. I'll never get seen. Why don't they have more doctors?'

'We'll just join the end of the line,' Jenna said. 'If we can work out where it is . . .'

We waited in the drizzle for three hours. It was like waiting in the food queue, or – in my dim memory – to get into Altiers. Every now and then we moved forward a few steps, and then we stopped again. It was horribly tedious and frustrating, and I couldn't help complaining. 'That woman's been in there for ages. What on earth are they doing? And the other nurse didn't need to go in too – how many nurses does one patient need? What about the rest of us?'

Jenna, usually patient to a fault, finally snapped and told me to shut up, there were other people much sicker than me, and if I didn't want to be left on my own, I'd stop moaning.

Furious at being told off, I sat mutinously silent for the rest of the time.

Eventually we did reach the head of the line, and a tired-looking woman with a grey headscarf invited us into a tiny examination room. It was a relief to get out of the rain, and I was so tired I nearly burst into tears. 'Hello, there,' she said. 'I'm Tasha, one of the nurses here. What are your names?'

'I'm Jenna and this is my sister Amina,' said Jenna. 'She's hurt her knee.'

'Right,' said Tasha. 'We'd better have a look, then. Sit on this chair, Amina.'

I showed her my knee, streaked with dirt and water. Tasha cleaned it briskly, which made me wince. Then she prodded it, and yellow pus oozed out. I yelped in pain. 'Sorry,' she said. 'It's infected.'

'I know,' I said. 'That's why I've come.'

Jenna shushed me. 'Is there anything you can give her?' she asked.

Tasha pulled a face. 'I can bandage it up,' she said, 'to try to keep it clean. But to be honest, she needs antibiotics and we haven't got enough. I can't give her a tetanus shot either; I've just used up my last one.'

I felt bitter that someone else had got the medicine I needed. 'So you can't help me?' I said, and my voice wobbled. 'Am I going to die?'

Tasha smiled kindly at me. 'I hope not,' she said, which was not very reassuring. 'You are young and you look strong. I think your body would be good at fighting off the infection. There are two things you can do, though.'

'Yes?' asked Jenna eagerly.

'Keep it clean,' said Tasha. 'That's really important.'

'And the second?'

'The second is even more important,' she told me. 'You have to want to fight. Do you have family you're looking for?'

'Yes,' I said. 'How did you know?'

'A lot of people are lost,' she replied. 'Or they have lost others. Who have you lost?'

'My mother, and my sister and my brother.'

She nodded. 'Then you must fight off this infection so that you can find them. You must want to stay alive.'

'I do,' I said, swallowing. 'I do.'

'Keep hold of that,' said Tasha, 'and you will get better.'

I didn't know what to say. 'All right.'

'I'll make sure she doesn't forget,' said Jenna, squeezing my hand.

Tasha bandaged my knee quickly and efficiently. Behind her, from somewhere else in the tent, someone screamed; a high-pitched sound of fright. I jumped. 'Who was that?'

'I don't know,' said Tasha. She sighed and rubbed the back of her hand over her eyes. 'This is not a good place at the moment.' Once she had finished, she stood up. 'Keep fighting,' she told me, 'right?'

'Thank you,' said Jenna, and I echoed her thanks, feeling emotional at Tasha's kindness. I lingered for a moment in the hospital doorway, my heart sinking again as I looked out at the mud and the straggling line of sick people waiting their turn. Tasha had been nice, but I hoped we didn't have to come back.

That evening, I began to shake. I couldn't tell if I was too hot or too cold. I lay down in the mud and tried not to be sick. It wasn't as though I had anything in my stomach to bring up. Cosima sat by my side and cast anxious glances at me every now and then.

Jenna came to sit by me too. 'Remember back

home?' she began. 'Remember how we used to play the stick game in the street? The game you made up, which we started as a joke – and soon everyone in our row was playing it?'

I said nothing. I was trying not to retch.

She went on determinedly. 'And remember that time there was a new seller in the market and he had rubber balloons that you could fill with water and throw at people? You hit Ruman with one, and he was so angry because he was wearing his best suit.'

I could hear the smile in her voice, but I couldn't smile back. Everything ached. I just wanted to sleep.

'You have to keep fighting, Mini,' Jenna said. 'Remember what Tasha said. You have to want to stay alive.'

But right now I just wanted everyone and every thing to go away.

I was ill for two weeks, though I didn't realize how ill until afterwards. I just knew that, for whatever reason, I couldn't think or care about anything. Everything was grey – the sky, the tent, and my mind. There were no thoughts beyond how wretched I felt.

I couldn't think about Mamie or Vivie or Ruman. I couldn't think about anything.

People came by the tent in a haze. I heard snatches of conversation; people asking how I was. Jenna and Cosima murmured to them in low voices. 'Tell her she must get well so that she can tell us more stories,' someone said, and if I hadn't been in a black pit of not-caring, I would have smiled. Imagination? Stories? What were they?

Maklam asked constantly how I was. Jenna became quite irritated by it, which again I would have found funny if I had cared. But my body was so full of pain that my head was empty. I was supposed to be fighting, but I just couldn't find the energy. Wouldn't it be easier to give up? Everyone was worried about me. I didn't want them to worry. Maybe it would be better not to fight any more. I lay in the tent with my eyes closed, and shivered and ached and groaned, wishing it would all come to an end one way or another.

Gradually I began to feel less wretched. The grey fog in my head lessened and I noticed things again. It took another four days before I felt strong enough to sit up and take an interest in things around me.

Jenna sat by me and stroked the hair out of my eyes. 'I'm so glad you're feeling better, Mini,' she said, in a voice that wobbled.

I had a vague memory of a grey world where Jenna had wrapped her arms around me and begged me not to leave her. 'I'm glad too,' I said, and made an effort to smile at her. My cheek muscles felt stiff and unused. 'What did I miss?'

She gave a short laugh. 'It's been raining.'

I looked up at the sky. 'It's not raining now.'

'No . . . It will again, I expect.'

'Are you sure? It looks a bit clearer to me.'

Jenna burst into tears. 'I thought you were going to die!' she cried.

I put my arm around her shoulder and she clung to me, her whole body shaking with sobs. 'I'm all right,' I said helplessly.

'What would I do without you?' she cried.

I didn't know what to say. Seeing how upset she was brought a swollen feeling to my throat. I hugged her back, blinking.

It took another week before I could walk steadily and not collapse with exhaustion after ten steps. I still felt tired but every day brought a little more strength. Jenna sat by me every moment that she could, sharing good memories from Talas, and I was touched by her compassion.

One morning, the sun came out. Jenna and I sat outside the tent as usual, but today things felt more positive. Aron came back from the water run smiling. 'You want to come for a walk?' he asked us.

'Yes,' I said immediately.

'What about Lemo?' asked Jenna.

Lemo was sitting in the corner of the tent. His fingers played with a piece of something grey that crackled slightly, but his gaze was as blank as ever. I held out my hand to him. 'I'm going for a walk,' I told him. 'Do you want to come?'

His gaze was fixed on the rug and he made no response. Something in me gave a twinge of pain. All that time I'd been ill, I hadn't been there for him. He must have felt as though I'd abandoned him. 'I'll be back soon,' I said, though he made no sign that he'd heard.

The camp was still grey and miserable but somehow, with the arrival of the sun, it didn't affect me in the same way. I felt absurdly grateful to be alive as Aron, Jenna and I walked slowly among the starving, ill and grieving people. My legs felt stronger than they had in weeks, so before long we'd walked quite a distance. 'How is Ghion?' I asked, suddenly remembering something. 'Did his family get more tins?'

'They left,' said Aron.

'Left?' I was startled. 'Why? Where did they go?'

He shrugged. 'Ghion's mother said they would be better off taking their chances outside the camp than risking death here.'

'Are things that bad?' I asked, though it was easy to see the answer. Before the rains, the camp had been a busy, bustling place, with children running around; adults sitting chatting; soldiers sharing a joke. Now everyone looked hollow-eyed, and so many of them simply sat, silently staring at nothing. I put my hand on my tunic; I could feel my ribs through the thin cloth. But I was still alive, I told myself. I wanted to live – now more than ever.

'Amina! You're alive!' a voice cried. I turned my head with an effort. A small child was running at me, and I had only a second to realize it was Tiger before he buffeted me in the middle. I swayed, out of breath.

'Don't do that!' Jenna scolded.

Tiger stepped back, his face split by a huge grin. 'Sorry. You all right now?'

I smiled, though I was surprised how breathless I was. 'I'm all right. Or I will be.'

'Excellent! You telling a story tonight, then?'

'No,' said Jenna. 'She won't be telling any stories until she's completely better. This is the first day she's walked this far.' I was glad that Jenna had spoken for me. I was starting to feel shaky.

Tiger's face fell.

'I will soon,' I said quickly. 'But I'm too tired right now.'

'You need to sleep,' he said helpfully. 'Then you can tell a story tomorrow.'

Aron laughed, a sound that made me blink. When had he last laughed? 'Maybe. I'll come and find you if she does, all right?'

Tiger nodded, grinned again and then bounded off.

I marvelled. So many people were depressed and silent, but Tiger was still bouncing around. I was pleased that he had come through the rains so well, especially as he had no parents. Seeing him made me think of our quest to find clues to our own family.

'Has there been any sign of Mamie or Vivie or Ruman?' I asked Jenna.

She shook her head. 'There have been fewer people coming to the camp in the past two weeks – I heard the soldiers say so. But I haven't really been out asking people, not while you were ill.' She looked guilty. 'I haven't made the most of the time. Not even when you started to feel better. I could have gone out then.'

'You shouldn't feel bad,' Aron told her. 'You were looking after Amina.'

I gave him a quick glance. Another reference to Jenna's self-sacrificing nature. Was he looking at her in an admiring way? Had something happened between them while I was ill? My head spun slightly and I stumbled.

'You've done enough,' Jenna said quickly. 'We should go back.'

But when we got back to the tent, Cosima announced that she had decided to leave.

# 21

'Leave?' We all stared at her.

'What, now?' asked Aron, clearly as taken aback as the rest of us. 'But you – you haven't said anything.'

'I'm saying it now,' said Cosima. 'Sit down, Amina, you're worn out.'

We all sat. 'When did you decide this?' Aron pressed her.

Cosima put her arm around Lemo, who was sitting quietly next to her, silent as a ghost. 'I've been thinking about it for a while, ever since Ghion's family left. They were right. There's nothing for us here. We're just sitting around waiting. Getting older and weaker. It's no life.'

I could see Aron struggling. 'But in here we're looked after. There's food and shelter. We're protected from the Kwana.'

Cosima shook her head. 'It's not enough.'

My head was whirling. Leave the camp? The idea was somehow exhilarating. I was so tired of all this grime and despair. In my mind, the land outside the camp was green and lush, with wide skies and opportunities.

'Have you forgotten why we came?' Aron's voice broke into my thoughts. He sounded furious. 'Have you forgotten how dangerous life is outside?'

'I haven't forgotten,' said Cosima, and there was a hard edge to her tone. 'I remember *every single day* why we came, Aron.' Her arm tightened around Lemo, who flinched slightly. 'But people are *leaving*. It's not just Ghion's family; there are others. I see them setting off, walking past, their belongings packed away again. Things are changing – there must be hope outside.'

'I've heard nothing.' Aron was stony-faced. 'And I am out and about every day – I would know if things had changed.'

'What about that news on the radio last week?' Cosima challenged him.

'What news on the radio?' I asked, curious.

Aron made a noise of frustration. 'It wasn't proper

news, I told you that. It was just one person's opinion – which doesn't make it true.'

'But you said people who were listening believed it.'

'Believed what?' I asked.

'There was a man on the radio,' Cosima told me, 'who said that the Kwana were losing control over some of their key cities. That the peacekeepers were moving in to set up local democracies.'

My jaw dropped. 'Where? How? Near to here?'

Aron rolled his eyes. 'You mustn't get so excited about it; it's nothing more than gossip. One of the old men listening said that the speaker was a rebel leader and couldn't be trusted anyway.'

'They mentioned Gharsad,' Cosima put in quietly.

My gaze swung automatically to Jenna. 'Gharsad! Jenna – oh my, maybe—'

'I know,' she said quickly. 'I know what you're thinking. But we mustn't rush into anything.'

I felt like jumping up and setting off home right away. 'But if Gharsad isn't under Kwana control, then maybe Talas is safe too? We could go home, Jenna! We could go and find Mamie and Vivie!'

'We can't be sure it's safe,' Aron interrupted. 'You can't just go rushing off.'

'It's not the same for you,' I snapped. 'You haven't got family out there!'

There was an intake of breath from Jenna and Cosima, and I could have bitten off my own tongue. What an insensitive thing to say! A chill swept through me. 'I'm sorry, I didn't mean that – the way it came out.'

Aron got up and disappeared into the camp.

I felt sick with guilt. 'I didn't mean it like that,' I said again. 'I just meant . . . if it's safe for us to go home, then . . .' I trailed off.

Jenna put her hand on my arm. 'I know what you meant,' she said.

'He'll come back,' added Cosima.

'I'm very sorry.'

Cosima gave me a sad smile. 'He's only upset because you're right. We only have each other.' She sighed. 'Which is why it's time to leave. We must make a new life for ourselves if we can.'

'If the Kwana are defeated,' I said slowly, 'then won't this camp be closed down? I mean, we'll have to leave at some point anyway, won't we?'

'Everything takes time,' said Cosima. She looked down at Lemo, who was staring at the ground. 'And I can't bear to see my boys vanishing.' She hesitated before saying, 'You would be welcome, you know, with us. If you wanted to come. I – I consider you both family now.'

I had to press my lips together to stop myself bursting into tears. The illness seemed to have taken all my self-control along with my energy. Cosima had looked after us as well as Mamie would have. She didn't have to take us in, and the thought of now saying goodbye to her frightened me. We would be without a mother again while we looked for Mamie. But what choice did we have? I was still weak; I couldn't walk for a full day. Even if I could, how could we go with Cosima and her family? We would never know if Mamie and Vivie were still alive. How could we live like that?

Jenna knew how I felt. She said, 'Thank you,' and I could hear the tremble in her voice. 'But we need to find our mother and sister and brother.' She hesitated. 'You could come with us, instead? Back to Talas?'

It was the perfect idea! 'Yes!' I cried, hope gripping me. 'Yes, come with us! We can all live together!'

A vision rose in my mind: Cosima, Aron and Lemo at our house in Talas, Mamie and Vivie sitting on the floor with us all, eating rice.

Cosima's eyes filled with tears. 'You are dear, sweet girls. But I want to return to a place I know well. We may not have family left, but I had friends. I had a house. There are things, and people, that we left behind . . . maybe they are still there.'

For a moment hope had filled me like a balloon. Now it deflated, leaving me empty and sad again. I nodded, wanting to say I understood, but unable to speak again.

'We know how you feel,' Jenna said.

'Home?' said Lemo in a voice so quiet it was a whisper. Something inside me ached to hear him say the word.

'Yes.' Cosima looked down at him, and tears fell from her eyes. She brushed the hair away from his face. 'Home.'

He let out a big sigh, laid his head in her lap and fell asleep.

Jenna didn't want me to, but I felt I had to go after Aron to apologize. I had hurt his feelings through my own temper, and I couldn't bear to have him hate me.

My head hurt and I still felt a bit dizzy, but I picked my way through the camp in the hope of finding Aron at one of the usual places – maybe by the water tap, or hunting through the rubbish piles at the edges. But there was no sign of him, and I stood still to think where else he could be. Perhaps by the man with the radio?

I heard the crackle before I could see the aerial, and then I turned the corner and almost walked straight into Aron. He was leaning against the side of a shed with his eyes closed, but my clumsiness jolted them open, and he stumbled. 'I'm so sorry!' I said automatically. 'I didn't see you – are you all right?'

'Oh, it's you.' He turned away. 'I'm fine.'

'I came to find you,' I said, before my courage gave out. 'I came to say sorry for . . . for what I said earlier.' The radio gave another crackle and then died completely. Two men started arguing over it. 'I didn't mean it like that – I mean, I should have thought before I spoke . . .'

The hint of a smile crossed his face as he turned. 'Thought before you spoke?'

'I know, I know,' I babbled. 'It's one of my worst

habits. You don't have to tell me. Always saying stuff without thinking about it. There was this time at the market when I told a stallholder that Jenna was a mute because she should have done the talking but I couldn't bear to stand there while people were being rude to us . . . er—' I caught Aron's confused expression. 'Anyway, it doesn't matter,' I added hastily. 'I just – it sounded horrible, what I said, and I never meant to hurt you or – or remind you of what you've lost. We've all lost a lot.' I stopped abruptly at the memory of Potta. Even after five months, it was as vivid and fresh as if it were still happening in front of my eyes. What did Aron remember? What did he see when he closed his eyes? Suddenly I really wanted to know. A part of him was still so closed off. 'You . . .' I began, without really knowing what I was saying. 'Your father . . . was it . . . bad?'

He turned shocked eyes on me. It was probably the first time anyone had asked him. Then he quickly looked away; up at the sky, down at the ground. A frown gathered between his eyebrows.

I thought he wasn't going to answer, and for a moment I regretted asking. He was going to leave soon, and what did it matter anyway?

Then he gave a huge sigh – the sort of sigh that went on for ever. And he said, 'It was night time. They came into our house. There was a lot of shouting, and it was hard to tell what was going on. All the lights were out, so I couldn't see how many of them there were.'

I held my breath.

'They said Father had done something wrong, but he started shouting back and it all got too noisy to work out what anyone was saying. Mother was screaming and begging them not to hurt us.' He took another breath. 'Then one of them grabbed me and another pointed a gun at me. They yelled at Father that he needed to confess or they'd shoot me. Lemo was holding onto Father's leg and crying, and I – I was just shaking and useless.' He sounded bitter. 'I didn't try to stand up to them or anything. I couldn't move, couldn't speak. I was too scared.'

I could imagine how much he hated the memory. We all wanted to be brave. But being faced with death changed everything. 'I'm sorry,' I said.

He went on as though he hadn't heard me. 'Father had his hands up; he was trying to tell them that he'd go with them, that they didn't need to hurt us.

But they got impatient, and then the one with the gun shot at me.'

I gasped, a tiny sound.

'Father got in front of me, and – and the bullet hit him instead. He fell down, and then the Kwana all shouted at each other, like they were blaming each other for killing him by mistake. And I still couldn't see anything, except the flash when the gun went off, and Father falling to the ground. In the end they all went away, still arguing – without even seeing if he was dead or anything. And when they'd gone, all I could hear was Mother crying and Father making these really horrible sounds, like he was sucking water through a straw inside himself. His eyes looked so white, and he grabbed my hand, and I just knew he was afraid, and that made me feel even worse because – because he got shot instead of me and I wished it had been me. And then he died. And ages after-wards, we realized that Father had fallen on top of Lemo, and Lemo had been squashed underneath all that time, in the dark, as Father died.' He swallowed.

My face was wet. I didn't know what to say. I wanted to hold his hand, but I didn't know if he would like it. 'I'm so sorry,' I said in the end.

He looked at me. 'Mother told me what you did when they pulled your father out into the street. You tried to save him. You told lies to keep them from killing him.'

'It didn't work—'

'But you tried. You said things – you thought of ways to save him.' He looked down at the ground again. 'I did nothing. I just stood there. And he put himself in the way. He saved *me*.' He sounded angry.

'He would have wanted it that way,' I said. 'He wouldn't have wanted you to die instead of him. And if you had, they probably would have killed him anyway – and then Cosima and Lemo would have lost both of you.'

His mouth twisted, as if he were trying to stop himself from crying. He gave a shrug.

'What would Cosima have done without you, here?' I asked him. 'She couldn't have gone to get food every day, not with Lemo how he was. You've saved *them*, you know.' My imagination caught hold. 'And I bet your father would have known that. He knew that saving you would mean that you could look after them.' I grabbed his hand. 'You mustn't feel bad about it,' I told him urgently. 'Just because you didn't fight back doesn't make you a bad person. Everyone's allowed to be scared.'

He looked down at our hands and nodded – short, jerky movements. Then he rubbed at his face with his other hand.

The radio crackled suddenly into life, making us both jump: '. . . *towards the outer boundaries of the town,*' came a voice, '*where the Kwana have gone into hiding . . .*' There was a loud outburst of hissing, and both Aron and I clapped our hands over our ears. Then there was silence again, and the men nearest the radio made exasperated noises.

'I've spent most of the past three weeks here,' Aron confessed.

'Really?'

'I knew you'd have been here. If you hadn't been ill. It felt like the only useful thing I could do.'

I felt touched. 'Thank you.'

One of the men at the front threw up his hands in disgust, and the group started to break up. 'Come on,' said Aron. 'I don't suppose we'll hear anything useful today.'

'Did you hear what it said about the Kwana being

in hiding?' I asked as we walked slowly back to our tent. 'Do you think it's true?'

'I don't know. But it ties in with what they said a week ago. Trouble is, no one really knows what's going on.'

I stopped and looked at him. 'So, do you want to go home?'

He looked back at me. I held my breath. What would he say?

'There you are!' Jenna's voice made me jump. 'Amina, you really should come back and rest now – I was worried about you. Aron, Cosima says please can you see if you can find any bits and pieces that might be useful for your journey.' She smiled. 'I'm glad you two have made up. Come on, Mini.'

That night the sky was clear for the first time in weeks. I looked up, marvelling at the number of tiny pinpricks, glowing and sparkling against the deep purple of the night. It was like seeing old friends again, and even though I knew things were all about to change, seeing the stars gave me comfort.

'Time for a story,' said Cosima softly. 'Our last one, perhaps.'

I swallowed. Cosima wanted to leave tomorrow. It felt too soon; too big a decision to make that quickly. I didn't want to tell a story. It felt as though, if I did, it would be like saying goodbye. 'Maybe tomorrow,' I said, grasping at the thought that they might wait if I promised to tell one then.

There was a gentle tugging at my tunic. It was Lemo. He looked up at me, his big brown eyes even more huge in his little face. The bones in his shoulders showed through his tunic, and his fingers shook. I thought of how terrified he must have been, crushed beneath his father's dying body, and I knew I couldn't refuse. I looked up at the sky, but inspiration eluded me. I didn't want to talk about warriors; about battles. We knew enough about soldiers and beatings and death and grief. Why had I ever invented an army in the sky? Why couldn't the stars be dancers or athletes, or children?

'I . . . um . . .' I said, swallowing again. 'I don't think I can.'

'It doesn't have to be about the stars,' said Jenna gently. It was as though she guessed how I felt. Her hand reached for mine and squeezed it. 'We could make up a story all together – about whatever we like. It'll be fun.'

I squeezed her hand back.

'Good idea,' agreed Aron. 'We've listened to your stories for so long, Amina – we must have learned something from you. Let's see if we can tell one as good as yours.'

'All right,' said Cosima, mildly surprised but smiling. 'Who's going to start?'

There was a slight pause before Aron said, 'I will. Once upon a time . . .' His gaze fell on his little brother. 'Once there was a small boy whose name was . . . er . . .'

'Paul,' said Jenna.

'Paul.' Aron nodded. 'And what Paul liked more than anything was . . .'

'Oranges,' said Cosima. She smiled, her eyes closed. 'Big, juicy, sweet oranges.'

Oranges! I couldn't remember the last time I'd tasted an orange. I felt my mouth water at the words.

'Right,' said Aron. 'And luckily for Paul, he lived next door to the biggest orange grower in the country. Every day when Paul went to school, he passed the fence that bordered the orange fields, and he breathed in the scent of the orange blossom, which bloomed at the same time as the fruit. Um . . .'

Fences made me think of the camp – and thinking of the camp made me think of the reasons we were here. My jaw tightened. 'But the man who owned the orange fields was a horrible man,' I said. 'And he kept fierce dogs to patrol the edges of his fields so that no one could get in to steal the fruit.'

'Why was he horrible?' asked Jenna. 'He was just protecting his business.'

'Because,' I said, warming to my theme, 'one day Paul found a large juicy orange lying by the fence, where it must have dropped from a tree. And he picked it up and put it in his pocket. But one of the fierce dogs smelled it on him and chased him down the street until it caught him and bit him on the leg.' *Injustice*, I thought. *That's what all this is about. Potta didn't deserve to die. We shouldn't have had to leave our home. All the people here in the camp – they'd done nothing wrong, had they? And yet they were the ones who ended up hurt.* I went on, feeling anger rise in my stomach: 'And the horrible man said Paul had stolen the fruit and he told the police to arrest him.'

'But Paul didn't steal the orange; he found it lying on the road,' argued Jenna.

'Yes, but the horrible man didn't believe him— We can't go on calling him "the horrible man",' I said, breaking off. 'What's his name?'

There was a moment's silence. 'Nero,' said Aron.

I screwed up my nose. 'Doesn't sound nasty enough.'

'Boran?'

'Hmmm.'

'Mister Orange,' said a very quiet voice. We all looked at Lemo. Cosima's jaw dropped, and she looked at me almost fiercely, as if to say, *Go on. Keep going. Stories make him better!*

'Excellent name, Lemo,' I said, as though his contribution were perfectly normal. 'Mister Orange it is. Well, Mister Orange was such a powerful man that he could practically do what he liked, and so the police arrested poor Paul and put him in prison. For . . . for . . .' Ten years? Was that really believable?

'Ten years,' said Aron, and I blinked at his words. Had he read my mind?

'For stealing an orange?' said Jenna incredulously. 'That's silly.'

330

Aron shrugged. 'He was a powerful man; he could do what he liked.'

'Yes!' I said. 'That's it, exactly! He was like the Kwana, he could make up the rules and get everyone to obey him.'

'I don't want to talk about the Kwana,' said Cosima sharply.

I bit my lip. I hadn't meant to refer to them out loud. 'Sorry.'

Maklam appeared in the entrance to his tent. 'You are telling a story,' he said, and smiled, though his eyes were tired. 'I would like to listen please.'

'Of course,' I said. 'It wouldn't be the same without you. What about your sisters?'

Maklam smiled, but his eyes overflowed. 'They have passed,' he said quietly. 'Together.'

'Oh, Maklam,' said Cosima. 'I'm so very sorry.'

He nodded. 'This is why I need a story.'

A lump had formed in my throat. I tried to speak but couldn't. Poor Maklam! All alone without his sisters. How awful for him. He was looking at me expectantly, and I couldn't think of a thing to say.

Thankfully Aron took up the story. 'Paul's family was very upset that Paul was put in prison,' he said, 'and they tried everything they could to get him out, but Mister Orange was simply too powerful. He told everyone it would ensure that no one else dared to try to steal his fruit. Which was true – everyone was too scared. But during the ten years that Paul was in prison, something happened to the orange trees. They began to wither and die, and all the scientists in the country couldn't work out what was wrong with them.'

'They had a disease?' asked Cosima.

'Yes. I don't know what kind, but every year, a few more trees shrivelled up and died. The people who bought from Mister Orange began to look elsewhere for their supplies because the quality couldn't be guaranteed any more. Mister Orange was losing money.'

'But he's not the real story, is he?' said Jenna. 'Paul's the hero. Let's go back to him. Mm . . . he's in prison, and as the years go by he finds a new interest – books. He reads and reads, and the more he learns, the more he feels he wants to do something to help people.'

I rolled my eyes. Typical Jenna! She *would* turn Paul into a helper! If it had been my story, he'd have spent his time planning his revenge against Mister Orange. 'Though the bite on his leg didn't heal properly,' I said, 'so he had a constant limp as a reminder of the injustice that had led to his imprisonment.'

'I like that he's been reading books,' Cosima said, in her soft voice. Her eyes were distant and she stroked Lemo's arm. 'Let's say he's been reading up on law and injustice – and by the time he leaves prison he's taken some exams and can practise as a lawyer. That way he can set up his own business to help people.'

'Yes,' I said, suddenly seeing a way to drive this story along. 'He has a burning desire to right wrongs and fight injustice. He calls his business "Righting the Wrongs".'

The others nodded, and I realized that even though we had different ways of looking at it, we all felt the same about our situation. If we could take back our lives, we would.

'It is a good name,' said Maklam with satisfaction.

'To start with he helps people for no money,' said Aron, 'which is a bit of a problem because he can't afford to buy food. So he lives on . . . uh . . . he lives on . . .'

'Potatoes,' said Lemo.

Again, we all jumped at his voice.

'That's right,' said Aron. 'Potatoes. And a bit of olive oil.'

I tried not to laugh, and ended up making an odd snorting sound instead. 'And then one day,' I said hastily, trying to cover up my red face, 'a man came to see Paul, and his story was a sad one. He had been the accountant for Mister Orange, until Mister Orange had accused him of stealing money.'

'Embezzling,' said Cosima. 'That's what it's called – embezzling money.'

'Yes, that. And it was all a complete lie, because the man hadn't done anything wrong. Well, here was the case Paul had been waiting for. Here was an opportunity to prove that Mister Orange was a horrible man who should be locked up.'

'So they went to court and Paul won,' said Jenna with satisfaction.

'You can't skip to the end like that,' I said, shaking my head. 'That's not the right way to tell the story!'

'It's a group story, isn't it?' asked Jenna mildly. 'I want to get to the happy ending.'

I looked helplessly at Aron. He would know how I felt.

He smiled at me. 'You're both right. Mister Orange had all the best lawyers and spent lots of money on the case, but in the end Paul was able to prove that the poor accountant was completely innocent. And when Mister Orange was told to pay compensation to him, he suddenly discovered that he didn't have enough money left, because his orange groves had lost so much in value.'

'And so he came, lost and broken, to see Paul . . .' said Jenna.

'To say he was sorry,' said Lemo.

'And Paul . . .' I looked around at the others. If it had been my story only, Paul would have turned Mister Orange out on the streets, or had him put in prison for non-payment of debts. That would have been justice. But as I met Maklam's milky gaze, it suddenly struck me that justice *wasn't* the most important thing in the world. It was important, of course – but there were other things that were *more* important. If I were given the opportunity to have revenge on the men who had killed Potta, could I take it, really and truly? Could I do what they did in the name of justice? Was 'justice' the same as 'right'? I wasn't sure, but suddenly I knew how the story should end.

'And Paul forgave Mister Orange,' I said quietly, and there was a kind of collective sigh from the others, and an approving smile from Maklam. 'And he told Mister Orange that people needed and loved his oranges and so he would help him get his business back on its feet.'

'And so he went into partnership with Mister Orange,' said Aron, smiling at me again. 'And eventually they discovered what was killing the orange trees and they were able to develop a treatment for it, and within five years the business was back on its feet and making more money than ever.'

'And they took down the fences,' said Lemo.

'The fences?' I said.

'The fences round the orange trees.'

'Oh yes, of course, the fences! Yes, Paul made sure the fences were taken down and the dogs taken away . . .'

'To good homes,' said Jenna.

'Of course. And the business made so much money that they were able to build a new school for the children, and a hospital, and Paul was still able to take law cases for people who couldn't afford to pay.'

'And people smiled at Mister Orange now, instead of being scared of him,' added Jenna.

'And Paul married a lovely young woman,' said Cosima, 'and they had five children . . .'

'And they were called Orange One, Orange Two, Orange Three, Orange Four and Orange Five,' said Lemo, in a satisfied this-is-the-end voice.

There was a small silence, and then the laughter burst out of us like water from a tap, bubbling and gushing. Maklam threw back his head and chuckled to the stars. Lemo giggled and giggled, his whole face transformed with glee. Aron caught my eye, and I choked suddenly, as though his gaze had stopped my breathing. Tomorrow – he would be leaving. And I was absolutely certain that I didn't want him to go.

In times to come, I would hang onto this memory, I was sure. The feeling of warmth and security, family and friendship. Laughter in grief.

The feeling that imagination could overcome every hardship if you just tried hard enough.

\*

The next morning brought a change in the air. The words seemed whispered on the new breeze, as though carried along by invisible beings. 'It's over!'

Tiger jigged from foot to foot as he told us the news.

'Over?' I said, my heart racing. 'You mean, the war? Over? Are you sure?'

'It's gossip,' said Aron, frowning at Tiger. 'No one knows the truth.'

Tiger looked him right in the eye. 'A soldier told me,' he stated.

Jenna and I gasped. A soldier! Then – then it must be true! 'What else do you know?' I demanded.

Tiger grinned impishly. 'The Kwana have surrendered. Bremir has fallen. Ranami is captured. It is over.' Then, unable to keep still any longer, he dashed off.

We all stood and looked at each other, jaws dropping. It seemed too big to comprehend. Could it really all be over? 'You see?' Cosima cried triumphantly to Aron. 'You see, my son? We can go home!' She reached out to him and to Lemo, and pulled them into her arms, hugging them with a fierce affection. I was astonished to see that Aron's face was wet. Was he crying?

And then Jenna was hugging me, and a new emotion swept through me, and we jumped up and down, shouting, 'It's over! It's over!' And everyone who went past saw us and smiled, and I felt happy inside, in a way I hadn't for a very long time. It was safe to go home! And maybe there we would find Mamie and Vivie – and even Ruman! Tears ran down my face too at the thought of seeing my family again.

'We must get ready to leave,' said Jenna.

I nodded. Of course we must. We must go home. I felt stronger by the moment. Surely I could make the journey. We could take it slowly . . .

I looked up to see Aron watching me, and I felt torn in two on the inside.

Once the decision was made, though, there seemed no point in waiting. In a remarkably short space of time, our few possessions were wrapped in sheets, the tent dismantled and the patch of ground where we had lived for the past five months was bare. I stared at it.

Maklam smiled as he sat alone outside his tent. 'Come with us,' Cosima had said. 'There is nothing for you here. Come with us.'

'I am too old,' Maklam had said. 'I do not wish to

make journeys any more. The only journey left for me is the one to my sisters.' He smiled as he said it, which just made it even sadder. Now he smiled again. 'Goodbye, storyteller,' he said to me. 'I have your stories locked inside my head, and I will tell them to myself every evening to keep myself company.'

On an impulse, I went forward to kiss his cheek. I'd never known a grandfather, but Maklam felt like one to me now. 'I wish you . . . good things,' I said, at a loss to know how to say goodbye.

Maklam nodded to the others and went into his tent.

'Right, then,' said Cosima, taking Lemo by the hand. Jenna took his other hand. 'Come on.' They started off.

I stayed behind for a moment, looking at the place we had called home for so long.

'Looks strange, doesn't it?' Aron stood beside me, staring too.

I shook my head. 'It's like it never happened. You know – the tent, the storm, my stories . . .'

He hesitated. 'I found this. It was in a pile of debris. I thought you should have it back.'

He held out an object, twisted and spattered with

mud, but bright and clear underneath. It was the ornament I had been given in return for one of my stories; the one that had hung on our tent until the rains washed it away. 'Oh, Aron!' I cried. 'Thank you!' He handed it to me, and I wanted to throw my arms around him but didn't quite dare. Instead, I beamed at him with all the warmth I felt.

'I wish *I* had something to give you,' he said, and then frowned, as if he were cross with himself.

'You don't need to give me anything,' I said. 'You and me, we're survivors, remember?'

He held my gaze and smiled. 'That's right. Survivors.'

'Come on, you two!' Cosima called. 'No point hanging around.' We would walk to the gate together, but after that, Cosima's road took her in the other direction to ours.

Aron and I looked at each other again and smiled. 'I'm ready,' I said.

'Me too.'

We turned away from our patch. I felt two things – excitement and hope about returning home; and terrible sorrow at saying goodbye to my friends. I couldn't decide which was the stronger emotion. But

I wished I had had the courage to hug Aron. Would it be against all the rules to do it at the gate? Surely no one would mind, if we were not to see each other again?

Then, just as I had decided that I would, no matter what anyone thought, Jenna let out a sudden scream.

I turned to her, and she was white and shaking. 'What is it?' I said in alarm. 'Are you sick?'

She couldn't speak, but pointed – and I turned to see a woman and a small girl staggering towards us. The little girl had lost her headscarf and seemed to be holding up the woman, who was on her last legs.

It was Mamie and Vivie.

# 22

I can't put into words my feelings at that moment. I think it's because part of me is ashamed – terribly ashamed – that my primary feeling was one of sickening disappointment. We were about to leave! We had said our goodbyes to Altiers! But I knew, from the moment I set eyes on them, that Mamie and Vivie would not be going anywhere. Mamie was sick – that was clear to see – and in no condition to undertake a further journey. Vivie was drooping with fatigue, and she was so thin her legs looked barely able to support her.

'Amina?' said Vivie, in a voice that was so quiet I barely heard it. I dropped my bundle on the ground and rushed to catch Mamie, before she toppled over. Jenna did the same.

Mamie felt as fragile as a bird, and her eyes were

blank. She stared at me without recognition. 'Mamie!' I said, trying to smile. 'It's me – Amina. And Jenna.' But Mamie just continued to stare at me as though I were a complete stranger.

'Get out the blankets,' I heard Cosima say to Aron, who was already untying his bundle. She came over and gently took Mamie from me. 'Mrs Ambrose, it's very nice to meet you. My name is Cosima. You're safe now.'

Mamie's eyes closed at the word 'safe' and she looked like she had fallen asleep in Cosima's arms. Cosima lowered her onto the blanket that Aron had spread out.

'Jenna?' said Vivie, and then burst into tears, her thin shoulders shaking and shivering with the sobs.

We both put our arms around her and sank to the ground, and the three of us stayed like that for some minutes. Tears ran down my face so fast that I couldn't see anything. There was a howling noise in my ears and a burning pain in my stomach – whether from relief or terror, I couldn't tell. Because we were none of us the same as we had been, and now that they were here, I had to admit to myself that I had honestly thought we would never see them again. It was a wonderful, terrible shock.

Vivie clung to us both even when she stopped crying. It was as though, having found us again, she was determined to glue herself to us. When Cosima called Jenna over to see to Mamie, Vivie wrapped her arms and legs around me so tightly I could barely breathe, let alone move. I stroked her hair and whispered soothing things to her. My poor little sister – what had she been through?

'I lost you,' Vivie kept whispering. 'I lost you.'

'You've found us now,' I said. 'We're here, it's really us.'

Jenna shuffled over to me. She looked frightened. 'Mamie's really sick,' she said in a low voice. 'Cosima says we should take her to the hospital tent.'

A lump formed in my throat and I nodded. 'How long has she been sick?' I asked Vivie, but Vivie either didn't hear or didn't want to answer. I pulled back so that I could look into her face. 'Vivie. Darling, you have to tell me. How long has Mamie been ill?'

Vivie shrugged. 'Ages.' Then she folded herself around me and wouldn't say anything else.

Cosima and Aron carried Mamie to the hospital

tent. Aron had said nothing since their arrival, but his eyes were kind and sad. I was grateful they hadn't left yet, but I couldn't think about anything except Mamie and Vivie. The hospital was, as ever, bursting at the seams with the sick and the dying, and we were told to wait our turn. 'But she's really sick,' I heard Aron tell a nurse.

'They all are,' was her response. Nothing had changed since our last visit.

I felt desperate. What could we do? Jenna got out her water bottle and poured a little into Mamie's mouth, though most of it dribbled out again. Vivie, on the other hand, grabbed my bottle from me with such force that I was taken by surprise, and before I knew it, she had drunk half the contents. 'Stop!' I said in alarm, but it was too late and she was immediately sick all over the ground and my feet. Then she burst into tears again.

We sat in a huddled group for a long time, waiting for our turn. When it eventually came, a doctor helped us to carry Mamie into the tent to examine her, though it was so full of patients she had to share a bed with another woman. I had not seen this part of the hospital when I had come with my bad knee, and it appalled me. People lay everywhere, groaning or crying or silent; desperately thin, curled over, plastic tubes hanging off the side of the bed.

Cosima, Aron and Lemo had to stay outside because there was so little room, but they let Jenna and Vivie and me in when we explained who we were. The doctor put a needle in Mamie's arm and attached a tube to it. On the other end of the tube was a bag of what looked like water, and this was hooked onto a tall pole. I could see the contents running down the tube into Mamie's arm. 'Will that help?' I asked, but the doctor ignored me. It was a stupid question, I realized.

The doctor handled Mamie gently, but when he pressed on her stomach, she let out a wail that made me turn cold with fright. Then she turned her head to one side, biting down on her lip as tears ran from under her closed eyes. The doctor looked serious as he continued, looking closely at her arms and legs – and even lifting her skirts, to my shame.

After he had finished his examination, he turned to us. 'You are her daughters?'

We nodded.

'Your mother is very sick. I am sorry. There may not be much we can do.'

'What – what's wrong with her?' asked Jenna in a small voice.

He hesitated. 'I believe she has some internal injuries. There is bleeding under the skin.'

'Can't you stop it?' I asked.

He spread his hands. 'If we were in a properly equipped centre, then possibly, but here there is too great a risk of further infection. We can give her antibiotics and painkillers, but if her organs are damaged, then they won't recover.'

I turned to Vivie. 'What happened to her?'

But Vivie shook her head and seemed unable to speak.

The doctor sighed. 'Your mother has been abused. Her body has been through a lot.'

'Was it the Kwana?' I asked Vivie sharply. 'Did they do this to her?'

Vivie burst into tears again.

'Don't ask her any more,' Jenna told me. 'Can't you see you're upsetting her?'

I felt frustrated. 'But if she knows what they did, then maybe the doctor could make it better.'

The doctor shook his head. 'I suspect it may be too late for that.' His gaze passed over the three of us, and he seemed genuinely sad. 'I am very sorry. You can stay with her, if you like.'

I gulped. Stay with her? Did that mean – did that mean Mamie didn't have long to live? How long? I couldn't find the words to ask – and I wasn't sure I wanted to know the answer. As the doctor went to deal with another patient, I looked down at Mamie. Somehow she was smaller than I remembered. Impulsively I reached for her hand and held it in my own. Her eyes were closed, but the lids fluttered slightly as if she knew I was there. 'Mamie?' I whispered. 'Can you hear me?'

There was no response. Her face was so familiar, and yet it was also different from how I remembered it. Had there been so many lines on it before? A small scar ran from the corner of one eyebrow into her hairline. It looked new. How had she got that? Was she protecting Vivie at the time? Had it made her life harder or easier to have Vivie with her?

I wished with all my heart that she would wake up so that I could ask her some questions, but her eyes remained resolutely closed, despite my whispered encouragements.

After a while Jenna said, 'One of us should go outside to tell the others.'

I jumped. Of course! Cosima, Aron and Lemo were still waiting patiently for news. They would be worried. But my gaze returned to Mamie.

'You go,' said Jenna. 'We'll stay with her.'

I left them and wove my way out of the tent, through people on beds, chairs and the floor. This was an awful place to be. Mamie would hate it.

I saw Aron first. He was standing up, looking towards the tent. Something inside me always felt better when I saw him, and I hurried over. 'How is your mother?' he asked.

Cosima and Lemo were sitting at his feet, and they both looked up expectantly.

'She's really ill,' I said, and bit my lip. 'The doctor says – he says she has internal injuries.'

Cosima's eyes closed as if in pain. 'I'm so sorry, Amina.'

'But they can help her, right?' asked Aron. 'The doctors?'

I shook my head. 'No. He says . . . it's too late.' My voice broke, and I swallowed hard.

Cosima reached up to touch my hand. 'After all this time. It's so unfair.'

This was exactly what I had been thinking. I burst out angrily, 'We should have gone back to look for them earlier! We should never have left them! It's our fault for not trying harder.'

'No,' said Aron sharply. 'It's not your fault.'

I looked helplessly at him. 'You don't know that. Maybe we could have done something.'

'Try not to think like that,' Cosima said gently. 'It's not good for you. Believe me. When my husband . . . died . . . I spent a lot of time wishing I had done things differently. Maybe I could have stopped it somehow. But I have made my peace with it now.' She reached for Aron. 'I have made my peace with all of it.' I remembered how Aron blamed himself for his father's death, and I saw tears in his eyes as Cosima took his hand. 'Your mother,' she went on, 'she would want you and Jenna to survive.'

Survive. That was the word Aron had used, way back before the rains came. He said we were survivors. Did that mean, though, that Mamie wasn't a survivor? That she hadn't fought hard enough? I wiped my eyes. 'Are you staying?'

Cosima glanced up at Aron. 'I don't think we can, Amina. Your mother is in good hands now, and you have found your sister. Your family can be repaired a little. But I still want to go home.' She smiled at me. 'This doesn't have to be goodbye. One day we can all meet again, I'm sure.' She rummaged in a fold of her tunic and held out a piece of paper. 'I've written down how to find us, so that once you have been home and found your brother, you can come and visit.'

It sounded so ordinary, so easy, when she said it like that. I took the piece of paper and glanced at it. The name of the village meant nothing to me, but Cosima had written down other things too: landmarks and roads and a city name. 'You are Amina from Talas, who tells stories,' said Cosima. 'We will be able to find you.'

'Yes,' I said suddenly. 'Yes, you could come to visit us too.' She caught my gaze and we both smiled. I was going to miss her terribly. She stood up and we embraced. Then Lemo squeezed me so tightly his thin arms trembled with the effort. I had to swallow hard. Lemo had been like a little brother to me, sharing the delights of our stories. And then I turned to Aron, and felt unsure again.

He smiled at me. 'See you again, survivor.'

'You too,' I said.

Some emotion crossed his face, but it was gone before I could be sure of what it was. The moment had passed.

'Ask Jenna to come out and say goodbye, will you?' said Cosima.

'Wouldn't it be better to wait until tomorrow morning?' I said desperately. 'It's nearly the afternoon now.' But I could see by her face that she didn't want to delay. 'All right. I'll fetch her.'

'Don't lose that paper,' Cosima told me.

'I won't.' I just couldn't bring myself to say goodbye, so I waved and turned away. Every few steps I glanced back, and Aron was always gazing at me until I couldn't see him through the tents and people.

The three of us lived the next few days in the hospital tent, taking turns to sit with Mamie. Sometimes we saw Tasha, the nurse who had treated my knee. She looked as tired as ever, and now I could see why. There was a constant stream of sick and dying people every day, and Tasha worked without a break from morning till night. She remembered us, and when she had time to stop for a moment, which wasn't often, she always asked how Mamie was doing. 'I am so pleased that you found her,' she said to me. 'It was worth fighting through that illness.'

'Yes,' I said, though I wanted to add that it would have been worth it even more if Mamie had been fit and well.

Fortunately for us, the hospital had its own food supply so we didn't have to queue for hours as we were used to. At night, when the doctors cleared the place of extra people, we huddled against the outside of the tent, using Cosima's blanket to keep us warm. Jenna and I lived in fear of Mamie dying during the night without us by her side.

Vivie said almost nothing for two days. And then, little by little, the haunted, tense expression on her face began to relax. 'Don't keep asking her things,' Jenna told me. 'You'll make her worse.'

So I held my tongue, and instead, I told story after story at night when we couldn't sleep for worrying. The skies were clear again now, and the stars shone brightly. Vivie hung on my every word. As I looked down at her – her painful thinness, her frightened eyes – it gave me an ache inside, and my stories became more and more about reconciliation and hope for the future. Alham's army still leaped into the sky, and the soldiers still did battle, but more than one found a way to return to his family, and in one story, the warrior's mother leaped into the sky after him. I couldn't help myself. We all wanted Mamie to recover; to be our mother again. Jenna and I had had to be independent while we were away from her. We had grown up a lot, but inside we were still Mamie's little girls and we couldn't help but want her to look after us again.

One night, about five days after Mamie and Vivie's arrival, the three of us were sleepily settling in our usual spot outside the tent. There was a chill in the air as the season was turning. I had told a story to warm us: the warrior had found peace in the sky near the sun, where he would be warm for ever. My eyes were closing, and Vivie was already asleep, her little hand peeking out from under the blanket. I saw Jenna tuck it in gently before my head nodded.

And then there was a soft whisper from nearby: 'Girls? Girls, wake up.'

I struggled to open my eyes. Tasha was crouching beside us, and in a second I was fully awake again.

'What is it? What's happened?' I said quickly, and my jolt awoke the other two.

'Come with me,' she said, holding out her hand. Her eyes were soft.

We followed her into the tent, past the sleeping families and the patients who groaned in their beds. Moonlight was pouring in through the windows like milk, lighting up Mamie's bed and the floor around it. One of the doctors was standing next to Mamie, her wrist in his hand. He looked at us.

'I'm very sorry,' he said. 'I don't think she has long. She is nearing the end of her journey.'

I couldn't speak. My lip trembled, and I clamped my jaw shut. 'No,' I heard Jenna whisper. 'No, she can't die. She's hung on this long.'

The doctor was sympathetic. 'It's always been a matter of time. But you can console yourself with the thought that she hasn't been in pain. And you have been with her.'

Those thoughts were not consoling in the least. I felt angry. This was a hospital! Why couldn't they do anything? But I was afraid to open my mouth in case I burst into loud sobs.

Jenna reached for Mamie's right hand, and I went

round the other side of the bed and took her left. Vivie stood and stared. Her eyes were dry, though her face was even paler in the milky moonlight. Tasha melted into the shadows, her face sympathetic.

'We should say something,' said Jenna, in a wobbly whisper.

I swallowed. She was right, I supposed, but I couldn't think of the words. What did you say to your dying mother? 'Mamie,' I whispered. 'Mamie, it's us. We're all here with you.'

There was a long pause. Mamie lay silent, her breathing so slight you'd hardly know it was there.

'Mamie, it's Jenna,' said Jenna. 'I wanted to tell you . . . we all love you very much. And we're so glad you came to the camp. Amina and I have missed you every day, and we looked for you all the time.'

'Yes,' I said. It was as though Jenna's words gave me strength. 'Yes, we did. We never stopped looking for you and Vivie. And we want you to know that we'll look after Vivie, just like you did.' I glanced at the end of the bed. Vivie's eyes were wide open, but tears now streamed down her face like an open tap. 'We're going home,' I told Mamie and Vivie, 'to find Ruman, so that we can all be together again.'

357

'And you can be with Potta,' said Jenna. She wiped her eyes. 'Just like you would have wanted. You needn't worry about us, we'll be all right. Three of us are together now, and we'll go and find Ruman and be happy again.'

Mamie let out a sigh; a huge, deflating sigh that seemed to seep through her whole body. Then, slowly, her eyes opened.

'Mamie!' I cried, though my voice was still a whisper. We crowded in closer. 'Mamie, it's us!'

Mamie blinked for a few moments, and then her gaze focused. She looked at Jenna, and then at Vivie, and finally at me. 'My girls,' she said faintly, and her mouth twitched up at one side in a very small smile.

'Yes,' Jenna said. 'It's us. We're all here.'

'My girls,' repeated Mamie, and then her eyes closed again. Another sigh, ending in a little raspy cough – and then she didn't breathe in again.

We waited a long time for her to take another breath, but she didn't. And even when I knew she wouldn't, I still waited, just in case.

And after a long, long time, the doctor came and covered Mamie over with a sheet.

# 23

We cried together, holding each other. I cried for everything we once had; for everything that had been taken away by the Kwana and the war. I cried for myself; and because Mamie would never know how much I had grown up and how people had loved to hear my stories. I cried for Jenna, who was head of the family now and who wouldn't have a mother to help her on her wedding day. I cried for Vivie, who had been through so much with Mamie and would now be without her for ever. I cried for Ruman, who, if he were still alive, would not know what had happened. And I cried because Cosima and Aron and Lemo had left and we only had each other.

But despite how I felt, there were only so many tears in my body, and when they were spent, I simply sat, exhausted, holding my sisters.

The doctor and nurses were very kind, but they needed the bed space, and so Mamie was moved within minutes of our leaving her side. They told us she would be buried in a special area for graves outside the camp. I felt bad; she should have been buried back home in Talas with Potta, but then, we didn't know where Potta was buried, did we?

'I'm glad she saw us,' said Jenna after a long time.

I nodded. 'Me too.'

'She knew us. She recognized us.'

'Yes.'

'Maybe – maybe what we said helped her to die happy. Do you think, Amina?'

'I don't know,' I said wearily. 'I hope so.'

'What are we going to do?' asked Vivie in a little voice.

We looked at her. 'We're going home,' I told her. 'To Talas. To see if we can find Ruman.'

'When?'

I shrugged. 'Soon, I suppose.'

'Today? Tomorrow?' We were back outside the hospital tent, and Vivie's gaze swept the area. 'I don't want to stay here.'

Neither did we. 'Tomorrow,' I suggested. 'We need to eat something today.'

'We shouldn't wait long,' said Jenna. 'It's getting colder.'

'Tomorrow, then,' said Vivie. 'Good. I've had enough of camps.'

Jenna and I exchanged glances. 'Were you in a camp before?' I asked, wondering if this was the wrong thing to say.

'Yes,' said Vivie. 'With the gypsies.'

'Why did they let you in?' I said.

'I pretended I was a gypsy too,' she told us. 'Once we were away from the checkpoint, no one knew any better.'

'Were there lots of people there?' asked Jenna. 'At the camp?'

'Yes. And Noori's family.'

'Noori's family!' I exclaimed. 'You saw them?'

'Yes,' said Vivie. 'And Mamie told me that they're sort of cousins of ours. Mamie's brother was Noori's uncle, or something. I can't remember.'

'That's amazing!' I stared. 'All that time we went to see them, and we never knew.'

Vivie shrugged. 'It was supposed to be a secret.'

'What happened to them?' asked Jenna.

'I don't know. We all left when the camp was shut down. The Kwana just went away one day. One minute they were there, then they weren't. There was no food, so we had to leave. And someone told us about this place. Though it's not as good as they said it was.' Vivie looked disappointed, and for a moment I thought I saw a flash of the old Vivie, the spoiled child I remembered. It gave me a sense of relief – she was still in there somewhere, our little sister.

'How did Mamie get hurt?' I asked.

But it was a question too far. Vivie's eyes filled and she pressed her lips together.

'It's all right,' said Jenna in a comforting tone. 'You don't have to tell us.' She put her arm around Vivie. 'You did really well to bring her here. It must have been a long way.'

Vivie nodded as her tears splashed onto the ground.

'We're so proud of you,' Jenna told her. 'Me and Amina – we think you did an amazing thing.'

'I don't know if I could have done it,' I added. 'Looked after Mamie all that time.'

Vivie flashed a startled glance at me. Then she put her small hand in mine and leaned on my shoulder.

*

When we told Tasha that we were planning to leave the next day, she managed to find us a parcel of food. Bread, cheese, some dried meat – I could barely speak for gratitude. I couldn't remember exactly how long it had taken us to walk to Altiers from Talas – four, five days? – but we couldn't do it on no provisions, especially Vivie, who was the thinnest of us all. I also managed to find an undamaged water bottle lying discarded on the ground. Such things were like miracles, and at first I couldn't believe that it wasn't broken. 'It's a sign,' said Jenna when I brought it back.

'A sign?' I knew what she meant. It was a sign that we were meant to be leaving; that this was the right thing to do. We began to speculate about who we might see when we returned home.

'We could stop at Lakma's sister's house,' suggested Jenna.

'No,' I argued. 'It's off the main track. We should go home first. Lakma might have gone home too.'

'I wonder what happened to Davir.'

'What do you mean?' asked Vivie, and so we told her about our journey and how we had spent the night round the back of Leilah's place. 'That was the first night you told me the story about the stars,' said Jenna, smiling. 'Remember?'

It seemed so long ago.

'That's how I found you,' Vivie said, almost off-hand. 'When I arrived, I asked if anyone knew you or Jenna. And someone said there was a girl who told stories. I knew it would be you.'

My throat closed up with emotion. They had found me because I told stories and people had heard of me! It was exactly as we had hoped.

'Lots of people came to listen to Mini's stories,' Jenna said, and I could hear the pride in her voice. 'They said it made them feel better. It gave them hope.'

'Well,' said Vivie, 'that's good, I suppose. Back in the camp with Mamie . . . maybe it would have been nice to hear some stories then.' She sounded wistful.

'Mamie would have been proud of you,' Jenna said to me, 'for making use of your gift to help other people.'

'She'd have been proud of you too,' I said. 'For staying so sensible and all that. Keeping me out of trouble.' I remembered Ghion and the food tins. 'And for being so kind.'

She smiled at me and I smiled back. 'Tell us a last story here,' she said, 'before we go to sleep. Tomorrow we're leaving, so let's have a last story here.'

'All right,' I said. 'A story just for us.' I looked up at the sky. The stars were just beginning to emerge. I pointed. 'Look. Can you see that little group of stars? Three of them, bunched together? That's the three sisters. They leaped into the sky to find their brother, who went off to fight a war, even though his father didn't want him to.'

'Did they find him?' asked Vivie.

Jenna laughed. 'You can't skip straight to the end, Vivie. Mini will tell you off if you do. She likes to tell stories the right way.'

I looked down at my little sister 'I don't mind this time. I'll tell the end first, and then we can go back and fill in the rest of the story. Yes, Vivie, they found him. Can't you see him? Look really hard.'

Vivie squinted up at the sky until her eyes watered. 'Yes!' she said finally. 'There's another star there, right next to the three sisters. It's much fainter, but it's there.'

'There you go,' I said. 'That's the brother.'

'Why is he so much fainter than the others?' Vivie wanted to know.

'Ah,' I said, pulling my knees in and tugging the blanket so that it covered all of us. 'That's the story. Are you ready?'

We huddled together as the air chilled and the sky darkened. Jenna put her arms around Vivie, who held my hand.

'Ready?'

Vivie nodded.

'All right,' I said. 'This is how it goes. Once upon a time there were three sisters . . .'

Amina's story has probably left you with lots to think about.
Read on to find out more about *Looking at the Stars* . . .

# Q&A WITH JO COTTERILL

**Where is *Looking at the Stars* set?**
Amina's country doesn't have a name. I didn't want to set it in
a specific place for three reasons. Firstly, it's likely that I would
have got some details wrong. Even when you've done lots of
research, errors can creep in. Secondly, countries change but
war is always the same: people dying and families torn apart. By
setting *Looking at the Stars* in an unnamed country, it could apply
to many places. Thirdly, I wanted to be able to tell a very specific
story. Therefore, I needed to have control over all the aspects of
the plot, including what kind of people were in power and how
the country was run. There isn't a country that is exactly like
the one where Amina lives, though there are many that share
similarities.

**What gave you the idea for *Looking at the Stars*?**
I wrote the first draft of this book in 2007. Back then, we were
in the midst of the Iraq War, a complicated conflict with many
confusing aspects. I was also aware of civil war in the Democratic
Republic of Congo and in the Darfur region of Sudan. The news
was full of the political wrangling and the discussions about what
other countries should or should not be doing. But in amongst
that were the stories of the ordinary people; people like me.
When we see people from other countries in the news, it's easy to
distance ourselves. We think, Well, they don't talk my language,
they don't wear the same clothes, they don't live in the same kind
of house. But those are all superficial differences. Underneath,

we're all human, and that's what touches us when we hear about children who've lost their father, or a very pregnant girl who's had to walk miles to get help for her little brother.

Seeing all these stories also got me thinking about how people always hope for the best. When they've been living unhappily, they're so grateful to see their rescuers – and then things go wrong all over again. I wondered what it must be like to have your hopes dashed again and again, and what kind of mental strength you must have to develop to get through that. *Looking at the Stars* began as a single line: 'The day the soldiers came, we cheered.' I had no idea who any of the characters were or where the story was going, but that was my starting point and the book grew from there.

**Is Amina based on a real person?**
No, but she has many qualities that I admire. She likes to think for herself and be independent (though her family is very important to her), and she isn't afraid to stand up for herself. She also has a great imagination and is a natural storyteller. I think stories are so important. They bring people together and they can bring hope and comfort in the darkest hours.

**How did you write the bits where Amina is making up stories about the stars?**
It sounds odd to say it, but I let Amina take over. I know I made her up; that she isn't real, but she has her own 'voice' and so I would slip into her voice and relax my conscious 'author' side. I never planned where the stories were going or what they would be about, but I think I was partly influenced by traditional folk tales and older stories from the Greeks and Romans, who were very keen on heroes and warriors.

**The women and girls all wear headscarves in this book. Are they Muslim?**

No. There is no specific religion in *Looking at the Stars*. However, the way women are expected to behave is similar to the way women have to behave in many Muslim countries. I deliberately didn't include a religious aspect to the war in *Looking at the Stars* because, to me, it is only one aspect of human nature. In the end, no matter how peaceful and positive a belief in god(s) may be, the darker side of human nature will find a way to corrupt it and use religion as an excuse to oppress others. Perhaps what concerns me more in *Looking at the Stars* is the way that men use and abuse their power to reduce women and girls to second-class citizens. Half of the global population is female, and yet males dominate every area of life. As a female, I know how lucky I am to be a UK citizen, where I have many more rights than women in other countries – and yet even in my own country, there are very few women in positions of power compared with the huge numbers of men.

**Where did you get the idea about the letters of heritage?**

They were inspired by the Star of David which the Jews were forced to wear during the Second World War. These stars marked the Jews out as being visibly 'different' and many people who had previously been friends turned against them.

**If you wrote this book in 2007, why has it taken so long to be published?**

Lots of other things happened during those seven years: I had two babies (not at the same time!), I was working as an English teacher, and I wrote six books in a series called *Sweet Hearts*. My first draft of *Looking at the Stars* wasn't good enough, so it took a lot of rewriting before it was accepted for publication. It would never have been published at all, though, if it hadn't been for my fantastic agent, Penny Holroyde, who read the first three chapters years ago and nagged me over and over again to finish the book. She has championed it every step of the way and I am very grateful.

**Is this a book about war or a book about stories?**
It's a book about hope and human resilience. We see it again and again in the real world with people who have been through terrible, unimaginable horrors. They can smile, they can tell jokes, they can be compassionate to others. They look to the future. The human spirit is amazing.

**Will there be a sequel?**
There isn't a sequel planned at the moment, though perhaps in the future . . . !

**If you're in a reading group, *Looking at the Stars* would be a brilliant choice. Here are some discussion points to start you off . . .**

Jenna 'just wants everyone to be happy'. Amina can't stop asking 'why' and 'what if?' With which character do you have most in common?

Do you think it's important to have pride in your family background or country? Why?

Mamie says that Amina shouldn't judge people by which letter they are wearing. Why is it important not to judge people by appearances? And why is it hard not to do this?

Do you think it's important to mix with people from different backgrounds or do you think people should stick to their own kind? Why?

In Chapter 4, Jenna says, 'Stories aren't important. Having enough to eat; keeping safe – those are the important things.' Do you agree with her? Do you think she's changed her mind by the end of the book?

Do you think Ruman was right to run off to join the rebellion? What would you have done in his place?

What skills do you have that might help you to survive in a camp like Altiers?

Is there a 'message' in this book? What do you think it might be?

**Even though Amina's country isn't a real place, there are plenty of countries in the world where this kind of thing has happened or is still happening today.**

In Amina's country, Ranami is the leader. He is a dictator and he rules with the help of the Kwana, a military political power. But many ordinary people don't like Ranami or the Kwana. They begin a rebellion. The Kwana fights back, often by killing people in public (like Amina's father) in order to stop others rebelling. Another (unnamed) country sends in armed soldiers to help protect the people, but their presence causes even more destruction for the residents.

**Civil War** – a war between people in the same country

**Dictator** – a person who rules over others by telling them what to do and not allowing them to disobey

**Rebellion** – when people openly disagree with the ruling power and try to get others to fight against the rulers too

**Refugee** – a person looking for 'refuge' or safety, usually because they've had to leave their own home due to war

**Revolution** – a rebellion that has succeeded

## Syria

As *Looking at the Stars* is published, one of the worst civil wars going on is in Syria. Syria is a country in the Middle East, and in 2011 some people started to protest publicly against the government. The protesters wanted democracy (where ordinary people have a say in how the country is run: the UK is a democracy) and they also complained that the people in power were corrupt. Instead of talking to the protesters to see if an agreement could be reached, the government army arrested and tortured many of them. This made people angry, so more and more of them joined the protests.

As the protests spread, the government reacted with greater force. Tanks and machine guns were sent into cities and towns where people regularly protested against the government. The soldiers fired on buildings and people, killing hundreds. Even those who weren't rebelling got caught up in the conflict, and many innocent people were killed. Some soldiers didn't like the way the government was responding, so they switched sides and began to fight with the protesters. The rebels were supplied with weapons by governments from other countries who were sympathetic to their cause. This meant that before long there was a civil war in progress.

Hundreds of thousands of people (mainly women, children and the elderly) ran away to escape the violence, taking only what they could carry with them. They knew that, to be safe, they had to be out of Syria completely. They hoped that the neighbouring countries (Turkey, Iraq, Jordan, Israel and Lebanon) would help them and provide them with food and shelter.

By August 2013, over two million refugees (half of them children) had escaped from Syria into other countries. But as

I write this there are huge problems in finding them all places to stay. International charities like the Red Cross and Save the Children have set up refugee camps, but they're not big enough to fit in all the people who keep coming. It's also easy to catch life-threatening diseases if you don't have a clean, spacious place to live. And during the winter months, many refugees die from the cold and from starvation.

The United Nations (which is an organisation made up of representatives from 193 different countries) says that the Syrian people need protecting. But because the UN is made up of people with different opinions, they can't agree on how best to do this. In the meantime, the refugees continue to stream out of Syria and thousands continue to die.

## Rwanda

In 1994, a terrible war began in Rwanda, which is a country in Africa. For a long time there had been two ethnic groups living side by side: the Hutus and the Tutsis. They had never really got along. The Tutsis had been in charge for many years (even though there were fewer of them): they had positions of power and they owned more property. But in 1973, the Hutus had taken over, and many of the Tutsis lost their jobs or were sent away. It was an ongoing feud, and both sides felt they had been hard done by.

Some of the Hutus were 'extremists' (that means they believed very strongly that Hutus were the only people who should be living in Rwanda and all Tutsis were evil). In 1994, the country's president, a Hutu, was killed when his plane was shot down. No one knows exactly who was responsible, but the Hutu extremists used it as an excuse to start killing Tutsis. Because everyone in the country had to have an identity card, it was easy to find out where the Tutsis lived. Groups of Hutu extremists went from house to house, village to village, killing the Tutsi families: men, women, children, babies – all of them were killed. Guns and bullets were expensive so most people were killed by machetes (a big chopping knife). Neighbour killed neighbour, and many Tutsis were betrayed by people they thought were helping them. Some Hutus were forced to kill Tutsi friends to avoid being killed themselves.

In only a few weeks, around 800,000 people were killed, perhaps as many as three-quarters of the whole Tutsi population. Thousands of Hutus were killed too, either for refusing to kill Tutsis or for actively trying to prevent the killings. The war only came to an end when a small group of determined Tutsi rebels overthrew the Hutu government and took charge. Many other countries around the world knew what was going on, and yet no one stepped in to stop it.